I TURNED TO WALK AWAY . . .

Richard was beside me in a moment, pulling me tightly to him. "So you were jealous, too—as jealous as I was," he murmured in my ear.

"I thought there was to be no repetition of last night!" I cried, struggling. "Let me go!"

"I have not finished explaining," he said, and there was something in his voice that stilled my struggles. I looked up at him and saw his eyes glinting in a frightening way. And then he bent his head to mine and kissed me.

All the world vanished in that kiss. I clung to him, dizzy with the sweetness of it. It held tenderness, yes; but there was a tightly leashed fire burning just beneath the tenderness . . .

ROMANTIC SUSPENSE WITH ZEBRA'S GOTHICS

THE SWIRLING MISTS OF CORNWALL   (2924, $3.95)
by Patricia Werner

Rhionna Fowley ignored her dying father's plea that she never return to his ancestral homeland of Cornwall. Yet as her ship faltered off the rugged Cornish coast, she wondered if her journey would indeed be cursed.

Shipwrecked and delirious, Rhionna found herself in a castle high above the roiling sea—and in thrall to the handsome and mysterious Lord Geoffrey Rhyweth. But fear and suspicion were all around: Geoffrey's midnight prowling, the hushed whispers of the townspeople, women disappearing from the village. She knew she had to flee, for soon it would be too late.

THE STOLEN BRIDE OF GLENGARRA CASTLE   (3125, $3.95)
by Anne Knoll

Returning home after being in care of her aunt, Elly Kincaid found herself a stranger in her own home. Her father was a ghost of himself after the death of Elly's mother, her brother was bitter and violent, her childhood sweetheart suddenly hostile.

Elly agreed to meet the man her brother Hugh wanted her to marry. While drawn to the brooding, intense Gavan Mitchell, Elly was determined to ignore his whispered threats of ghosts and banshees. But she could *not* ignore the wailing sounds from the tower. Someone was trying to terrify her, to sap her strength, to draw her into the strange nightmare.

THE LOST DUCHESS OF GREYDEN CASTLE   (3046, $3.95)
by Nina Coombs Pykare

Vanessa never thought she'd be a duchess; only in her dreams could she be the wife of Richard, Duke of Greyden, the man who married her headstrong sister, Caroline. But one year after Caroline's violent and mysterious death, Richard proposed and took her to his castle in Cornwall.

Her dreams had come true, but they quickly turned to *nightmares*. Why had Richard never told her he had a twin brother who hated him? Why did Richard's sister shun her? Why was she not allowed to go to the North Tower? Soon the truth became clear: everyone there had reason to kill Caroline, and now someone was after *her*. But which one?

Available wherever paperbacks are sold, or order direct from the Publisher. Send cover price plus 50¢ per copy for mailing and handling to Zebra Books, Dept. 3665, 475 Park Avenue South, New York, N.Y. 10016. Residents of New York and Tennessee must include sales tax. DO NOT SEND CASH. For a free Zebra/ Pinnacle catalog please write to the above address.

THE
RUBY TEARS OF
EDGECLIFF
MANOR

ELIZABETH CARROLL

ZEBRA BOOKS
KENSINGTON PUBLISHING CORP.

ZEBRA BOOKS

are published by

Kensington Publishing Corp.
475 Park Avenue South
New York, NY 10016

Copyright © 1992 by Elizabeth Carroll

First printing: February, 1992

Printed in the United States of America

Chapter One

London 1862

London lay under a thick pall of mist that day in early March, mist that smelled strongly of chimney smoke and soot, mist that rose from the river. A fitting backdrop for the day that was to change my life forever.

Though it was early afternoon, the glass-fronted drapers' establishments I was hurrying past had already lit their ornate gas lamps, which glowed in yellow circles in the dusk. The establishments were stately marvels of ornamented stone and brick work, decorated with illuminated clocks and gilt lettering in curved glass windows. But I was in no frame of mind to admire the glamorous shop fronts as I passed them, handkerchief pressed over nose and mouth, as much a preventative against disease as to shut out the smells. The dreadful cholera epidemic of 1858 still lived in everyone's mind, and there were other diseases rampant.

I was shaking, glistening from head to foot with mud and water, with a pounding heart and trembling knees. The wind of a London spring was catching at my wet cloak, which was none too warm even when dry. The curious crowd of passersby which had gathered momentarily was moving on. The coach which had soaked me, nearly running me down, splashing me from head to foot with muddied water, had already turned the corner.

"Bloody stupid trollop! Orter mind where yer goin'! Now ye've ruined yer fancy clothes. Wot will the customers say? Not even a draman'd look at you now!" a jeering, rough voice said from behind me and I jerked up, cheeks burning.

I met the sardonic gaze of a fat baker, standing in his doorway with his arms folded, an apparent witness to the whole incident. It was evident what he thought me! But I checked the hasty words rising to my lips and merely stared at him a moment, trying to match his insolent, coarse gaze with one of frigid disdain. What use was it to argue, or gasp in shocked insult? It was only natural that he should think me a woman of the streets.

No other kind of ladies would walk unaccompanied through the street. Ladies had chaperones, maids, grooms, escorts—a veritable retinue of followers when they descended from their shining carriages. With the strict example of Queen Victoria setting the mode, it would be an unthinkable impropriety for a lady even to take a turn in St. James' Park alone.

Poor working girls might walk alone here, marked by toil and poverty as they were, thin creatures with ragged shawls. But I was young, pretty, and until the coach had soaked me, I had been nicely dressed. In this part of London, there was only one kind of woman who fit that description.

I looked grimly down at the sheet music I still clutched in my hand—ruined now. Tears started as I thought of the long hours I had worked to pay for the music. My clothes might perhaps be washed, salvaged, but the music! The ink was running, staining my hand, smearing madly across the pages. With disgust, I flung them in the river of mud they called a street and silently cursed the careless coachman.

I looked down at my clothes. They might be salvage-able, but they certainly weren't fit to be seen in now!

I rounded the corner, half running, forgetting the cold in my panic at being late, in my anxiety over my appearance. As I hurried along, my hands were frantically wringing out my wet curls, wiping the mud from my face.

I slowed my steps to a respectable walk when I reached the wealthy neighborhood near Belgrave Square, so that the passersby would not think that a raving madwoman was running through their midst. Still from the stares and heads turning as I passed, my heart sank even further about how I must look.

At last I reached the great cream-colored facade of Heathfield House, a masterwork in stone that faced the green and tree-filled square. Everything here was neat, orderly, shining with luxury. I almost turned and ran.

But I squared my shoulders and walked to the service entrance, smoothed my skirts, wiped my cheeks with a handkerchief, and rang. The door was opened in a few moments by a little maid, smartly turned out in the neatest black and crisp starched white. Her eyes grew round as she took me in.

"I am Miss Woodstock, the music teacher," I began. "As you can see, I have suffered an unfortunate accident on the way here. I desire to speak with the butler or housekeeper, so that they may convey my regrets to Lady Heathfield. I am unable to give this morning's lesson."

"Yes'm," she said, still staring roundly. "Wait here."

In a few moments the butler, all frigid dignity, was before me. He drew himself up and peered down at me in the coldest manner imaginable.

"And what is this all about? A mishap?" he inquired.

"I was almost run down by a coach on the way here, sir," I replied, bowing slightly, "and as you can see, I was splashed from head to foot with muddy water. If you

7

would be so good as to inform Lady Heathfield of this occurrence, and convey to her my most sincere regrets and apologies for being unable to conduct Miss Heathfield's lesson this morning. Please tell her that I will wait on her at her earliest convenience, and would not dream of charging her for the next lesson, as I have so greatly inconvenienced her this morning."

He stared at me coldly for a moment, then said, "Very well. I will deliver your message to Her Ladyship. Wait here."

So I was left shivering in the drafty hallway, from fear as much as from cold.

Lady Heathfield was the first among the gentry to engage me, and I had high hopes that if she found me satisfactory, she would recommend me to her friends. One could charge the gentry so much more! And I needed the money desperately. But it was hard. Most of the blue-blood families preferred to engage men as music teachers—preferably French or Italian men, with names like Monsieur LaPoulet or something equally ridiculous. Unless they were families like the Heathfields, which had only daughters. Daughters without any pretensions to musical talent, daughters who just wanted to be able to play and sing adequately in the evenings at social gatherings—an extra talent to display, along with their bosoms, in their unrelenting search for a husband. And Lord forbid that a *male* teacher, a foreigner no less, would be hired to teach nubile young women, unchaperoned. Well, thank goodness they were not!

Having Lady Heathfield's daughter Cynthia as my pupil was an entrée into a better life, but now I feared it might be jeopardized.

The butler returned. "Lady Heathfield desires to see you. Follow me."

I only took a step before he stopped me. "Your cloak, miss," he said, eyebrows raised.

Embarrassed, I handed him my dripping cloak, which he took with one finger and hung on a hook near the entranceway.

I wiped my muddy shoes on the mat and I followed him over fine woven carpets, through white and gilt halls appointed with mahogany and enormous landscape paintings, before I was ushered into the morning room. Lady Heathfield awaited me, erectly poised at her desk, fashionably gowned in the shade that was all the rage that season, squirrel gray.

"And she looks exactly like a squirrel!" I thought as I stood before those beady black eyes that held not a trace of sympathy. She raised her lorgnette from her jutting breast and fixed me coldly.

Though she looked unwelcoming, I dared to speak. "Lady Heathfield, please forgive me—"

"Silence!" she snapped. "How dare you come here like this? As filthy as a street Arab, and half an hour late as well! I ought to have known that you were little better than trash, but for the sake of your family name— enough! You are dismissed from your post," she concluded, turning her attention from me finally.

"But Lady Heathfield, did the butler not explain my accident? I—"

"Insolent chit! Did I not say you were dismissed? Heavens!" she gasped, turning red and pointed at my feet. "You have ruined my Persian rug!"

A growing puddle of blackened water had indeed formed around my feet. I looked in horror at the damage I had done.

"My Lady, I apologize—"

"No more from you!" She picked up a silver bell and rang it furiously. The butler appeared so quickly that I knew him to have been listening at the door. "Take this this . . . *person* out of my sight at once!"

Cheeks crimson, I followed the butler down to the

kitchen and out the service entrance. I tried to avoid the curious eyes of the maids and footmen, who had gathered, as if by magic, to watch me leave in disgrace.

The door was shut with a bang. A fine, cold rain was falling as I trudged down the walk, turning my back on Belgrave Square. Now that Lady Heathfield had dismissed me, I would probably never find another post among the gentry. Word traveled fast in such social circles, as I well knew.

Though I had never known the crimson and gold luxury of a house such as Heathfield House, still that was the class I was born into.

And yet its doors were closed to me—now even as a teacher. It did not matter to Lady Heathfield that I had been raised to be a lady; I was still beneath her contempt.

The winds had quieted some and the fog had almost lifted by the time I reached Regent Street.

I looked longingly at the scones in the baker's window and continued home, knowing that I would probably not have one for a very long time. I would have to count my shillings from now on. My bright future as a tutor to Cynthia Heathfield and the doorway to the gentry were memories now.

At last I turned wearily onto my street. I paused a moment, looking down it. Soggy gray clouds floated in veiled streamers, seemingly just over the roofs of the buildings, which were as gray as the clouds. A few weak lights flickered yellow in the mist, but gave no warmth or life. The houses were all in a row, grim and dismal. Usually I loathed this street, for not a rose bloomed there, if anyone had a thought to plant such a thing. Yet after today, I was relieved to have reached it at last. I almost had a feeling of homecoming.

I picked up my skirts and hurried down the street, dodging broken paving stones, morasses of mud, and piles of refuse. The sidewalks were crowded. Returning workmen, black with the grime of the mills and the factories, shouldered roughly past me, some carrying a mite of fish wrapped in newspaper for the evening meal. Carts drawn by broken-winded horses, whose lives were as hard as their masters', made their way slowly down the middle of the street, the drivers shouting and cursing. Ragged children darted everywhere and seemed always to be underfoot. I clutched my reticule closely, for many of these children were adept at cutting purse strings and vanishing into the crowd before you had a chance to shout.

The rain began to spatter down again. I passed a woman standing in her yard, a thin shawl over her head. Our eyes met. Though she was probably not more than thirty, hers was the face of an old woman, lined with toil and worry, thin with hunger and disease. I gathered my cloak tightly about me and ran the last few yards to my door. Not as much from the rain but from the vision of the woman's face. I saw a reflection of my own ten years into the future.

I had come a long way since that day, two years ago, when my father had died so suddenly. I had been barely eighteen then, still so sheltered and innocent, totally unprepared to make my own way in the world. I had been happy before he died, alone with my father in our small neat house. It was not in a fashionable quarter, but the garden was lovely and the furnishings good. It had always been just my father and me ever since I could remember. My mother had died of cholera when I was very young, and I had never even seen a portrait of her. Mrs. Hall, our housekeeper, was like a mother to me, and watched over my father and me affectionately.

But when he died, I found I was left penniless. When the lawyers told me that the bailiff would have to come, that we must sell up and leave, I was too numb with shock and grief even to think what it would mean to me. But at

11

the funeral, I heard snatches from the mourners: "No relatives . . . such a pity! What can the poor girl do now? Imagine, such a disgrace. Everything lost at the gaming tables, and he had a modest income, I understand. It might have been enough for her if he had not gambled it all away . . ."

I had fled from the room, my cheeks burning. Gambling! I could not believe it and yet it explained so much. The periods of poverty and of wealth. How could my father have gambled away everything we had, and left me so defenseless against the world?

I flung myself on my bed in tears, and Mrs. Hall found me there some minutes later.

"Now, now," she said, her kind face full of concern and sorrow. "Cry if you want to, but don't think ill of your father because of what you just heard. He did it out of love for you, I reckon. He thought the world of his little Emily, and I think that's why he kept going back to the tables. He hoped to win a fortune, to see you secure and married . . . and he loved your mother so. She was a real lady, your mother, and when she died, he wasn't ever the same. He gambled to forget. Men are like that—they can't take the sorrow the way a woman can. I'm sure he gambled to win enough to settle the debts once and for all. He wasn't to know he was going to go so soon, before his time . . . he thought he had years to see you settled. And never a kinder or better father ever breathed. You remember him like that."

Her words had comforted me, and taken away the sting of being left on my own. And because of my father's insistence that I get an education, he hadn't left me completely defenseless after all.

Thinking about my father had made me feel better. I could do without the starched upper class. If the aristocracy would not have me teach their children, then I would make do with the merchants' class, where I was very well accepted and looked up to as a lady.

And at least, though the neighborhood was poor, I lived in the most respectable boardinghouse on the street. I let myself into the brown building, and paused once inside to shake out my cloak and wipe my boots, muddy and drenched as I was. I usually rushed up the stairs. My landlady, Mrs. Beade, was one of the most inquisitive and long-winded women I had ever known. If she caught me, she would keep me twenty minutes with tales of my neighbors' scandalous doings: Who was drinking; who was beating his wife; what unfortunate unmarried girl was with child.

Mrs. Beade was not malicious, just bright-eyed and noticing, kind though miserly. Usually I listened to her gossip, but today I felt I must be alone, locked away from the world, as soon as possible. I meant to take the stairs at once before she caught me. But since I was not teaching Cynthia Heathfield, I had arrived early this day and the scents of Mrs. Beade's afternoon tea overtook me. So I paused in the vestibule to savor the delicate smells.

I could hear the crackle of the fire coming from the drawing room and the sound of the more monied boarding home guests as they sampled Mrs. Beade's delicious homemade scones. I hung up my wet cloak and sighed. How I longed to join them and I stood by the bannister a moment, picturing myself by the fire, warming my cold hands, sipping the steaming tea. Then I pushed the wish from my mind and started to climb the creaky stairs to my cold room. Afternoon tea was extra and I knew I could barely afford the basic room and dinner from now on, now that I had lost my post at Lady Heathfield's. Dreams of afternoon tea were past me now.

I took the steps slowly and about midway I heard a voice call to me.

"Emily! Emily *Woodstock*." It was Mrs. Beade. "Don't run off now, child."

13

I paused. I could not in good conscience pretend not to hear her this time. She had caught me, but how strange for her to call me at teatime. I could not pay, so she never intruded upon me at this hour of the afternoon.

I turned. Something about Mrs. Beade seemed different this day. She was wearing her gray hair as usual, tied up into three small buns on the top of her head, her round eyeglasses perched precariously at the end of her nose. And her dress, a serviceable woolen brown, was a mere decade out of date. There was nothing new about this. It was well known that fashion was not Mrs. Beade's concern. Costly it was to follow those rules, and although far from poor, Mrs. Beade pinched pennies tighter than the greediest miser.

It was her face that was changed this day. Her normally inquisitive expression was replaced by a broad smile that seemed to transform her. Her pale plump cheeks were blushing pink and her blue eyes glittered. What juicy piece of gossip did she have this afternoon? I wondered.

"What is it, Mrs. Beade?" I asked, hoping that whatever it was she would make short work of it.

Mrs. Beade crossed her plump arms across her ample bosom. "Well, let's not talk with the staircase between us, child. Come down and have some tea."

"But Mrs. Beade, I—I cannot come down to tea. You know it is a luxury that I cannot afford."

"Shhh," she whispered and put her finger to her lips. "Don't say a word. I want you to share tea with me by the fire. I have set a table for the two of us, and worry not about the expense."

My eyes opened wide. "Why, thank you, Mrs. Beade," I replied and started down the stairs slowly, hardly believing my ears, wondering what had caused her to offer this treat to me. Mrs. Beade never bestowed kindness without expecting something in return.

I was soon alone with Mrs. Beade in the drawing room.

14

"Look what we have here, Emily." She beamed. There before the fire was a small round table, set for two, and with her finest china, no less. "Some of my very own scones, cucumber sandwiches, and even strawberry preserves. A proper tea, for a change."

I could hardly believe my eyes, cucumber sandwiches and strawberry preserves! "And what is this occasion, Mrs. Beade?" I asked skeptically. "Has a relative died and left you a legacy?"

"I have not been left a legacy, but *you* . . . you have cause for a celebration!"

"A celebration? In honor of what?" I sat gingerly in the wooden chair. Fortunately now, though still damp, my dress had dried enough so it would not damage anything, and sitting by the fire, I would very soon be completely dry. "I am afraid I do not feel like celebrating. I have had bad news today."

"I will not hear any bad news until you open this!" She reached in and pulled from her bosom an envelope. "*This* is the cause for celebration. A letter for you from the solicitors of Carrington and Phyfe!"

I shook my head. "Mrs. Beade, how can you think that a letter from the solicitors of Carrington and Phyfe is a cause for celebration? In my experience, solicitors only bring trouble."

"Perhaps. But letters from the law are almost always about crime or money. And since you are not a criminal, I decided it must be about a legacy. So, I quickly ran out to purchase a proper tea for a celebration!"

"Mrs. Beade, you have gone to all of this trouble for no account. I know no one with any money. And I am in no state to celebrate now, because I have lost my post at Lady Heathfield's." The words came out with a quaver despite my intentions to be cheerful, and Mrs. Beade put her arm around me while placing the letter on the table.

"No! But you're too good for that sour old woman. I

15

have heard stories. But Emily, please open the letter! Perhaps it *will* be good news. Maybe the mother of one of your pupils, like Mrs. Sommes, has remembered you in her will. She was a patroness of the arts, and always spoke kindly of you. But don't let's speculate. Open it at once!"

Snatching a cucumber sandwich from the tray, I complied. Not reading more than a few lines, I moaned in disappointment.

"This letter can't be for me," I said. "Listen to this:

> 'Dear Miss Woodstock,
> On behalf of Sir Ralph Woodstock of Edgecliff Manor, Cornwall, we have been charged with the task of locating his niece, an Emily Woodstock who would at this time be approximately twenty years of age.'"

I looked up. "You see. It isn't even for me. I have no relatives, and no Uncle Ralph Woodstock. They are merely searching for someone with my name."

"Oh." Mrs. Beade sounded disappointed, then looked determined. "But you are twenty, Emily, so perhaps it *is* you. What else does it say?"

I shook my head at her foolishness. I had no relatives. Why else would I live in a boardinghouse? But to humor her, I read on:

> "'If you are the said Emily, daughter of Thomas and Amelia Woodstock, originally of Cornwall, please wait on us at your earliest convenience, at our offices. We would like to discuss with you a matter of some importance. Respectfully yours . . .'"

I broke off, dropping the letter as though it had burned me.

"Emily! You are white! What is it, child?" Mrs. Beade demanded.

"Mrs. Beade," I said slowly, in shock, "perhaps this letter *is* meant for me. Those are my parents' names! And they did come from Cornwall, long ago! But it is too absurd. It can't be. Because I don't have an uncle."

"Emily," she said abruptly, "are you *certain* you don't have an uncle?"

"Yes, of course! My father never spoke of *any* relatives. Surely if I had had them, he would have told me! It must just be a case of another Emily Woodstock, that's all, whose parents were named—"

"Do you hear what you are saying?" she cried, jumping up and snatching the letter from the floor. "Who also happens to be twenty years old! It's too far-fetched a coincidence! Besides did your father ever *tell* you there were no relatives, or did he just never mention them?"

"He . . . just never mentioned them . . ." I paused, trying to remember. Before I could think clearly, I blurted out. "Wait—he did say something once. It was on his deathbed. Though I thought him delirious."

"What was it?" she asked.

Though I could not tell Mrs. Beade everything that transpired that day, I felt bound to tell her something. I spoke slowly, choosing my words carefully. "He gave me a box and said that someday it would bring the family together."

"A box, what was in it?" Mrs. Beade's eyes grew wide, but I did not answer. The overly inquisitive Mrs. Beade asked so many questions that if one wasn't answered immediately, she would usually ask another. I did not want to say what the box contained and so I waited.

"You say he spoke of family? Don't you see, Emily? I'm sure it means that the letter is true. I think that this Sir Ralph *must* be your uncle!" She raised her arm to the

17

ceiling, waving the letter in the air. "In any case, you cannot in good conscience ignore this letter! Perhaps you are not the Emily Woodstock they are looking for. But the burden of proof is up to them! They are the lawyers, and they would not have contacted you unless they were already reasonably sure. And if you *are* the right one . . ." She stopped, dazzled, clutching the letter to her breast dramatically. "Sir Ralph Woodstock! He must be rich! You must go tomorrow to see the solicitors, this could be a stroke of the greatest good luck!"

"Yes, or a dreadful letdown," I reminded her and breathed a sigh of relief. The box and what it contained was quickly forgotten. "Even if he is my uncle, what could he possibly want from me now, after all these years? To ask me to live with him as some sort of poor relation—or even a governess to his heirs! In any case he must be a very bad man if my father never mentioned him to me."

"Emily, I cannot sympathize with your doubts. It is a good deal better to have any relative, even a wicked uncle, than none at all. And a lord! Perhaps he lives on a great estate!" Mrs. Beade's eyes took on a dreamy expression.

"Or perhaps on a mean farm," I interjected into her rapture.

"Baronets do not live on mean farms," she said irrepressibly. "Or have firms of solicitors who have handled the family business for many years. I will miss you, child." And then her eyes took on that strange glistening quality before she said, "I hope you do not forget poor Mrs. Beade in all of your good fortune."

So this was the reason for Mrs. Beade's kindness. I could have laughed aloud, but I should have guessed it sooner. Never before had she treated me to afternoon tea. But I did not speak my true thoughts. "Miss me? What nonsense is this?"

"You're bound to enter society now, meet a rich young man and marry. You are the niece of a baron! Oh no, whatever will you wear?"

"Wear?" I gasped, truly laughing now. "I assure you I do not have a satin gown for my wedding to this rich young man!"

Mrs. Beade's cheeks turned crimson, as annoyed with me now for laughing as she had a moment ago for my seriousness.

"Wear to the solicitors tomorrow, of course! You simply cannot wear any of those rags you call dresses! What if they are to report to your uncle whether you have been raised a gentlewoman or not?"

"Oh, but you are right." I was struck by her logic. Though I was reasonably sure that there must be some mistake, that the Emily Woodstock the solicitors were searching for was not me, I must still go to their offices. And I would want to be presentable. "But I have nothing decent, and not a shilling to spare." I sat back in my chair dejectedly. "Perhaps I should not go."

"Nonsense!" Mrs. Beade wagged her finger at me. "I have an old friend, Mrs. Goodrich. She has a dress shop not far from Regents Park. Go there tomorrow, mention me, and tell her of your circumstance. Perhaps she will give you a price," she finished, eyes sparkling.

"I could not begin to hope for so much," I replied, wondering indeed what price I would eventually pay for Mrs. Goodrich's kindness, if she were anything like Mrs. Beade. "Thank you, Mrs. Beade, we will see what tomorrow brings."

"Perhaps a future for you, my child." Mrs. Beade relaxed in her chair and smiled smugly. Whatever she hoped to gain I did not speculate about now. I was enjoying the tea and warmed by the fire. Even if the letter was a mistake, it had at least inspired Mrs. Beade to this afternoon's treat.

We shared some more tea then and finished the petite sandwiches, along with not a little of Mrs. Beade's latest gossip.

Afterward I climbed the stairs feeling contented, in much a better mood than I had been in scarcely an hour before. Though my circumstances had not changed, for a moment I felt at peace. I let myself into my lodgings. My room was small but I kept it immaculate. I had a small bed and a bureau with an oval mirror. As I looked into the glass, large gray eyes looked back at me from under straight brows. My thick dark hair had come undone from its pins and hung in long strands below my shoulders. My cheekbones were high, but too gaunt, my mouth too wide. My nose was what my father called patrician. Yes, I looked like a schoolteacher. What nonsense that the solicitors might think me a lady.

I glanced at the small oval miniature of my father that rested on the bureau and an irrational surge of hope filled my bosom.

Could it be true? I thought of that day my father spoke so deliriously. I opened the drawer to my bureau and rummaged a moment, then took out a small case. Sitting down on the bed, I opened the black leather casket.

There on the red velvet rested a ring. "This ring belonged to your mother," my father had said. I looked down at the rubies and diamonds, sparkling in the heavy, old-fashioned setting, and remembered his words as if it were a moment ago. He told me not to show the ring to anyone—I had thought he was afraid the creditors would take it. "Keep it hidden until the time is right, Emily," he had said, and I often wondered what those words meant. But I remembered telling him the ring was a beautiful memento. "How the ruby glows," I had said.

"Like blood," he answered me. I was sure then it was the fever that made him rave. He said the ruby symbolized the blood shed, and that the diamonds were

20

the tears. He just kept saying it over and over again, "the blood and the tears." I didn't understand, and when I questioned him he became even more delirious. "The blood and the tears will bring the family back together," he had raved.

But perhaps my father wasn't delirious, I thought now, as I gazed upon the ring. Perhaps I *do* have a family, in Cornwall, awaiting my return to its fold. I almost didn't dare hope, and yet I did. It was all I could think about that evening as I ate my solitary dinner and the last thing I thought of as I rested my head on the pillow.

"The blood and the tears will bring the family back together." My father's words echoed in my mind until I was fast asleep.

The next morning I arrived at Mrs. Goodrich's shop. It was not yet unshuttered, it being far too early for the ladies of fashion to be abroad. I banged for a few moments at the door before it was answered by a short woman with graying hair, pinned up fashionably. Around her plump waist was a dark apron that contained a tailor's measure, scissors, and hemming needles.

"Good morning, Mrs. Goodrich," I began, and then explained my predicament.

All at once she was all business, running a practiced eye over my frame. "Mrs. Beade is a dear friend. And you may be in luck, Miss Emily. You can't imagine how fussy these young ladies are when it comes to their gowns. They describe to me what they want, and sometimes I work on a dress for weeks, and then they moan and say, 'Why that's not what I asked for at all!' It's enough to drive a body mad! Now just last week a young miss had a regular tantrum over three gowns, called me a clumsy idiot, and refused them all. Seems they weren't as grand as some her friend had just fetched home from Paris. She

21

was a mite bigger than you in the frame, Miss Emily, you're too thin, if I may say so, but I could have my seamstress take them in, nothing easier."

"But I could not pay the extra expense, Mrs. Goodrich, I am nimble with a thread. If one of them is suitable, I can take it in."

"Very well, then, have a seat and I will fetch them."

One was a sea green, a shimmering confection of silk, low in the bust, trimmed with lilac ribbons and tiny flowers, undoubtedly a dinner dress. The next was a yellow and white afternoon dress awash with lace. Neither were suitable for a visit to a solicitor, though I sighed over them.

"This is probably more appropriate, eh, Miss Emily?" Mrs. Goodrich held a suit in front of me before the mirror. It was a deep red traveling suit, with a collar trimmed with black velvet and a smart black hat to match. "And see how the color suits your dark hair and eyes!"

Indeed it was perfect, too perfect. "Mrs. Goodrich," I said and frowned. "It is lovely beyond my imaginings, but I am sure it is too costly, even at a bargain price."

"But it is worthless to me now and it will be out of style in a few months to boot. Tell you what, lass. I'll let you rent it for the day. And if fortune shines upon you, then we can speak of a price. You can't say fairer than that for the both of us."

"No, you can't say fairer than that." I said.

"And if you decide you want the other two dresses, Miss Emily, why I'd do the same again."

I smiled weakly as I paid for the rental of the traveling suit, using all the money that was in my reticule. If this was her "bargain rental price," I wondered, what inflated price would she charge the Baronet's niece, Emily Woodstock, to purchase it? If indeed this proved to be true.

Still, with many thanks I left the shop and rushed

home. My fingers flew as I took in the traveling suit and I had it ready by noon.

As I was leaving, Mrs. Beade caught me at the door. "You look the perfect lady now! And so beautiful," she said with that smug expression. "Don't forget your Mrs. Beade, *Lady* Woodstock."

I laughed. "I will not. Thank you so, Mrs. Beade."

"And hurry home. I cannot wait to hear the news."

I clutched tightly to a pound note as I went down the steps to the street. This was the last money I had saved for an emergency. I would hail a cab. I would not ruin my new skirts in the mud of the streets. I must look as good at the solicitors' offices as I did at this moment.

Even on our sorry street, I had no trouble hailing a cab in my new clothes. I supposed I looked like a lady who could pay.

I directed the driver to the address on the letter and settled back into the cushions. I tried not to think about what lay in store, happiness or disappointment. I smiled, shaking out my skirts, admiring the deep crimson.

"Even if I am the wrong Emily Woodstock," I said aloud, "it is wonderful to wear a new dress again!"

Chapter Two

The cab halted. I looked down at the letter for reassurance, then stepped out and paid the driver.

I saw that I was near Lincoln's Inn Fields, a square near the Royal Courts of Justice, where solicitors had hung their signposts for hundreds of years. The square was lovely, surrounded by brick buildings decorated with wrought iron, white shutters, stone lions, and plaster mouldings.

I stood beneath the brass plaque proclaiming the offices of Carrington and Phyfe and took a deep breath before ringing the bell, trying to suppress the wild nervousness that was all at once overtaking me. The door was opened by a gangly youth in clerk's clothing, who became very respectful when I told him my name and showed him the letter. He ushered me into a small waiting area, then disappeared into the back.

After only a few moments, a tall elderly man with stark white hair stepped out through a mahogany door inset with leaded glass. He was dressed in a costly black suit. His pink face held a mild expression, but his blue eyes were sharp behind his spectacles. His mouth was open to say something, but when he saw me, he shut it abruptly and stopped as though he were greatly taken aback. His eyes were wide, almost in amazement. His expression startled me.

Recovering himself almost immediately, he smiled and said,

"Miss Woodstock? I am William Carrington. I have handled the affairs of the Woodstocks for over twenty-five years now. This is indeed a pleasure. Perhaps you would care to step into my office?"

He held the heavy door open for me and then he followed me inside, closing it behind him. The office was simple and yet elegant in its appointments. Smooth polished brass lamps and a cherrywood desk and chairs. A thick Oriental carpet was below my feet and I was glad I had not had to walk through the muddy streets this day.

Mr. Carrington sat into his leather chair and shook his head, on his face an unmistakable trace of amusement. For some reason I felt at ease, so much so that I blurted out my first questioning thought.

"Mr. Carrington, I apologize, but is there something about me that amuses you?"

He hesitated for a moment and then smiled. "No, no. I am just very pleased. I know now that my search has come to an end." He leaned forward. "Quite amazing." He shook his head again and his eyes took on a faraway look. "You look exactly like her."

"Like who?" I asked, wondering how he could be so sure that I was the Emily Woodstock he was searching for by just one glance.

"Amelia. Amelia Woodstock. That was your mother's name, was it not?" he asked me lightly, as if he knew the answer already, and opened a folder that was before him on the desk.

"Yes, it was. You say that I look just like her. Did you know my mother, then?"

"Yes, indeed. The resemblance is remarkable. We shall still have to locate the documents as proof, of course, but there is no doubt in my mind that you are Sir Ralph's niece. So I feel I can inform you of the business at hand with a clear conscience. I am sure you are curious as to why you were called to my office." He pulled from the file a thick pile of official-looking papers.

"Miss Woodstock, can you tell me your birthdate?" He smiled at me as if to reassure my nervousness, which evidently was obvious to him.

"Yes, it is April 20, 1842. But Mr. Carrington—my father never mentioned that he had a brother, so I cannot possibly have an Uncle Ralph. You must be mistaken about me. A family is not something that a father would keep secret from his daughter, especially when he is dying and leaving her alone in the world." I felt a strange anger well up inside. I didn't want to believe my father could do such a thing to me. So it must be a mistake. All I wanted at that moment was to correct it straight away.

The solicitor regarded me gently with his wise eyes. "I know this will all come as quite a shock to you, since your father never told you that you had living relations, but I assure you that you just named the correct birthdate. I myself do not know all of the details, but your father and his brother Sir Ralph had a bitter quarrel after your mother . . . died. Since that time there was no correspondence, the silence was absolute. It did not make my task any easier in locating *your* whereabouts, Miss Woodstock."

"Mr. Carrington, you say my father and this Sir Ralph quarreled after my mother's death? Where did this quarrel take place? Here in London?" I asked, bewildered.

"No, my dear," he said with great sympathy. "At Edgecliff Manor."

"But I don't understand." I shook my head. "My mother died of the cholera, here in London, when I was but a year old."

He coughed, looking disconcerted. "Your father told

26

you that?"

I nodded.

"I wonder . . ." He paused to clear his throat and then continued slowly, as if he were carefully weighing each word. "Perhaps he was reluctant to speak of something that must have been very painful to him. Your mother fell to her death from the cliffs of Edgecliff Manor. It was a terrible tragedy."

I felt stunned, unable to decide whether he was speaking of *my* mother or some other Amelia Woodstock. "But Mr. Carrington, that would mean that I was born at Edgecliff, and—"

"Yes, you were." His voice was gentle.

"But . . . why did my father never tell me this? And that my mother fell from the cliffs, you say? How?"

"As to why your father never told you any of your family history . . ." He shrugged delicately. "But yes, your mother went walking one evening along the cliffs. It was very foggy. Some speculate that the cliffs simply gave way beneath her feet, others that she merely missed her footing in the fog."

I sat in silence, thinking of the terrible story . . . wondering why my father had never told me the truth.

"I am sorry to have disturbed you with such news," Mr. Carrington said softly. "I pray this will not dissuade you from my request. How soon will you be ready to travel to Cornwall?"

"What?" I asked, the shock of it all just barely invading my consciousness.

"Sir Ralph is in poor health. He is greatly sorry for the past and wishes to atone it with you, his closest relative. He wishes you to come to Edgecliff Manor, on the Cornish coast. It is one of the richest estates in all of southern England."

I felt a dizziness overtake me. *Richest?* "I am his closest relative? Surely, he must be married and with children?"

27

"No, but the estate is now occupied by your four third cousins, once removed. Sir Ralph made them his wards on the death of their parents. In any case, Sir Ralph has expressed a strong desire to see you and it would be a great act of charity for you to go. I know that he wishes to make his peace with the world before he departs it. He regrets the quarrel with your father, and your separation from the family."

All at once, it seemed, my fortunes had changed. From being a penniless music teacher and alone in the world, I was suddenly niece to a wealthy noble, and even had cousins as well.

"Of course I shall go. I shall leave as soon as I can arrange it with my pupils," I heard myself saying, as if in a dream. "Perhaps in a week's time."

"Good," he said briskly. "In a few days all the necessary documents as to your identity shall be in order. Parish records and so forth. But you may take my word, Miss Woodstock, that I know there to be no mistake in this matter. Sir Ralph will be very pleased when he learns you are coming."

I left the office in a daze, hardly remembering the ride home or climbing the stairs. Mrs. Beade was waiting in the doorway.

"What is it, Emily?" she cried, pulling me inside into the drawing room. "You look in shock. It's not bad news?"

"I *am* his niece," I said, sinking down into a chair. "Sir Ralph Woodstock is one of the richest men in England—and I am his closest relative."

She poured me a cup of tea and I had to go over every detail of my meeting at the offices of Carrington and Phyfe.

The next few days as I prepared for my departure, I felt I was caught up in a dream. It couldn't possibly be true. I was convinced that something would happen at the last

28

moment and I would go back to plain Miss Woodstock again, Cinderella back to the ashes.

But nothing of the kind happened. And to my great surprise, I actually found myself setting off very early one morning in a fine coach, wearing the red traveling suit, now mine, not rented. I had a draft from my uncle's bank, traveling money for the journey, the two other dresses from Mrs. Goodrich, and a few other necessities. I even had enough to pay Mrs. Beade the remainder of that month's room and board, with a little extra besides, which she pocketed with a smile.

The first light of dawn lit the street, making a halo of Mrs. Beade's silver white hair. I hung out of the coach window, waving at her. As we turned the corner, I lost sight of her.

The cab rumbled on through the slowly awakening streets, crowded with wagons on their way to the market. London sprawled everywhere around me, full of life and movement. The great gray edifices of the city loomed in the morning light, imposing monuments to the prosperity of our age, to the fact that Britain was queen among the colonies, the queen of trade. Then I caught a glimpse of the Thames, the houses of Parliament, and the famous outline of Westminster Abbey set against the pink of the morning sky.

And as I gazed at the crowded narrow streets of London, I wondered about the place I was going to, and the people I would meet there. The place where my mother had died. The thought cast a shadow. I reflected that I never showed Mr. Carrington the ring that had once belonged to my mother—I had forgotten in his offices, and later events had moved too quickly. Should I have told him about it? I wondered uneasily.

I looked down at the ring, the case open on my lap. The rubies and diamonds sparkled at me and I was mesmerized by their brilliance. But I also felt a foreboding. The blood

29

and the tears, my father had called it, an heirloom of the Woodstock family, which would bring it back together.

What did it all mean? I wondered, as I climbed into the coach that would take me to Cornwall. What was the tragedy that had caused my father to turn to drink and gambling? And why did the brothers quarrel?

I was going to the place where I might find answers to the secrets of my past. And I was bringing the ring—the ring that was to unite the family again—back where it belonged.

Edgecliff Manor.

Chapter Three

It was late afternoon, the sun beginning to wester, when we reached the Cornish town of Truro. The slanting rays touched the hills with golden light, and warmed the walls of the gray stone cottages clustered steeply over the harbor. I caught a glimpse of the sea, gray and turbulent.

The coach halted and I was glad to be leaving the cramped compartment. My muscles felt stiff as I stepped gratefully out for some fresh sea air. I took a deep breath, my eyes going to the curtain of green hills that rose behind town. Suddenly, I passionately hoped that I never had to go back to London.

I had loved every moment of the journey, viewing the countryside through my window. I was awed by the moors of Devon. To one whose life had hitherto been bounded by buildings, paved by streets, and fenced about by noise and dirt, the tumbled and broken moors, the endless hills of deep green moss, shrouded in mist against gray sky, were almost frightening. The shaggy denizens of the moor—the ponies and grazing sheep—were the only life. Now and then a thatched cottage or a church spire was the only indication that man dwelt there too.

I had fervently hoped there would be no moors near

Edgecliff, for those wild and untamed vistas, though fascinating, filled me with trepidation.

And I was not disappointed when we reached Cornwall. From the moment we crossed the River Tamar, I leaned forward, my nose glued to the window. I had heard that its folk believed it was a land of mystery, peopled by piskies, as they called them, and mischievous spirits. There were endless legends here, but to me the magic was in the green hills, so different from the grimy walls of London, the airy space of the soft sky above, the black rocks that crowned the steep cliffs, and the silver beaches where the waves broke like lace.

I looked around me to the streets of Truro. I admired the spires of the great cathedral and the many new and elegant buildings erected by rich tin and copper merchants. Although the narrow, tilted streets about me were crowded, they were so charming compared to the poverty-stricken streets I was used to. Already the earliest of flowers bloomed in the gardens.

Across the street, a housewife, scrubbing her front steps with a brush, looked up at me and smiled. I smiled back, thinking that I already loved it here. All at once a hand touched my elbow and I jumped.

"Aeer," I heard behind me. A small wizened man stood at my elbow. He touched his cap deferentially, his eyes growing wide as he leaned forward, peering up into my face. "You be Miss Emily. There's no mistaking that. Just like 'er you are. Aeer," he repeated and scrutinized me for a moment. "They won't be glad. I'm Polker. Come to fetch you out to the big house. I'll see to your bag."

"Polker, wait!" I cried after his retreating back. "Who won't be glad?" But he didn't turn, just made his way into the station. He shouldered his way back through the crowd to me, managing my bag easily for such a small man. I followed him to the carriage and asked him how far it was to Edgecliff as he handed me in. I knew the manor to be near the town of St. Just on the coast, but I did not know the distance we were to travel.

"Not o'er far," was all he replied. He seemed to have reached his conversational limit, so I gave up and settled back into the seat.

". . . Just like 'er you are," I mused as the carriage jounced off. He must mean my mother. So Polker knew my mother as well. But who won't be glad, and of what? Could he mean my cousins? I was already apprehensive about meeting them, afraid they would look down on me as a poor relation.

How I hoped not. I tried to picture them and reviewed in my mind how I would present myself, what I would say. And there was much that I wanted to know.

I grew more entranced by the countryside with every passing mile. We rode alongside the Truro River, and finally crossed it on a ferry. I watched the gulls wheel overhead and was enchanted by the beauty of the small fishing villages clinging precariously to the steep hills. The hours flew by, for Polker's idea of "not o'er far" seemed rather modest.

At last the trap made a sharp turn and we came upon a great gray stone gatehouse, and carved in the stone were the words EDGECLIFF MANOR. My heart started to beat at a rapid pace. A woman with a small child at her skirts curtsied as we passed, staring curiously.

We were passing through rolling parkland, green and beautifully kept. The elms and oaks had girths wide enough that they must have been standing for hundreds of years. Under them, the lawns stretched smooth as emerald, dotted with bright white sheep. I glimpsed neat borders and a mist of bluebells beneath the forest of rhododendrons that grew along the drive.

All at once a wizened old woman, wrapped in a dark shawl, jumped into the road in front of us, frightening the horses. Involuntarily, Polker drew rein so that we

33

stopped beside her. It was me she spoke to, fixing me with her dark eyes: "So ye come to complete the circle. Beware the curse. Go back before it's too late!" Her wild gaze took mine and held. I felt a chill pass through me.

"Get away, ye old witch!" Polker yelled, flapping the reins and starting the trap again.

The old woman let out a cackling laugh, shook her long, tangled gray hair with a toss of her head, and disappeared behind an ancient tree.

"Who is that, Polker?" I asked, trembling, as we continued up the drive.

"Er? Ah, 'ers Malvina. The witch-woman she be called. Lives in a cottage by the sea. Folk go to her for herbs and potions. But she be a bad one. You stay out of 'er sight if ye don't want t'evil eye put on you."

I shivered, feeling her intense glance again. "I fear she already has," I murmured. Her warning was directed at me. How strange. For surely I could have no connection to a curse in a place where I had never been. Her words were nonsense by all counts. It was 1862, after all, and no one believed in witches or curses any longer. Except, I thought, my good humor restored, evidently Polker still did.

I smoothed my hair nervously as I stared out the window. There was a curve in the road. I caught the smell of sea air, and then I remember gasping.

"One of the richest estates in southern England," I had been told, but that description didn't prepare me for Edgecliff.

Green cliffs gave way suddenly to black rock, tumbled cliffs that dove to meet the sea. Perched on the cliffs, seemingly at their very edge, stood Edgecliff. It seemed enormous and overwhelming in its beauty. It towered like a gray castle, with a wing on each side, jutting crenellated towers and many-windowed walls. At first glance it almost looked like a jagged outcropping of the cliffs themselves. But sunset mellowed the gray of the ancient walls with warmer, softer shades, and the windows glittered like topaz and rubies. Spread on both sides were intricate formal gardens of roses, rhododendrons, and sculptured trees.

Soon the coach drew up with a flourish on the gravel sweep in front of the house. My heart leapt with excitement. I sat back, took a deep breath, and waited for Polker to open the door.

I stepped from the coach with some trepidation. And I stood uncertainly a moment, feeling the gravel through the thin soles of my shoes, as Polker unloaded my bag. Should I walk forward and ring? I wondered. Or wait in the wind for someone to notice that the coach had arrived?

The carven doors opened then, much to my relief, and I began to walk forward, trying to hold my head high and my shoulders straight, awkwardly conscious of the sea wind whipping through my hair unmercifully. I could hear the breakers on the beach, a low thunder that must be an unceasing sound here. Once this was my father's house, I thought, in a kind of wonder. Why had he never let me know of such origins?

A butler was standing in the door, all in black, stiff and formal. All at once a young man brushed past him, starting down the gray stone steps toward me. The setting sun caught his hair and turned it to gold.

He took my hand and gave me a dazzling smile. But before he smiled, his eyes widened for only a moment, or was I mistaken?

"Cousin Emily!" he said, bowing. "I am Charles, the second eldest." He laughed disarmingly. "By George, I'm glad you've come! We were worried you might hold it against Uncle and not come. He is so anxious to see you. But come in! I must not keep you out in the cold. The damp sea air can be a cruel thing if one isn't used to it.

35

Polker, bring in Miss Emily's bags!" He led me up the wide stone steps. "The others are chafing at the bit to meet you."

All at once he made me feel as if he were a long-lost friend who could share his utmost confidence. His blue eyes were warm and appreciative. But I caught a slight glimpse of calculation in them when he spoke of being worried whether I would come. The tiniest flash of ice, perhaps, at once melted by a rush of tropic warmth?

When we reached the door, the stiffest and most pompous-looking of butlers stood waiting to receive us.

Charles took my cloak and handed it to the butler, saying sunnily, "Cousin Emily, this is Penwillen, been with the family forever."

Penwillen took my cloak with just a brief nod. His heavy florid face held no more expression than a block of wood.

"It's just teatime," Charles said. "I'm sure you would love a cup after your long journey. We shall go to the drawing room and meet the others and then you can rest a bit before dinner."

I followed him into the entrance hall, a large room with a beautifully laid mosaic floor that formed a square around a thick exotic carpet in the center. Directly in front of me was a massive stone fireplace. An intricately carved rosewood staircase flanked the room on either side, leading up to what looked to be another two stories.

"How beautiful it is!" I could not help exclaiming. "I feel as if I've stepped into a castle!"

"Hardly," Charles laughed, his blue eyes sparkling. "But it is quite grand, forty-one rooms, scads of acreage, and a chapel as well." His voice betrayed no sense of boasting. He seemed to feel almost the same excitement as I with Edgecliff.

"How old is the house?" I asked.

"That is where looks deceive. Edgecliff Manor was

36

built a mere century ago. Until then the Woodstocks were not much more than country squires, I am afraid. We have no long lineage of nobility to brag about," he said, crossing the room. "In any case, Emily, your direct ancestor William Woodstock came into some money in the 1720s, just how being the disputed fact—though most agree it was by disreputable means."

"Are you saying that we are the descendents of a criminal?" I stepped up alongside him and we entered a long hallway in the East wing.

"No one knows for sure, but most likely William Woodstock was a smuggler. In these parts an almost respected way to make money. Some say it was the foundation of the Woodstock fortunes. And here he is." Charles stopped before a small portrait of a man in the prime of his life, his rich black hair gracing the collar of a fine green velvet coat. His eyes held a devilish quality.

"He does have the look of a pirate, does he not?" I could not help remarking.

"That he does. But William invested wisely, land, tin mines, china clay, and shipping. By the time he died he was a rich man, knighted for his contributions to the crown, no matter that he was a smuggler." Charles turned to look at me then, his eyes brilliant with mischief. "How does it feel knowing you are related to a pirate?" he asked and gave me a devilish smile.

The impact of it took me off guard and I stepped back. "How does it feel indeed?"

"I rather like it," he teased. "Pirates are well known to cut a dash with the ladies. I hope I have inherited some of that charm."

It flowed from him so naturally that I didn't doubt it to be true. "I am sure you are quite practiced at being charming to the ladies."

"But it's easy to be charming to someone as pretty as you are," he said, blue eyes sparkling. "But as pleasant as

37

it is, I must not keep you to myself any longer. I'll give you a full tour later. I shall enjoy it. And I am the natural one to do it. Richard is far too dour to care about being charming to the ladies. Now, the drawing room is the next room down the hall, and we must make haste, the others are waiting. Annabel in particular will have my head if I keep you much longer."

The charm flowed from him so naturally, so secure he was in this that I felt guarded. Something about his manner seemed too kind to a stranger in his household and words of compliment flowed too easily to his tongue. For no matter how smart I looked in my new red traveling suit, I knew that I must pale in comparison to the fine ladies of distinction that he was used to.

As we made our way down the hall, I inquired after Uncle Ralph. Charles told me that I should not be able to see him until the following morning, for he had spent a restless night and the doctor had been summoned. "He is at his best in the morning after a good night's rest. You will be shown up to see him directly after breakfast tomorrow."

We reached a large door at the end of the hallway.

"We are all here except Richard, the eldest. He is off on business to Penzance—seeing Uncle's lawyer, I believe. For some reason Uncle keeps sending for him, poor devil. Perhaps he plans to cut us all off without a shilling!" Charles said and opened the door with a laugh as if he found the idea amusing. But what I saw flash in his eyes betrayed something other than good humor.

Two pairs of eyes stared at me as I walked in and I managed what I hoped was a friendly smile at them. My first impression was confused and I didn't even notice the lovely drawing room until later. I stood fixed, speechless in the doorway until Charles took my arm and led me forward.

38

"This is our long-lost cousin Emily, dear brother and sister." They were a handsome family, all of them. "Let me present them in order of age. First, this is William, my younger brother."

William I liked immediately as he took my hand and smiled at me. Although he looked only to be about twenty-three years of age, his face bespoke a steadfastness that made him seem much older. He had dark brown hair and calm blue eyes and was good-looking, though he had none of Charles's flash. Later I learned that he was, in fact, twenty-four, while Charles was twenty-seven and Richard, the oldest, was thirty-one.

"Welcome to the family, cousin Emily. It's very good to have you with us after so long." William seemed shy and solid and his tone much more sincere and less practiced than Charles's. I found this comforting.

The girl seated on the sofa was as unlike her two brothers in looks as possible. She was a green-eyed beauty with straight black hair that was as dark and shiny as jet.

"This is Annabel," Charles said. "The youngest in the family, a mere sixteen."

Annabel gave a little bounce in her seat, saying, "Cousin Emily, at last! I've been so curious about you and London! *I'm* glad to have you as a cousin." She smiled up at me, the emphasis implying that perhaps not everyone was as glad. She was slender and brimming with mischief, a wild little pixie. I smiled back, liking her at once.

"And I'm nearly seventeen, Charles, and I'll thank you to remember it!" she reprimanded.

"At seventeen little girls turn into ladies," Charles replied. "When you begin to act as such, we will all remember."

"Perhaps Cousin Emily will be a good example for her,

Charles," William said, then turned to me. "I do hope you are not too fatigued from your journey to partake in a cream tea. Cornish cream is famous."

"And most fattening!" Annabel chimed in. "But then you would look better if you gained some weight, Emily."

I shot her a curious look, and saw that Charles was frowning at her almost forbiddingly. "I am not in the least fatigued and would enjoy some tea," I answered, feeling provisionally encouraged by my first impression of my cousins. At least, they showed no signs of assigning me to the servants' hall.

I took the chair Charles offered me. Just then Penwillen and two footmen entered with the tea, creating a confusion that was welcome to me. For a few precious moments, I was not the center of attention and could gather my composure. The tea was poured to the accompaniment of Annabel's and Charles's amicable bickering.

Charles seated himself near me, lifting his brows with a good-natured exasperation at his sister. I felt more at ease and my mental image of my haughty cousins was fast disappearing.

"How do you find Cornwall?" William addressed me as he handed me a cup of tea.

"It must seem quite wild and lonely after London," put in Charles.

"London, tell us about London!" cried Annabel eagerly.

"Really, Annabel," Charles said. "Let Emily answer one question at a time. We don't wish to *confuse* her."

Annabel quieted and looked away from me.

"I . . . I do find it very different than London. But it is a welcome change," I answered Charles's question, not wishing to appear *confused*, though his emphasis did confuse me. "London is tedious, so constantly gray and grimy, one longs for a glimpse of green. I think I have fallen in love with Cornwall already."

"London tedious?" Annabel asked in a disbelieving tone. "I shouldn't think it would be tedious, not with all the shops and theaters and balls to go to! I should love to visit London."

"Well, I am glad to be free of it." I sighed. "After all, a music teacher doesn't often get a chance to do those things. I am afraid it's been several years since I've been to the opera or a play."

"Well, you are the most beautiful teacher I have ever seen," said Annabel, not quite to the point, as though this fact alone should have guaranteed entrance to the opera for me. "You should have seen my governesses! Positive horrors, every one!"

"Emily was not a governess, Annabel," reproved Charles, as though that would have been a great social blot indeed. "She taught music, did you not, Cousin Emily? Much more refined. And you are the only Woodstock I know of with musical leanings, except your mother. She played, did she not?"

There was a sudden silence.

"Yes, she played, although . . ." I paused, bewildered at their faces. For a moment I felt compelled to ask my cousins about my mother, if they knew anything more. But I remained silent. Only the mention of her and there seemed to be a dark curtain drawn upon their expressions.

"We may not play, but we all ride," broke in Annabel, and there seemed to be a general sense of relief. "I hope you ride, Emily. It is the only way to see the entire estate."

Immediately the conversation became fixed on riding. Everyone was shocked when I confessed I could not ride and vowed that I must learn.

"Then you will need a proper riding habit," William said.

"But until then," said Annabel, "you can wear one of

41

mine, for I have many more than I know what to do with."

"Indeed she does," Charles laughed. "And it's all that we can do to get her out of them and into a dress for dinner."

"Now Charles, I'll hear no more!" she said. "For you're always teasing me about my riding and calling me a tomboy!" Then she offered to show me to my room and I accepted. I suddenly found myself quite tired.

"I don't think I'll come down to dinner tonight," I said. "I think the journey is catching up with me."

"Quite, quite," Charles said, following us to the door of the drawing room. "We will have many nights to enjoy your company at dinner, I hope. I will have a tray sent to your room."

Annabel took me up to my room, chattering all the way, and I had a chance to see more of Edgecliff. It was vast, and I was sure I would need a map to find my own way through the twisting passages to the dining room in the morning.

Annabel opened the door to my room with a flourish and then took her leave. It was grander than any place I had ever imagined staying. The windows overlooked the cliffs and the sea. There was an enormous fireplace and a huge four-poster bed that I thought I would be quite lost in. My bags had been unpacked and a fire was crackling. There was even a steaming bath ready in the adjoining dressing room. After soaking in the bath, I climbed under the heavy covers and thought about my cousins, and speculated about Richard, the eldest, the "dour" one as Charles had called him.

What manner of man was he? I wondered. Would he welcome me into the family as the others had? I hoped that I would find in him someone to speak with me frankly about the family and about the past.

But most of all I wondered about my uncle, Sir Ralph

Woodstock, my closest living relative. What manner of man was *he* that could leave his brother to die in poverty?

Tomorrow, I should learn the answers to my questions. At last I drifted into a fitful sleep, filled with dreams of crashing waves on black jagged rocks and the cold stone walls of Edgecliff.

Chapter Four

I will never forget my first day at Edgecliff. The singing of birds awakened me. None of their songs was familiar. How different and beautiful this was! It seemed as though a hundred songbirds were vying with one another beneath my window. I rose, enchanted, and crossed the room to open the window and lean out.

It was barely dawn of a lovely spring morning. The world was bathed in delicate light, and the heavy dew of the night before had drenched the lawn with sparkles. The cliffs were not as close to the house as they had appeared from the front. Gardens and lawns sloped gently down to the rocks, and a footpath ran along the cliff's edge. The sea was calm, a brilliant turquoise that deepened to sapphire farther out.

Although I had been told that breakfast was early, I was certain the household wouldn't be up and about yet. Only a faint clatter below my window told me the servants were busy in the kitchen. I was seized with a desire to be out and walking on this glorious morning. How free I would feel, slipping the shackles of the city at last! A bath in the pure air would cleanse the grime of London once and for all.

Hastily, I dressed in my red traveling suit, only

44

pausing before the glass long enough to make sure my hair was smooth. I was momentarily arrested by the sparkle in my eyes. Country air and excitement were agreeing with me.

Once in the hall, I paused to think of how to find the way downstairs and outside through the seemingly endless maze of Edgecliff. I slipped quietly along to the main staircase, and down. Though the clatter in the kitchens at the back was still evident, I met no maid or footmen as I walked across the wide, echoing entrance hall and let myself out.

I circled around the formal gardens in front of the house to the wild and tumbling gardens I had spied from my window. I noticed the sloping lawns beyond were blocked by a high wall. But there was a gate in the wall, and to my relief, it was unlocked.

Through the gate, and then I was alone with the morning. The air was fresh and bracing as I walked over green fields toward the sea. The earliest flowers peeped from the turf, larks and sea gulls spiraled upward in the strengthening sunrise, and I was surrounded by the smell and the sound of the sea. Such a soft and vibrantly colorful sky was something I had never imagined, accustomed as I was to the sooty pall that hung over London. It felt wonderful to be walking on deep, springy turf after a lifetime spent on pavement, and I couldn't resist. Impulsively, I bent to take off my shoes and stockings, and picked a tiny flower and stuck it behind my ear.

I paused and looked at the cliffs, so beautiful on this morning. But they must be treacherous in the dark, in the fog. Had this been where my mother had gone walking, that tragic day? The thought brought a poignant sadness that tinged my mood, but I felt an almost mystical rightness to being here. It was almost as if my mother were at my side, in the wind, touching me with her love, telling me she was happy I was here now.

"I have come home, Mother," I whispered. "To heal the family quarrel."

I felt quite clearly it was what she would have wanted.

Drawn, I came to the cliff's edge. I could suddenly understand why early peoples worshipped the sun. The sea moved endlessly below in wild majesty, stained with rose and gold. The beaches shimmered, untouched by footprints. If I didn't turn to see the house, I could fancy myself alone at the dawn of time.

I walked along the cliff path at the edge of the plunging black rocks. Suddenly the path branched, one part leading down the steep cliff. I considered it for a moment, having a fleeting momentary fear, wondering if *this* was where the tragedy occurred. I shivered and then looked around me. The cliffs stretched for miles on every side; surely it was not here. It was a clear path and looked well used. I decided to go down the path, for the spirit of adventure was running strong in me that morning.

I started down, leaving my shoes and stockings at the top. I wanted to walk near the sea on those inviting beaches.

"Stop!"

I was arrested by the sound of a masculine voice breaking into the peaceful morning. I could not have been more startled. I turned and climbed a little way back, straining to see over the rocks who the owner of the voice was.

"Don't you know it's dangerous there?" the voice went on. "Here—I'll help you back up."

A brown hand was extended over the top, and I grasped it, for the climb back was steeper and harder than I would have thought. I had to give my attention to where my feet were placed, as the owner of the hand hauled me strongly over the top.

A man was standing there, regarding me with some amusement. I had never seen him before. He was dark,

46

with hair as black as I had ever seen, and strong brows against a bronzed face. His jaw was square and sharp, his cheekbones high, his nose well marked. And his eyes were green, unusual in a face that might otherwise have belonged to a gypsy. Grass green, and laughing now. I was at once painfully aware of my state.

Barefoot, my hair flying in the wind, mud on the hem of my dress. He was handsome. Meeting those eyes sent a strange jolt through me.

"I am sorry to interrupt your excursion," he said, his eyes crinkled with amusement. "But the tide is just coming in, and it's not a place for the unwary to go walking. I misdoubt you could have made the climb back up without a great deal of difficulty and not a little damage to your clothes. There is an easier path further on I could show you, and you could try it this afternoon when the tide is out."

"I—thank you." I was at a loss what to say. My eyes went over his rough tweed coat and spattered corduroys. From his clothes and the breadth of his powerful shoulders and work-roughened hands, I realized he must be an estate worker. A farmhand, perhaps, or a stableman. "I realize now it was foolish to attempt the climb down, but I am new here."

He smiled, a flash of white teeth against tanned skin. "I know that, for I know everyone on the estate and we don't often get strangers here. But I think I can hazard a guess as to who you are." His eyes traveled over my clothing to my bare feet, then came to rest on the flower behind my ear. "You are, perhaps, a nature lover? Or even a wood nymph?" His green gypsy eyes brimmed with amusement.

My cheeks flamed. "I am—"

"Whoever you are, we have not been properly introduced. I am Richard Woodstock."

Richard Woodstock! I gaped at him. I had met my

cousin at last! No farm worker or gypsy lad, but the virtual master of the domain of Edgecliff.

"I am Emily Woodstock," I replied, summoning all the dignity I could gather, barefoot and disheveled as I was. I remembered his sardonic glance at the flower in my hair, and I moved to take it off. But his hand stayed mine, and lingered a moment on my wrist.

"Don't. It looks lovely. But of course I know you are my cousin Emily. You have the Woodstock look."

I thought of Mr. Carrington. "I have heard this." I looked over my shoulder, at the steep and jagged cliffs and they mesmerized me for a moment. I could almost see my mother lying there, at the base of the rocks, still and ghostlike.

Richard broke the silence, shaking me from my imaginings. "I am happy to meet you at last—and delighted to have met you in such an unconventional way."

"I . . . you must forgive me," I said. "I wanted to get outdoors, breathe the sea air. I didn't expect to meet anyone."

"Of course." He smiled. "Dryads never expect to meet anyone, do they?"

"You tease me so!" I could not help laughing. "It is too bad of you. I assure you, a dryad I am not. I am very sedate generally, and observe the proprieties as well as anyone else, but this spring dawn was too bewitching to resist. I find I am falling in love with the country already. A lifetime here would not be enough to make me feel clean of London."

"Bewitching indeed," he replied gravely. "But can I believe my ears? Do I really find before me a young lady of fashion who actually prefers the country to the city, and does not pine for the glitter of London?"

"You do," I replied with some decision. "But I must also confess you do not find before you a young lady of

48

fashion, cousin. If you saw the quarter I inhabited in London, you'd not wonder why I was glad to quit it."

He looked at me thoughtfully then. "Come, if I might escort you back to the house? Breakfast should soon be on the board, and I think you'll find the country air lends a noble appetite. For you are too thin," he added nonchalantly.

"Is everyone in the country so fond of plumpness, then? For I have been told this before."

"Let us just say that we have a clear picture of how you would look were you to . . . fill out a little."

I puzzled over this remark as I bent to pick up my shoes . . . and over the man at my side. Charles had described his brother Richard as dour. This could surely not be the same man! He was warm, polite, charming, his green eyes brimming over with laughter and teasing. Yes . . . he had certainly charmed me.

I wondered what it was about him that so instantly fascinated me. Charles was as handsome, more polished, elegant. Richard was taller than Charles, with broad shoulders that made him look as if he were no stranger to manual labor. His frame was slender, and even in his rough work clothes, he moved with an easy grace. I wished I had met him in better circumstances. What would he think of me? Doubtless that I was uncouth, common. I resolved to show him the opposite was true, that I was worthy of my breeding.

As if he'd read my mind, he smiled and said, "Emily, don't worry about this morning. I can see by your frown that you are embarrassed. But I'm happy to meet a fellow lover of the outdoors. When I arrived home early this morning, I put on my working clothes for a ramble along the cliffs. It's what I love best, and I wouldn't trade it for anything on earth. The family abhors this ungentlemanly trait in me. That, and the fact that I barely have time for social pleasures. I find Edgecliff and its concerns as

49

absorbing a society as I could wish for."

"I can well understand that," I said quietly. "For I begin to feel it myself, lately though I am come."

His eyes approved me. "Then it will be our secret, this morning walk." We were approaching the house. "There is a side door there you can go in. I promise to be properly surprised when I meet you at breakfast." He smiled at me.

I smiled back. "Thank you for being so understanding. I shudder to think what this encounter would have been like if you'd been as you were described to me."

"Ah, the family gossips already?" He laughed. "Charles, I would hazard. He simply cannot understand the fact that I enjoy work. He thinks it makes me a terribly dull fellow. But poor Charles. Think of what he misses—such beauty—by not being up with the sun." His eyes gave his words a double meaning, and I suddenly felt breathless. "I shall enjoy being fellow conspirators, and having a secret to share with you. And I'll dare to tell you a secret. I take a walk at this time every morning along the cliffs, and now I hope that sometimes I will meet a dryad on my walk."

Flustered, I could feel pink staining my cheeks, and I couldn't meet his eyes. I felt like a schoolgirl rather than a staid schoolteacher. Confused, awkward, I murmured a jumbled thanks and goodbye, and turned to go to the side door he'd pointed out.

And felt his eyes on my back the whole way.

I changed quickly once I reached my room, choosing a dark blue skirt and pale blue shirtwaist that I was sure made me look most demure. My head was awhirl. I never thought a single meeting could so affect me. It had been an enchanting few moments. Standing before the glass, I smiled at the blush on my cheeks and reached into the bureau for the leather casket. I removed the ruby ring, speculating if *now* was the time to produce it. The *time* that my father had spoken of with his last breath.

Suddenly, I was startled by a knock on the door and I slipped the ring into my skirt pocket. "Come in," I called.

A woman with the coldest face I have ever beheld on this earth entered. All in black she was dressed, black was her hair, and black her impenetrable eyes. Her skin was as white as a winding sheet. I had not encountered the dark Cornish yet, but later I realized she was a perfect example of the Spaniards who had long ago raided these coasts. I felt an unbidden chill when I met her eyes, which widened when she saw me, but then became more shuttered than before.

"Good morning, miss," she said. "I am Mrs. Kerrenslea, the housekeeper. I have come to show you down to breakfast. The family awaits you. Sir Ralph will see you directly after you have breakfasted. I care for him as well as the house. For thirty years. This way, please, if you are ready."

I found her words strange, as if there was a veiled threat in her manner. "How nice to meet you, Mrs. Kerrenslea," I said. "I am Emily Woodstock."

"This way, please," she merely repeated.

I followed her tall, black back in silence. Presently we heard a babble of voices. She opened the door to the breakfast room and left me without a word. I saw at a glance that all the cousins were there.

"Good morning, Emily," cried Charles, leaping up from his seat. "I see you have met our pet horror."

"Shush!" giggled Annabel. "What will Emily think?"

"Well, she is, but for all that, she nurses Uncle Ralph with great devotion," answered Charles, unabashed.

Richard and William had risen on my entrance. My heart beat faster at the sight of Richard. He was now quite splendid in a dark suit, impeccably cut, but sober in com-

51

parison to Charles's checked shooting jacket and drab breeches, pale yellow waistcoat, and snowy cravat.

I was conscious that I also looked impeccably severe, every inch the music teacher. My hair was drawn back into a smooth knot, and my high-collared blouse was very plain. Suddenly, as I met Richard's eyes, I hoped I didn't look too plain.

"I am pleased to finally present your cousin Richard to you, Emily," exclaimed Charles, radiant with good humor. "Richard Woodstock, meet our long-lost cousin, Miss Emily Woodstock."

We exchanged formal bows. "Pleased to meet you, Cousin Emily," he said gravely, not a hint of our morning meeting on his face. "Welcome to Edgecliff." He was almost stern. None of the morning's sparkle remained in his green eyes.

"Come, Emily—grab a plate. I'm sure you're famished!" piped Annabel. "Now that you've been welcomed to the kingdom by the Lord of the Manor and all that. She went without dinner last night, Richard! Something I could never do."

The moment's tension of my second meeting with Richard was broken, and I went to the food-laden sideboard as chatter broke out all around me.

"Good morning, Cousin Emily," said William, managing to look both kind and slightly abashed. "If you skipped dinner last night, I am sure you must be hungry. Let me get a plate for you."

"Watch out, Emily! William eats like a farmhand! He's Richard's right-hand man, and they both spend their time mucking around with the pigs all day, so no doubt he'll give you too much!" laughed Annabel.

It seemed she was right, for though William reddened at her teasing, he piled a great plate for me with bacon, eggs, kippers, toast, marmalade, fried tomatoes, and mushrooms, and I managed to shake my head at the kidneys. The men were drinking ale, but I accepted a cup of tea and took my place at the table.

Talk soon turned to when I would take a tour of Edgecliff. They all seemed anxious to escort me, except Richard, who took little part in the discussions. Now and again, he threw a repressive look at Annabel or Charles when they argued, and I was interested to see it was enough to stop them. In a few moments, he rose. William hastily put down his napkin and rose too.

Everyone looked up at him. "I will take Emily on a tour of Edgecliff this afternoon," he said. "William, we must meet with the steward."

"But . . ." Charles began to say.

"It has been decided," Richard said flatly and there was no arguing with his tone.

He strode from the room, William at his heels, and the door closed behind him, leaving me with a sense that a strong presence had vanished.

"The heir apparent." Charles dabbed his lips with a napkin. "He fancies himself the crown prince," he added with a light malice that surprised me.

"You know he runs things excellently—better than they've been in generations," protested Annabel. "I'd like to see you try your lazy hand at it, Charles. You know you'd hate it, as you do all work!"

Charles laughed, his sunny nature never clouded for long. "You are quite right, Annabel, I must agree with you. We should all count ourselves fortunate that the family produced such a hard-working devil as Richard to take over the reins when Uncle fell ill. I am glad Richard is so passionately concerned with Edgecliff, so I don't have to be," he concluded with a glance at me.

"Edgecliff is not his only passion," said Annabel mischievously, but I heard no more of this interesting subject.

Just then, Mrs. Kerrenslea appeared like a shadow in

53

the doorway. She waited silently for me to excuse myself from my cousins, and then with a "This way, please, miss," she led me up the stairs, to meet my uncle at last.

I followed Mrs. Kerrenslea's black back up the great staircase, putting a hand to my hair to smooth it. I was apprehensive, my heart beating too rapidly. At last I was to meet the man I had come so many miles to see. My closest relative.

Yet would it be a happy meeting? He had quarreled bitterly with my father. Apprehensive as I was to meet my uncle, I was at the same time eager. Perhaps he would tell me about the quarrel, why the brothers became enemies. And perhaps he would speak to me about my mother's death. I longed to hear more than the bare details Mr. Carrington had told me.

Mrs. Kerrenslea opened two great dark doors near the head of the stairs. She regarded me coldly.

"I shall not be far, if you need me. As you may. It will be a great shock to him, to see you. He is not strong. Be sure to call me if you need me." She turned and walked down the hall without waiting for a reply, leaving me standing in front of the yawning doors.

Why should seeing me be a shock to him? Surely he had been told of my arrival.

I paused for a moment, my hand on the door handle and suddenly it came to me that *now* was the time. All during breakfast the ring seemed to burn inside my pocket but the moment never came for me to show it. This, I decided was the perfect opportunity. I would wear the ring and Uncle Ralph would see it and it would bring him pleasure.

Taking a deep breath for courage, I walked through the doors. It was gloomy, hard to see at first. Dark red curtains had been drawn across all the windows, shutting out the daylight. A single lamp burned by his bedside. The rest of the massive room was dim, filled with looming

54

shapes of heavy furniture.

I approached the great bed slowly. It, too, was hung with dark red curtains, and seemed to be a piece of furniture from another age. A bed of state, fit for royalty to sleep in, to give birth in, to die in. The very size of the bed seemed to invest the scene, the dying man lying in the middle of it, with a certain grandeur and solemnity.

My uncle's eyes were closed, and I stood a moment, looking down at him. He seemed not to have heard my approach over the thick Oriental carpet. Once, he must have been a magnificent figure. But disease had wasted him. Command was etched in his firm lips and chin, but so was suffering. His skin looked grayish in the feeble light, his cheeks sunken. Yet his iron gray hair was immaculately brushed, and he wore a rich maroon robe over his pajamas. Clearly, he was well cared for, and giving in to his illness as little as possible.

"Sir Ralph," I said softly, after mastering an urge to turn and leave the room before he opened his eyes.

He stirred. "Kerrenslea?" he asked, turning his head, and opening his eyes, he fixed them on me. Then he gasped and all color fled from his face.

"Amelia!" he cried. "You have come to trouble my rest?"

I was shocked to hear him utter my mother's name. "No, Uncle, it is Emily, your niece—Amelia's daughter," I said gently. "I have come to see you, as you wished. Are you all right, Uncle?"

He stared at me for some time, his face still alarmingly white, then seemed to collect himself. "Of course . . . Emily," he said at last. "Forgive me, child. I thought for one moment . . . Come closer. I am not so strong as I once was. Bring a chair and sit beside me so I can look at you."

I obeyed, and sat as near to him as I could.

"So lovely," he mused, seeming lost in thought as he

stared at me. Then he roused himself. "I am glad you have come, Emily. Welcome to Edgecliff, child. You should have been here long ago." He shook his head, his eyes full of regret, then went on more briskly, "But enough of that for now. Tell me about you, and your father, a little of all the years I have missed."

I hesitated, not knowing exactly what to say. I wanted to spare this wreck of a man's feelings. Yet—he must have known how it would fare for us, left with so little to live on. I decided to be honest, but tactfully, if possible.

"As I believe you know, Uncle, my father passed away just over two years ago. The doctor said his constitution just gave out, and he succumbed to a fever." I did not add that the years of worry, of drinking and of gambling, and the unhealthiness of the poor quarter we lived in, took their toll and had taken him too young. "Fever is common in London," I added, thinking, commoner still where we lived, in a neighborhood where the doctors rarely come, and then all they do is shake their heads and go away, saying "It is with God."

I forced myself to shut the door on such thoughts, and went on, "We lived in a small house near St. Paul's until my father died. At times we prospered and were gay, but much of the time we were poor. He never spoke of any relations at all to me." I saw the frown on my uncle's face, and sought to put a bright cast to my words, something to lessen his guilt. "But we were happy, Uncle. There was much love in our house, poor though it was. My father always had time and a smile for me. He would come home and take me up on his lap and tell me stories, and spend hours walking with me through the markets. And he always saw to it that I had the finest education."

My uncle was still frowning. "His annuity kept you, then? It should have been enough, I thought, and yet I understand that when he died, it was all gone."

He gambled. I left the words unspoken, but they rang

loudly in my mind. "Yes," I answered, uncomfortable, not wanting to blacken my father in my uncle's eyes. "I believed I was alone in the world. Everything was sold to pay the debts, but some friends were kind, and found me some positions teaching music to their daughters." I stopped, not wanting to reveal my great poverty, not willing to say any more.

"I see." Suddenly my uncle's gray eyes were keen, and I had the feeling he saw all too well. I guessed that my Uncle Ralph knew more than he let on. Perhaps Mr. Carrington had told him the truth about my father's gambling.

I looked at him, wondering what more to say.

"It should not have been so, Emily," he said after a few moments. "You have Woodstock blood and should have been treated as a Woodstock. I shall never forgive myself for what happened so long ago. Nor for not finding you sooner. But I only learned of my brother's death recently. Now you are here, Emily, and you must regard Edgecliff as your home forever."

With those words I knew my chance had come. I raised my hand purposefully, to brush away a strand of hair. Uncle Ralph had not yet noticed the ring and I had wanted him to see it before asking what I longed to know. "Thank you, Uncle," I began. "If I may I ask why you and my father—"

"No!" he interrupted with a sudden choke, again turning deadly pale. His eyes were fixed on my hand. He stared as if transfixed, his face a ghastly color.

"Uncle!" I cried, leaning forward. Then I jumped up and ran to the door, calling for Mrs. Kerrenslea.

She appeared almost instantly from a nearby door, and brushed quickly past me to my uncle's bedside. With scarcely more than a glance at him, she spoke some soothing words and readied a draught of medicine at the bedside table. She held his head while he drank it, and he sunk back into the pillows, looking gray and drained. I still stood in the doorway, my hands clasped anxiously before me, watching helplessly.

Mrs. Kerrenslea turned and saw me then, and came to my side in one swift motion, her pale face virulent with anger—or perhaps it was hatred.

"Get out of here," she hissed. "Can't you see you've done enough harm? He mustn't see you again. You should never have come here!"

I stood frozen for a moment, then turned and fled that darkened room.

Chapter Five

My heart was beating wildly when I stopped at the top of the stairs, clutching the newel post for support. I could hardly catch my breath.

When I'd first come in, Uncle Ralph had mistaken me for my mother. Could it have been a shock to see a lost face from his youth, the dead seemingly come back to life? Or was it something more?

I looked down at the ring. Had the sight of it brought on his attack? What mystery did it embody, the nature of which I was unaware?

I shook my head. I was becoming as fanciful as the Cornish. But then—my Uncle Ralph was Cornish, and he was ill and old. Maybe the sight of the ring, my mother's ring, made him forget who I really was, made him believe that a ghost stood at his bedside.

I shivered. It was unnerving to be taken for a ghost.

Just then Mrs. Kerrenslea came gliding out of my uncle's room. She stopped before me, eyes black and icy as a tarn in winter.

"Young lady, I must forbid you to enter his room again. You cannot see him again until his doctor has come. It is too great a strain on him to see you, and he is too ill to stand it. I am sure the doctor will put an end to visits by you in order to protect his health. I will see that he does."

She turned on her heel and went back into his room. The door closed. As I stared after her, I was forced to admit that, as cold as she was, she was loyal to my uncle, and greatly concerned about his health.

Depressed and feeling very alone, I went slowly to my room to change for the lunch hour. I thought about what my uncle had said. With a kind of wonder, I looked around me, deeply moved. So I was to live here then. Accepted as a part of the family—not a poor relation. So Edgecliff Manor was to be my home.

Hastily I changed into the yellow-and-lace dress with the endless tiny pearl buttons up the back. I was struggling with them when there was a soft tap at the door. I quickly removed the ring and put it on my locket chain, then closed it under my collar so it was hidden. I would show it to no one until I learned whether it had been the reason my uncle had become so upset.

"Come in," I said calmly, and a young girl dressed in gray with a white apron entered.

She bobbed a curtsy. "Oooh, miss, yer oughter waited 'til I was 'ere to help you," she cried in dismay, hurrying behind me to help me loop my undone buttons. Her accent was so thick at first I had some difficulty deciphering her words. "I's Nan, I've been sent to maid for ye." Nan was a plump, brown-haired girl with a friendly but shy face. She stood waiting. I realized I was expected to do something but had no idea what.

At last, looking as embarrassed as I felt, Nan said timidly, "Sit down afore the glass, and I'll do up your hair. I'm that good with hair," she added anxiously, as though I might refuse her, and I saw that Nan was over-awed by me. Perhaps she had worked in the kitchens and this was a great promotion for her. But I didn't mind that.

With Nan, I thought, I wouldn't be subjected to a critical eye.

"Thank you, Nan, I am sure you are very good with hair," I said warmly, and was rewarded by her pleased blush.

I sat down and let her brush my hair out. "Ooh, such nice hair ye got, Miss Emily," she remarked, losing some of her shyness. "Thick-like, and shines ever so, even if the color just be brown. It'll be a pleasure to work on yer hair, Miss Annabel's is ever so wild, and takes a deal of coaxing before it'll curl."

I smiled and decided to put myself in the hands of this expert. It had been on the tip of my tongue to tell her to draw it all back into a knot on the nape of my neck, but I admonished myself that the music teacher was gone now. I was Miss Emily Woodstock, about to take my place at a grand table in a great house.

I watched in admiration as Nan deftly worked wonders on my hair. It was true, as she'd said, that my hair was thick and easy to work with. I'd often thought it was my best feature and regretted the matronly chignons I'd had to keep it in. Now it was being coiled and braided into a coronet on my head, and a few ringlets were being coaxed to curl down in back onto my shoulders.

"Thank you, Nan. You've done wonders."

She was finished, and I stared a bit amazed at the stranger I saw in the mirror. A young lady of fashion. And the hairstyle flattered my face. Even the afternoon dress didn't look quite so plain anymore, and the yellow and cream of the lace warmed my coloring.

When I reached the top of the stairs, I met Mrs. Kerrenslea coming up them, carrying a tray. She paused for a moment.

"Sir Ralph must take his lunch in his room because of the illness you brought on. It's the first time he's not

61

been strong enough to come down in the afternoon."

"I am sorry that my visit affected him so deeply," I faltered, not sure what to say. She didn't reply, just continued up the stairs and past me without another word.

I sighed as I made my way to the dining room, my happiness over my new hairstyle evaporating. Just as I reached the door, I heard them all talking, and I was arrested by the sound of my name being spoken.

"Cousin Emily is extraordinarily like her mother." It was Charles. "I wonder if she is like her mother in *every* way?"

"She seems most sensible to me," Richard's voice cut in, repressively.

"Still, one can never tell, can one?" said Charles. "Doctor Fielding was saying just the other evening that some of his maddest patients appear to be sane . . . most of the time."

"Brrr! Imagine if she were as mad as her mother?" Annabel said, with a note of delicious fear in her voice. "We should have to lock her in the West wing, and feed her gruel through a locked door, and listen to her screams!"

"Don't be a fool, Annabel," Richard said roughly, but Charles laughed. "There is no proof she was mad at all."

"I would think committing suicide evidence of madness," said Charles.

"That is quite enough of this subject. William, did the mine's foreman call this morning?" Richard said.

I stood at the doorway, feeling cold. My mother—they were saying she had been mad? And that she had committed suicide—not perished accidentally? And how . . . how did they all know what she looked like?

I waited for some minutes before I went in, to calm myself and to prevent them from wondering if I had heard what they had been saying. I must find someone to

62

ask about all this. But who?

Richard was at the head of the table, in the place Uncle Ralph would have had if I had not made him ill. I felt uneasy as I entered the room. I sensed Richard's eyes on me as I sat down, and Penwillen came forward to fill my glass with cider. The table was magnificent, decked with hothouse flowers arranged in cut crystal bowls.

It was everything I had dreamed of during those lonely, comfortless evenings when I had walked home through the London streets and gazed with longing at the passing carriages bearing the rich to tables such as this. But now that I was here, I felt ill at ease. Yet my cousin's first words seemed designed to assuage me.

"Good afternoon, Cousin Emily," said Richard from his place at the head of the table. He looked magnificent in a dark gray suit, very much the Lord of the Manor. "It is good to see you grace our table."

"Thank you." I looked at him shyly. I was unused to such compliments.

"Indeed, Emily. You look lovely," said Charles, gracious as ever. "You make a welcome addition."

I smiled at Charles. "Thank you, Charles. I see that Uncle is not joining us—I am afraid my visit upset him rather badly. He was taken quite ill, and I had to summon Mrs. Kerrenslea." I was suddenly conscious of Richard's attention. I looked up to find him watching me closely. "I hope to see him again tomorrow—if I am allowed."

"If you are allowed?" questioned Richard brusquely.

"Why, yes—you see, Mrs. Kerrenslea said that his seeing me puts too great a strain on his health, that this is the first time he has not been able to come to the table for luncheon. She intends to ask the doctor to forbid my visits—until he is better," I added, to soften what I'd said, for Richard was glowering.

"Nonsense!" he said forcefully. "Kerrenslea is known for her hasty words—at times. She is not the mistress of

63

the house. Though she may have served Uncle for years, she does not make decisions for him. For months he has talked of nothing but your arrival here. It would do him more harm not to see you. I shall speak to the doctor myself. And to Mrs. Kerrenslea."

This last was said in a tone that boded no good for the housekeeper. At last I had seen the masterful side of Richard's personality that everyone spoke of. There was no doubt who was the true master of Edgecliff. I glanced at Charles.

"How odd of Kerry to say such things. Uncle has not joined us for quite a long time," Charles said. "Since his illness began, in fact."

I spoke up quickly. "I am sure Mrs. Kerrenslea meant no harm—she was only concerned for Uncle. Perhaps I should not see him for a day or two, until he adjusts to the idea of my being here. I have no wish to aggravate Uncle's illness." I had no wish, either, to aggravate Mrs. Kerrenslea further.

Richard was about to answer when suddenly Annabel demanded, "Oh, do let us speak of something more cheerful! I am sure the doctor will say what is best for Uncle. I am as sorry as anyone that Uncle is ill, but we have had nothing but talk of illness for months now! Emily will think us a bunch of gore crows. She has just arrived, and we should make a better effort to entertain her." She smiled as she spoke, making her words seem more charming than selfish. "That is a lovely dress, Emily," she went on, eyeing Richard defiantly as if daring him to interrupt her. "Is that the latest style in London?"

I was grateful to Annabel for changing the subject. I answered, "It is the style just now, but I have it on my dressmaker's authority that it will not be next season." I noticed Richard's eyes were on me, and they seemed to mock me slightly when I said "my dressmaker." What did a poor music teacher know of dressmakers, I felt he was asking, so I added, "You see, lest you think a music teacher's life is a very fashionable one, I bought these gowns only after they had been refused by other ladies. The dressmaker is a friend of my landlady, and let me have them at a reasonable cost, they being unsalable. Young ladies, it seems, often change their minds about gowns once they are made—which is fortunate for me."

"How clever of you, Emily," cried Annabel, tossing her colt's mane of black hair. "I think it was brave of you to be so poor, and go out and teach horrid little children the piano. I should have hated it, I'm sure, and never have known how to go on!"

"Brave it was not," I replied, and smiled, "for I had no choice in the matter."

"Well, I shouldn't have borne being poor with such equanimity as you!" she rejoined decidedly. "No, teaching would never have suited me. I'd have become an actress, perhaps, and dressed in feathers. Or run away to join the gypsies! It would be a grand life, to dance on the stage and be admired, or travel all over with the gypsies, free as a bird!"

I smiled as she said this, at the romantic notion the very young have that poverty is a great liberator from conventions, and allows one to live a fancy-free life.

"The gypsies are the more likely of the two," teased Charles. "As you can't sing a note and have never mastered the simplest dance step!"

"Foo! Dancing!" cried Annabel. "How dull to be whirling about the room in the arms of a horrid boy! I'd far rather be on horseback!"

William smiled. "You won't always find boys so horrid."

"I should think not," put in Charles. "If she'd ever grow up, which I begin to doubt! Are we having the Trewithians and Alsops to dinner this week? Emily should meet some of the county society. We could have a small dance after dinner, or a few tables of whist—"

"Oh, but I have nothing to wear!" Annabel interrupted and then went on about the dreadful lack of good dressmakers in Cornwall, ignoring Charles, who cast his eyes to the ceiling on this feminine diversion into fashion.

I lost track of what she was saying, for Richard was still staring at me. I began to be uncomfortable. He had not spoken a word, and the look in his eyes was hard to decipher. Was it admiration—or speculation? I tried to avoid his eyes and listen to Annabel's prattle about the neighbors, but my gaze was drawn again to his. It was as though we were alone at the table. He raised his glass to his lips and, in slight gesture, lifted it to me. I looked away, coloring when I saw that Charles had caught this bit of byplay. But Charles was not looking at me. He was staring at Richard with narrowed eyes.

Just then an influx of servants entered, bearing covered dishes. I turned my attention to the food with relief. I was beginning to feel I was sailing in very uncertain waters. The less I said and did, until I mapped out the undercurrents, the better.

I was just finishing my last bite of fresh Cornish crab pie when Richard spoke. "Emily, let us tour Edgecliff, shall we? We will start with the grounds, the fresh air will do us good after such a meal. It's best to see the estate by horseback, so I'll find you a gentle mount."

He stode out, William at his heels, not waiting for my answer but taking it for granted, which, I was learning, was very much Richard's way. I stared after him, dismayed.

"I . . . he must have forgotten that I cannot ride," I said worriedly.

Annabel laughed. "He probably just doesn't believe you. I am sure Richard finds it impossible to imagine

66

anyone who cannot ride. Don't worry. I'll see Tomkins gives you Persimmon, she's twenty if she's a day, and never goes at more than a walk. With a sidesaddle all you have to do is sit there and hang on. You won't fall off. But you really should learn to ride, Emily. I'll teach you myself in the afternoons!" Annabel's green eyes sparkled with delight at this project.

"That would be very kind of you, for you are right, I should learn to ride," I said. "But I do not have a habit."

"Easily solved. Annabel has thousands," said Charles.

"Yes, and even though you're taller than me, it won't matter so much on horseback. Otherwise, we're much of a size, for you're so thin. If only my boots will fit you!"

"I'm sure they'll be miles too large, for Cousin Emily is delicately built, and you have the feet of a Hessian trooper," said Charles.

I rose, laughing. "If I am to try on a habit, I must do it now, for Richard is awaiting me."

"Come to my room. I'll have to show you the way. Otherwise you'll get lost and become the ghost whose dragging footsteps haunt the West wing!"

Annabel laughed as I followed her up the stairs. But I wondered about her words. The house was vast, and the family occupied only the East wing, or so it appeared. I wondered if a ghost truly haunted the West wing, perhaps the ghost of my mother. I fancied seeing shadows in the stairway and then I chastised myself. Never in London had I had such imaginings. Perhaps it was the Cornish air, or the "evil eye" that the witch woman gave me. I smiled at the thought.

"What a hornet's nest you've stirred up with your coming," Annabel suddenly remarked. "No one talks of anything else except what it will all mean. *I* say it's all for the good. It was getting terribly boring around here under the iron hand of Richard, since Uncle's been sick!" She smiled at me mischievously, obviously trying to

67

gauge the effect of her words.

I smiled back, pretending to be amused, but inside I felt a tiny twinge. I knew they had all been talking about me. Some, she'd implied, fearing the changes I might bring? It was only natural that they would talk about me. It was true. I *was* a change in their lives. I had not thought what my being here might mean to them. I had only been dwelling on the great change that had occurred in my life since coming to Edgecliff. But the words I had overheard about my mother concerned me greatly. Could I dare ask my cousins openly? I feared not.

In her room, Annabel ransacked her armoire and emerged with an armload of habits that she threw on the bed. "I thought the blue would look best on you," she said without preamble. "Most of my habits are dark blues and greens, or black, for they look best on me, but I wish I had one in cranberry or maroon. It would look so well on you!"

With an exclamation of pleasure, I held "the blue" against me. It was a rich and deep shade of ultramarine, trimmed with military black braid. I loved it.

In a few moments, we had it on me. As Annabel had predicted, it fit fairly well, though it was a few inches too short.

"But that won't matter, as you won't be showing your ankles, but only your boots," she pointed out. "Here— try the hat!"

I set the hat on my head. It was styled like a small bowler, blue to match the dress, with caught-back black veiling that trailed onto my shoulders. The white lace of the stock at my throat looked brilliant against the black braid and the severely elegant tailoring of the habit suited me as no dress ever had. I stared at the elegant lady in the mirror. My gray eyes almost looked blue, and if not beauty, the habit lent me a certain strikingness.

"It's perfect!" crowed Annabel. "Now try on one of

68

my boots." She bent down and groped under the bed, coming out with a pair of black boots. I tried one on.

"A tiny bit large—but it will do fine."

"Charles was right. I do have feet like a Hessian foot-soldier."

"Then so do I, for we are almost of a size." We smiled at each other delightedly, pleased with our newfound friendship.

The friendship gave me the courage to ask her, "Annabel, what did you mean when you said that everyone's been talking about my coming here? Are they—I mean, aren't they glad I've come?"

She flopped on her stomach across the bed and cupped her chin in her hands, staring at me seriously. "Glad? Oh, no. Of course they aren't. I mean, they do like you, Emily, now that you're here and everyone has had a chance to see you're not a monster or a heathen or anything terrible, but they're all nervous."

"Nervous about what?" I pursued, hoping she could be the one to clear up all the mysteries.

"About the fortune, of course! A new heir turns up—the old heirs are turned out on the street!" she said dramatically. "But I don't mind. I'll be a gypsy, as I said. Or run the stables here. I can earn my keep."

I smiled. So it was all just Annabel's dramatizing, after all. Or was it? "Annabel, has anyone *told* you they are nervous?"

"No. But of course they all would be, because that's all they think about, morning, noon, and night—the Edge-cliff fortune! Why, Richard and Charles have been at each other's throats since birth practically over who would be the heir, but of course Richard is the eldest, and in any case, Charles won't work so he has no hope of cutting him out. And they both want me to have lots of money for clothes so I can marry the catch of the century. No doubt some moldering old Duke. As if I

69

cared about being a Duchess. William and I are the only ones who don't care about being heirs. All William wants to do is manage the mines—he loves them, and a good thing, because Richard really only cares about the farms. And all I want is to be left alone to ride." She grinned at me.

"But no one has said anything to you about me?"

"Oh, of course they talk about you, but not like that."

I knew all too well in what manner they were speaking of me. "What do they say?" I ventured.

"The servants all say you're very much more ladylike than they expected, and Charles that you're prettier than he expected. William says you're a good sort, and Richard doesn't say anything—it's beneath his dignity— but he must like you very much or he wouldn't be taking you riding today. Besides, I can tell he likes you by the way he pays attention to you, for he never pays the least attention to the rest of us. Maybe he thinks you're pretty, too, and you'll be some competition."

"Competition?" I knew it was beneath my dignity, but I could not resist the question.

"Oh, yes, Richard's the apple of all the girls' eyes for miles around. They practically stumble over each other at dances fighting their way to his side. Of course they all want to marry him . . . he's a great catch here in Cornwall, since he's the heir. Charles gets his fair share of girls after him too, because he's so disgustingly romantic with them, and because he'll have money someday too, but it won't be as much as Richard so it's Richard who is the catch . . . even though he is so stern all the time, at least with *most* of the girls."

She smiled at me, pleased with the effect of her gossip. *Most* of the girls? So there must be one he cared for. She had hinted as much before. I dared not pursue this for fear she would see the interest I felt in Richard. Then she added, with a touch of the devil that was in her, "And, of course, there is Mrs. Kerrenslea. I think she dislikes you."

"Oh?" I asked sharply. "How do you know?"

She laughed. "Because she and I were watching you from the house when you arrived! I was much too curious about you to wait . . . and so was old Kerry. We were on the upper landing at one of the windows."

So I *had* been watched. My feeling when I first arrived had not been wrong. "What did she say?"

"It wasn't what she said as much as what she did. She went quite white when she saw you . . . and dropped the vase she was holding."

"She did?" I said, feeling disturbed.

Annabel's eyes were glowing, and she went on in a playfully ominous voice, "She gasped, and when I looked at her, she whispered, 'So you are back to make my life miserable again.' That was all she said, and in a moment pretended as if nothing had happened at all. So you can see, Emily, she believes you are going to make her life very difficult. She hates change of any kind, does old Kerry."

"It seems a very odd thing for her to say about me."

"Oh, Kerry's always saying things that have the ring of doom. You don't know the Cornish yet. Filled with fancies we are. It must be the sea mists, and these cold old stone houses that drive us over the bend and make us believe in omens and piskies."

"But what did she mean by 'again'? I have never been here before," I said uneasily.

"But you have! You were born here, have you forgotten? You must have been a dreadful baby to have imprinted yourself so on her memory!"

I laughed with her at the thought.

Annabel suddenly sat up. "But come on! You should hurry, Richard is waiting!"

As I left her room on my way to the stableyard, I

wondered about Annabel's impressions. The incident that she had described seemed too close to my uncle's fit when he saw the ring. Had Mrs. Kerrenslea known my mother? Had I been taken for a ghost again?

Ridiculous, I chided myself. She must have been referring to my stay here as a baby. But it still made me uncomfortable to hear that she disliked me. Why did she? It seemed extravagant. But then, she had an air of strangeness about her manner at times.

Perhaps the Cornish were all mad.

Including, I wondered, my mother? I resolved then that I had to find someone who could tell me the truth.

It was then that I became lost. I must have taken a wrong turning; I found myself in a hallway quite unfamiliar to me. I walked down the hall to a window, and it took me a moment to realize that the view I saw below me, the formal hanging gardens with their subtropical plants and two palm trees, were on the other side of the house. Lost in thought, I must have wandered into the West wing.

Much of the West wing was shut up now. They had explained that it was a mirror image of the East wing, but that most of the furniture was shrouded in dust sheets.

I shut my eyes, trying to picture where I was. But to no avail. If only I could get high enough to see in which direction the sea lay. I walked to the end of the hall, where there was a dark door.

I opened it, and saw a set of stairs climbing before me. They were dark, but the room at the top should be high enough for me to see from. I started climbing, wishing I had brought a candle.

The darkness enclosed me, and suddenly I felt unaccountably frightened. I quickened my steps and reached the top of the stairs. Putting my hand on the handle of the door, I turned it.

It was locked.

How strange. None of the doors at Edgecliff were locked. I tried it again. And then I heard a sound in the darkness behind me.

A long and whispering sigh, barely audible.

I went cold, freezing at the door. Annabel's words about the ghost that haunted the West wing came back to me all too clearly, and suddenly I felt, unmistakable and palpable, a sense of menace. It seemed that the shadows were reaching out to enclose me, that the darkness was filled with an implacable threat.

And then, quite clearly, a dragging footstep sounded on the stair below me. To my horror, that disembodied sigh, almost a whispered wail, was repeated.

"Who is there?" I squeaked, terrified.

In answer, the footsteps retreated.

For a long time, I stood trembling in the darkness, before I made my way down the stairs. It was a relief to come into the lighted hallways . . . which were empty. Almost running, I tried one hallway after another until I found my way to the East wing.

But I was unable to shake off the chill of those moments, when I had felt surrounded by a danger . . . a danger no less menacing for the fact that I knew nothing about its source.

Chapter Six

"So—are you ready for your tour of Edgecliff?"

Richard smiled down at me. The sea wind ruffled his black hair, and he looked magnificent in his working clothes, corduroys, and mud-spattered boots. Overhead, a scattering of high clouds were gathering, threatening the sun, but in the stableyard it still shone, light as my heart. Immediately on joining him, the dark shadow that had oppressed me vanished; in the sunlight, it all seemed a figment of my imagination.

The low slate roof of the stable was covered with lichen, and its long gray stone walls with their small dark windows were brightened by splashes of pansies and pinks growing in whitewashed boxes. There was an air of neatness to the cobbled yard. No weeds straggled, buckets and tools were neatly stacked along the walls, and horses grazed in the paddocks beyond. Though the stone paddock walls must have been very old, they were in good repair. The stables looked both ancient and lovingly cared for, and I suspected that this prosperous look was the result of Richard's untiring work.

Aloud, I said, "I am ready for the tour. But shall we not see the house first?" I hoped my voice did not betray my happiness at being alone with him.

"Ah, but if we began with the house, I am afraid we would be joined by Charles and Annabel. I have planned this campaign carefully. First the grounds, then the house, and all without company."

How happy those words made me! And how many foolish times I was to remember them in the weeks to come, taking them out again and again to examine as a woman would take out cherished jewels to watch them sparkle.

"Then—you were at pains to assure we would not be accompanied by your brother and sister?" I ventured, disbelieving it could be true.

"I was. I think you have an interest in Edgecliff. Perhaps a feeling for it already. First impressions often stay with us all our lives, and I thought you might like to see it without being distracted by useless chatter."

"Yes," I said. "It is true that having to make conversation with too many people can be very distracting. For though I am finding my new cousins very amiable, at times . . ." I stopped, realizing there was no tactful way to complete my sentence.

His eyes mocked me. "And I believed you always spoke your mind quite bluntly. I am disappointed at this sudden delicacy. All of us at once are overwhelming," he added dryly. "No one is more aware of it than I. That is one of the reasons I spend so much time at my work."

I smiled. "It would have been intolerably rude of me to have said such a thing. After all, I am the newcomer here, and must wait to make up my mind about all that I find. Yes, first impressions can stay with one, though they are sometimes mistaken. Such as yours that I invariably speak my mind."

"Perhaps it is the teacher in you that gives me that impression. The impression that you are a most decided young woman."

"Perhaps. And perhaps it is the fact that I believe it is

75

natural for women to have opinions as well as men, and to express them."

He laughed then. "And, I expect, to enjoy arguing as much as any barrister. But you mistake me. I enjoy a woman who speaks her mind."

Something in the way he looked at me stilled any reply.

"But come," he said, breaking the small silence. "Let us start. Otherwise we may be found soon. We can continue our sparring on horseback."

He walked to where two horses stood tied. One, obviously his, was a black and gleaming stallion that looked gigantic to my untrained eyes. The other, of a russet brown color, looked almost as large. He led the russet one to a mounting block.

He must have noticed my hesitation. I was beginning to learn that very little escaped him.

"Afraid?"

The single word was a challenge. But I was afraid. Afraid of the size of the horse and afraid of looking like a fool.

"No," I said, and approached the horse.

I could see from his expression that he knew I was lying, and admired me for it.

"I don't believe you would be afraid of most things," he remarked, letting down the stirrup iron.

"And what gives you that idea?"

"The first time I saw you, you were intrepidly climbing down the cliff path. Not the act of a coward."

"Perhaps the act of a madwoman," I said lightly. I was startled by the intense glance he gave me, and then remembered the conversation about my mother. He, at least, had taken my part. I blushed slightly, confused.

To hide my feelings, I climbed the mounting block. "I have never been on the back of a horse before. You must tell me what to do."

He held out his hands, clasped together. "Here. Put

76

your boot in my hands and I'll toss you up."

I was trembling. "Toss?"

His eyes danced with amusement. "A mere figure of speech. I promise to be quite gentle."

In the end, it was easier than it looked. He boosted me neatly aboard the mare's back, and she didn't move an inch, though I landed rather hard on her.

"Oh!" I gasped, half for breath and half for shock, and clutched the pommel of the saddle. But that was from fear alone. He'd set me firmly sideways on the saddle, and I was in no danger of falling.

I found my apprehension quickly vanishing as he adjusted my stirrups, then told me the right way to hold the reins. A new feeling had taken the place of fear. It seemed strangely intimate to have him cupping my boot in his hand, or placing his hands over mine as he showed me how to hold the reins. I was aware that my cheeks were reddening again, and I hoped he didn't notice it.

My embarrassment receded as he finished arranging me like a mannequin. "I feel quite stiff," I remarked.

"Wait until tonight," he said wickedly, then strode to his own horse. In a single fluid motion that seemed effortless, he was aboard, the reins neatly gathered in one hand.

He read my mind again. "In a month, you'll be doing the same thing. Now, just give her a tap with your heels."

"I very much doubt that I shall ever be able to leap onto a horse's back in that manner." Tentatively, I tapped the horse with my heels and she started forward. I was tempted to clutch again at the pommel, but she had an easy, rocking walk that was really very slow.

I looked up to find him watching me. "It isn't as bad as I thought it would be," I admitted.

"So you didn't believe me. I suspected as much. You are one to always make up your mind for yourself."

"You are attributing many qualities to me on such

77

short acquaintance. Do you always judge people so quickly?"

"I admit, my dear teacher, to that fault. And I have also been accused of always believing I am right. Annabel terms me a tyrant."

We rode across the stableyard toward the gate that led to the soft green fields behind the house, away from the sea.

Richard went on. "And here I am, showing you the domain of Edgecliff. The stables antedate the house itself by two hundred years. When I came here at eighteen, the roofs were still thatched. Picturesque, but in danger of fire. I had the thatch replaced with slate. Now that I am thirty-one, the lichen has mellowed their look enough that I don't miss the thatch every time I ride by here."

So at eighteen, I mused, he was already working. "I see that a farmer must be practical, rather than allow sentimentalities to rule him."

"I am glad you attribute a sentimental side to me. Even a tyrant likes to be thought to have some good qualities. The stone was quarried here in Cornwall in the days of Henry the Eighth—many of the village cottages are of the same stone. Now there was a man who also had the bad habit of believing himself infallible. A good trait for a king, but hard on his wives."

I laughed. "You are doing your best to paint a black picture of yourself, for what reason I cannot imagine."

"Perhaps it is because I am used to being obeyed. Not admirable, but true. And now comes the newcomer to the kingdom, who speaks her mind and makes her own decisions. I must do my best to intimidate her so she will not stand in my way. Through this gate, and we will be past the paddocks and into the fields of the home farm."

Was he being sardonic at his own expense—or was he truly warning me not to make trouble here? I could tell nothing from his face.

With the easy gypsy grace so characteristic of him, he bent down and unlatched the gate, swinging it open. Beyond, a much-used grassy path next to a track of cart ruts stretched over a rolling green pasture. In the distance, some sheep grazed.

I kept silence as we rode across the field. Was he teasing me? There was an edge to his words that puzzled me. The newcomer . . . standing in his way. First Annabel, now Richard, intimating that my presence here might be a threat in some way. I was beginning to feel that I was being watched by everyone, my actions weighed. Maybe they did not want me here. Uncle Ralph spoke as if this were now my home. But was it? Or was I the interloper, not welcome, perhaps resented?

I shook these doubts from myself. Why was I always so serious? A few light words and I was constructing castles of fancy. I glanced back over my shoulder and saw we had climbed high enough so that I could see Edgecliff dreaming below in the sun and shadow, with the blue of the sea beyond.

Richard told me much about the estate of Edgecliff that afternoon . . . and, without meaning to, more about himself. His deep and abiding love for Edgecliff was apparent.

It was an afternoon I shall always remember. At every cottage we passed, people came out to greet us. They were all very kind; I could see they admired Richard. And they were all curious about me. It was obvious that word of the long-lost niece was the talk of the estate, and that the cottagers, at least, were glad I had come home. "It's right and fittin' that you are back with us, Miss Emily," was how most of them put it.

Two incidents from that ride have never left my mind. The first was when we were passing a small gray stone cottage with a thatched roof. A profusion of roses grew over the doorway, and a buxom, white-haired woman

79

hurried out, waving anxiously.

"Mister Richard!" she called. "Ye must come in and stop for a glass of my elderberry wine."

He smiled. "Dame Polgrian, we would not see a tenth of the estate if we stopped in every cottage along the way. Perhaps some other time, I shall bring Miss Emily back for a glass of your famous wine."

She curtsied to me. "Ah, Miss Emily, it's welcome you are, back to your home. But Mr. Richard, it's little enough I can do to repay you for your kindness."

For once, here was a tenant less interested in me than in Richard.

Richard was scowling. "Now, Dame, I'll have none of—"

"None of my thanks, Miss Emily, is what he'll not have, and him who has been like a father to my family. Why, didn't he see to the new roof when the old one was falling to pieces? And didn't he himself ride for the doctor when our Rose was so sick, the poor child, yes, and pay the doctor himself? And here he's gone and sent our Tom off to college, to study agricultural methods, and we being one of the poorest families in Cornwall . . ."

Richard's scowl had deepened. "Now, Dame, I said I'd hear naught of it. If Tom is taught proper farming methods, it is to my benefit as landlord. He's one of the likeliest lads hereabouts. You see I act only from selfish motives," he said for my benefit. "And Rose has become an invaluable maid at the house. We could not do without her services."

"Oh, Mr. Richard, you are always too modest! Why, you sat up with the cow all night when she was ill—our only cow, Miss Emily, and—"

"And quite too valuable an animal to lose. We must take our leave, Dame." From Richard's very abruptness—for he was the soul of graciousness with the cottagers—I could see he was uncomfortable at being caught out in his kind acts.

So this was the self-described tyrant, I thought, as we rode away.

He was still frowning. "I hope you do not think—"

"That you are a kind man, who acts from unselfish motives? I would not dare to say such things aloud, after the reception you gave the dame."

But I can think them, I thought.

"Perhaps," he said enigmatically, "you will eventually learn the truth about my character."

It was a short time later that the second incident happened, one that was to be very important to me. We had left the farms and were riding along the cliff paths, back to the house. In the distance, I saw a tall, oddly shaped building at the cliff's edge, near a small forest.

"What is that?" I pointed. It had a romantic look, alone at the cliff's very edge.

"That? A folly. Useless thing, and in the worst state of disrepair," Richard said shortly.

I was about to ask more when the old woman I had seen near the gatehouse the day I arrived stepped out into the path.

"Oh no—Malvina," Richard said in a low tone. "We shall have to stop for a moment, but we won't linger. She is a trifle mad—or at least, it is good for her business as a wisewoman to appear that way."

"Good day, Dame Malvina," Richard said politely as we reined in near the old woman. As before, her gray hair was long and tangled on her shoulders. She had eyes only for me. "This is my cousin, Miss Emily Wood—"

"I know who she be," said Malvina, staring up at me with those wild dark eyes. "She be here to start it all again. The hawk at the eagle's throat, tearing each other over the dove. Just like it were when Amelia was here. You be her echo in time, child." She cackled, and I wondered if she were truly mad, or if this was an act to

81

impress her customers, as Richard had implied.

"We must be going, Dame. We wish you good day," Richard said.

But I lingered, unable to look away from those compelling eyes. "What do you mean, Dame?" I asked. "Do you speak of Amelia Woodstock—my mother? Did you know her?"

"That I did. And as you are her child, have a care."

"Come, Emily. We must be going," Richard said repressively, and started his horse. Mine obediently followed. I nodded at the Dame, then rode away, resisting the urge to look back.

"It seems that every time I see that woman, it is as if she has cast a very spell on me," I said.

He frowned. "You have seen her before?"

"Yes, when I first arrived. She gave me a warning at the gate. She mentioned a curse, and told me to go home. And how strange her words were just now."

"Don't listen to anything she says. It is all part of her act. She makes a tidy sum telling fortunes and selling potions. I'm sorry to say the Cornish are a superstitious lot, and most every village boasts a wisewoman. But I have always believed Malvina should have gone on the stage."

"Where does she live?"

He raised a brow at me. "Thinking of having your fortune told? Her cottage is near the cliffs, not far from the old gazebo. But you will only waste the silver you cross her palm with. She is a fraud. And I wouldn't have thought you'd go in for fortune-telling. I see you are not as practical as I supposed."

I only laughed, but during the ride back to the house I was thoughtful. Though her words were nonsense, of course, she had known my mother. I could ask her questions—about my mother's supposed madness. About the accident. But could I believe what she told me?

When Richard and I dismounted, I could feel stiffness from riding. But I was looking forward to seeing the rest of the house at Richard's side.

However, it was not to be. William and Charles awaited us on the front steps. It seemed there was a matter at the mine that required Richard's attention at once. Some of the miners were demanding to see "the master."

Did I imagine I saw regret in his eyes as he apologized to me for having to postpone our tour? It quickly vanished, if it was ever there, when Charles stepped in.

"I shall be happy to take Emily through the house. Go ahead, brother, since duty calls. You may be sure you are leaving her in the best of hands."

For a moment, the air between the brothers seemed to tingle with challenge. And then it was over as if it had never happened. Richard shrugged, the familiar bland look descending over his features. "As you will, Charles. Goodbye, Emily."

It was as if he were angry at me . . . or at Charles, I thought, as he strode away, William at his heels. I tried to mask my feelings and turned to Charles with a bright smile. "I am looking forward to seeing the house."

"And I am looking forward to showing it to you. What luck that Richard was called away to the mines." Charles's blue eyes were sparkling, and there was no mistaking the meaning of his words.

To cover my confusion, I asked quickly, "Where shall the tour begin?"

"As you have already seen the drawing room and the dining room, we shall start with the grandest room in Edgecliff," he said as we entered the house. He led me across the entrance hall toward a set of double doors I had not yet been through.

"Which room is that? I cannot imagine anything more magnificent than the drawing room."

"The ballroom." There was not a little pride in his

voice as he spoke.

"Edgecliff has a ballroom?"

"Said to be the most magnificent in Cornwall," he informed me, and opened the doors with a flourish.

I could not suppress a gasp at the sight before me.

"The ballroom of Edgecliff," announced Charles, clearly enjoying my wide-eyed stare. I had never before seen such a magnificent room.

"Marvelous, is it not?" he was saying as we walked into it. The polished wood floors reflected the waterfalls of shining crystal chandeliers over our heads. Across the room was a wall of French doors, opening into the garden, which I later learned was the center courtyard and surrounded by two wings of the house. A large carven staircase swept into the room at one end, with a balcony running along the top—a minstrels' gallery.

"That's where the orchestra plays during balls," Charles said, his fingers tightening on my elbow. "I hope that we can dance someday soon. The house has been so dull since Uncle fell ill. It is nice to have some excitement in our household again." He gazed at me with an unmistakable meaning.

I blushed, ignoring his remark, and turned away, looking at the ceiling of the ballroom. It was lighted by a mural of tumbling gods, goddesses, and cupids, with gilt borders.

"Apollo and Diana," Charles said, waving an arm to indicate the ceiling.

"It's so lovely!" I exclaimed. In the corner of the room I saw a suit of armour. "And how medieval. I never dreamed the house would be so grand." I turned toward him again, smiling a little. "I suppose that sounds terribly naive, but after my last lodgings, it is almost overwhelming." I had decided to be open about my past, and not put on airs. After all, I had nothing to be ashamed of.

"On the contrary, I'm delighted by your honesty," he

said, grinning. "I'm so glad you don't try to pretend to be unimpressed. You've no idea the number of young ladies taken on this tour who do their best to appear bored, trying to show how worldly they are. And *that's* such a bore!"

"Numbers of young ladies?" I inquired. "And do you personally conduct all these tours?"

"Oh yes, I am a natural for it. Richard is too busy to bother with guests, and much too grim. I, on the other hand, am a man of leisure, and always ready to be an escort to young ladies."

"I'm sure you are quite practiced at being charming to guests. You have been most kind to me."

"But you are the one who is charming." Before I could protest, he clasped me around the waist, though at a respectful distance, and whirled me once about in a waltz step. "Rather grand for smugglers, is it not? Come on. I'll show you the gallery where your villainous ancestors are captured for posterity."

I was laughing as he released me and as I followed him up the stairs. Oh, he was impossible! But quite, quite appealing.

The minstrels' gallery was long and narrow, with a waist-high balustrude that overlooked the ballroom. "Our smuggling ancestors had delusions of grandeur," Charles was explaining in a light, ironical tone. "Minstrels' galleries were popular in medieval houses, though naturally Edgecliff is rather new. But old William wanted the castle look when he built this place, doubtless to bolster his respectability. There he is again. A much later portrait."

He'd stopped in front of a large dark portrait of a man in eighteenth-century dress, with graying hair. The painter had managed to hint at a certain craftiness beneath the grave expression.

"I don't think he looks quite respectable, does he?"

Charles said at my elbow.

I smiled. "I am learning that my newfound family is most anxious to blacken itself in my eyes. First Richard was trying to convince me he is a tyrant, and now you are downgrading my ancestors. I begin to believe you all fear I shall get above my station."

"Richard is a tyrant. And our ancestors were black-guards. So—you and Richard got along quite well this morning?"

I could not help coloring slightly. "Well enough."

Hands in his pockets, he sauntered to the next portrait. "William's bride. Not a beauty, I'd say. And rather a tragic story. She died in childbirth when bearing their second son. That was the start of the legend."

"Legend?" I said absently, not really seeing the portrait I was staring at, too busy wondering about Charles and Richard. Wondering why they both seemed bent on charming me. It could not be my great powers of attraction. Yet I was all too ready to believe I had captured Richard's attention, I chided myself.

"Yes, the legend of the Edgecliff brides. It is thought to be unlucky to marry into our family. At least, to marry the heir. Many of the mistresses of Edgecliff have died young. But perhaps now the curse, if there ever was one, has ended. Some of the folk say it was the ring that brought the bad luck."

"The ring?" I was all attention now.

"Yes, the ring of the Edgecliff brides. All old houses have their ghosts or legends, and we are among them," he said with ironic pride. "And in Cornwall, coincidences like a few brides dying young quickly become superstitions. You see, old William had a ring made, a ring of diamonds and rubies, for that first bride. And it was passed down as a betrothal ring for all the mistresses of Edgecliff to wear. But now the ring is lost, and some

86

believe the curse on the brides went with it."

My eyes flew to the portrait in front of me. The ring was on her finger.

The same ring that was on a chain around my neck. "But—when was it lost?" I whispered. "How?"

Charles shrugged. "No one knows. I can show you the last bride to wear it—your grandmother. Uncle's mother. She was killed in a fall from her horse. Sometime after her death, it disappeared. By then, the legend that the ring was cursed was firmly established, and I think it was a case of good riddance. Perhaps someone even deliberately got rid of it. Or stole it . . . and now some other family bears the curse."

Numbly, I followed Charles to the portrait of my grandmother. I had eyes only for the ring on her finger. I barely glanced at her face.

Suddenly Charles was quite close to me, looking at me anxiously. "But Emily, you seem to be taking this legend of the brides to heart. You are quite white. Are you ill?"

"I—I am just a little faint. Perhaps it was all the riding today. If we could just sit down for a moment?" I smiled weakly up at him, trying to cover the way my mind was racing.

"Come with me." He took my arm, concerned, and led me to a bench set in the stone window.

Stolen.

The ring seemed to burn me where it lay against my skin.

We sat down and Charles kept my hand locked on his arm. I felt his hand cover mine. I was beginning to lose my shock and I was glad he was there. How very kind he was.

"Feeling better?"

I nodded. "I am. I don't know what came over me."

"That's my girl." Charles' finger came gently under

my chin, tilting my face up so he could examine it. "You do look better. You had me quite frightened for a moment."

Then his expression of concern changed to a tender and warm look.

"I would not want anything to happen to you. I cannot believe how important you have become to me in such a short time."

His voice was low and caressing. No man had ever looked at me in this way. Before my father died, I was too young, and after . . .

I turned my head away and dropped my eyes, feeling the blush in my cheeks, and at once, he dropped his hand from my chin. He stood, and I did not look up at him.

"Charles, please—"

"Emily, I didn't mean to embarrass you. It's just that I was worried about you. And I'm afraid . . ." He paused.

I looked up to see him standing with his back to me, his hands jammed deep in his pockets.

"I am afraid I don't feel very cousinly to you after all." For a moment, his voice was rough, serious. Then he turned back to face me, a crooked, devil-may-care grin on his handsome face. The light coming in the window turned his hair to burnished gold. "But don't fear I'll make a spectacle of myself. You've set me back on my heels as much as I seem to have set you back. I am not used to feeling protective about women, and I'm not sure I like it. I think you may have gathered I am normally a rougue where women are concerned. But only to experienced women. Not innocents like you. This feeling is new to me, I admit. And I intend to run a mile from it."

He grinned, and I had to smile back at him, amused and touched by his outrageous confession. It was so like Charles to be completely honest with me! How could I reprimand him?

"Then—a truce?" I asked lightly.

His smile held relief. "I shall make you no promises," he said gallantly.

We both laughed then, at ease with each other once more. I rose.

"And now, I think I shall retire. I shall blame it on being tired. But I will be honest with you, as you were with me. It is your practiced charm I am running from."

As he escorted me out of the gallery to the staircase, I wondered how I could have changed so, so quickly. Was that really the prim Miss Emily Woodstock, teacher, flirting lightly with a man?

But as I climbed the stairs, it all came rushing back. The ring.

Dear God, had my mother and father stolen it?

I fought against believing it. But perhaps . . . perhaps I had found the root of the quarrel.

I shut the door and sat on my bed. What should I do? I could not ask my uncle, when the mere sight of the ring, I now suspected, had brought on his attack.

But I had to know. Even if it meant tarnishing the images of my parents. There was only one person I could ask.

That was when I decided to visit the wisewoman.

Chapter Seven

After visiting the minstrels' gallery with Charles, I had retired to my room for what seemed only moments when a discreet knock on my door woke me.

Nan entered, carrying a tea tray. "Why miss, everyone's been asking for you. Dinnertime in less than half an hour and you've even missed tea in the Blue salon!" She set the tray by my bedside. "Now, what shall I put out for you?" She opened the wardrobe with a flourish.

"Heavens," I cried. "Dinnertime already?"

Annabel had told me that dinner was a formal affair and that they changed for it. The yellow dress was a tea gown, suitable for only the afternoon, and I had worn it earlier besides. The other dress I'd bought, the sea green one, was a dancing dress, not a dinner dress. It seemed there were many rules to follow when one was part of the gentry.

"I believe my yellow afternoon dress is the only choice, I am afraid," I said, alighting from the bed.

"And a fine dress it is," she replied. "What a color, and with the right ribbon in your hair . . ."

Nan rattled on, but I barely heard her. As she helped me dress, I realized that I was a little nervous going down to my first formal dinner. I hoped that my cousins didn't find my manners lacking. Though I was brought up to be a lady, I was sure there were proprieties that I did not know. And I was still tired, even after my long rest. I had only been at Edgecliff for one full day and already I felt as if I had been here for weeks, with all of the new experiences I had had.

When I reached the dining room, I found all of my cousins seated at the table. The long mahogany dining table was covered with white lace. Two large silver candelabras graced each end and in the center was a silver centerpiece of palm trees and camels.

The china was trimmed with gold and each place setting had three crystal glasses and eight pieces of silver.

"Good evening, Emily," cried Charles with a welcoming smile, leaping up to help me into my chair. "I hope that you are feeling better."

"Yes, thank you. It seems that I needed a rest. I am afraid I am not used to riding. I apologize for being late to the table."

Richard regarded me warmly. "No need to apologize, you have arrived in time."

I flushed under his gaze, realizing for the first time just how important the approval of *this* cousin meant to me.

I watched in amazement as the servants brought in the first course, followed by more dishes of the most elaborately prepared food I have ever eaten. There was fish, followed by a blanquette of veal and roast pigeon. There was a baron of beef and rack of lamb. Every course was served with a variety of vegetables, and two desserts were offered, a rich trifle and a creamy blanc mange. I tried small portions of everything, wondering if they ate this way every night.

I was apprehensive at how my stomach would react to all this rich food and wine, but for the moment, it was like being in paradise. Did the servants dine on the leftovers? Or maybe the meat was made into pies and pasties for the next day's lunch? Edgecliff was a manor farm, and clearly, the land was bountiful.

A voice broke into my thoughts. "What are you thinking about, Emily? I fear you've gone a thousand miles from us."

I smiled and looked up at the speaker—Richard. "I am just overwhelmed by a meal of these proportions." Then I bit my tongue. Why was I always harping on my poverty?

"I am glad you're enjoying it—at least, I think you are. Or do I detect a note of disapproval?"

"It just seems a bit—much, for five people."

He laughed. "But how shocked the neighbors would be, to hear you say that. I assure you, Edgecliff is not renowned for its table. It's even said we are rather mean. Now if you dine at Tregarth—"

"Mean! Richard, no one has ever said we set a mean table!" said Charles indignantly.

William was laughing. "But it's true we don't have a French chef in the kitchen."

"Yes, and you know Lady Tregarth once called what we serve 'farm fare,'" said Richard, with a sardonic glance at Charles.

"Well, I say Emily is right! It's perfectly disgusting that we have to have pigeon, when no one eats it, ever!" said Annabel. "It is just for show, and a criminal waste! Thank goodness we don't have a nasty French chef, for then we'd probably get nothing but pigeon, morning, noon and night!"

The corner of Richard's mouth lifted in amusement. "I can see I have been remiss in my running of matters. It seems I should have been taking more interest in the menus and spending less time on the farms. Very well then, tomorrow I shall no longer leave all to Mrs. Kerrenslea. I shall consult with her on menus. I vow no more pigeon," he finished solemnly.

"Hah! *You* decide menus? We'd have nothing but pasties and cheese if you had your way—and probably beer at the table as well! For you are always eating such laborer's food when you're out mucking around the farms," sniffed Charles. "If anyone should change the menus, it should be me, or—"

"But with you in charge we'd have nothing but cream sauces, and those I can't abide," protested William, pretending horror.

"Emily, as you can see, on your very first night here you have discovered a problem," Richard said. "Edge-cliff is sadly in need of a mistress. William is right, Charles. I fear for our digestions if you take a hand in the menus."

His eyes and Charles's locked for a moment across the table. Then he looked at Annabel and me as if the challenge between the two brothers had never happened.

"Very well then, it's settled," he said. "Starting tomorrow, I suggest Annabel and Emily go over the menus with Mrs. Kerrenslea. It's high time you started learning to run a house in any case, Annabel—and Emily should also know how things are run here."

My head reeled. A light comment and now—Richard had spoken! And clearly he meant to be obeyed. It was not that I objected to learning something of how Edgecliff was run, but that I dreaded the encounter with Mrs. Kerrenslea. I was so new here, and what right did I have to start changing things? Although it made me feel slightly better that Annabel would be at my side.

But she came to my rescue. "As if I have not been doing just that all these months, Richard, while you are in the fields! For there are many things about running a house that escape your attention! But old Kerry will lay a Cornish curse on my head if I meddle with the menus!"

"I doubt Mrs. Kerrenslea knows any curses," Richard said dryly.

"Maybe not, but Malvina does and you know they are friends!"

This started, of course, a spirited altercation between Annabel and Richard, Annabel vowing she was never going to marry but was going to run a racing stable in Ireland, so she had no need to learn to run a household.

"You may trust me to handle Mrs. Kerrenslea tactfully, Annabel. And perhaps Emily will help us restrain what she sees as our tendency to extravagance," Richard said with a slight hint of mockery.

The thought of debating *my* ideas on the daily menus with the cold housekeeper sent a chill up my spine.

"You are most kind," I interjected. "But I do not wish to impose my ways in any manner. I find this meal delightful, truly."

Richard looked at me speculatively, "Very well then," he said. "We shall keep with Kerrenslia's extravagance, for the present."

"Extravagance!" Charles raised his glass. "That is what we *need* in this dour household! We haven't had guests in an age."

"Charles, you know that Uncle is ill," Richard said harshly.

But his seriousness did not snuff Charles's enthusiasm. "It is time for a ball! Surely Uncle would approve. Annabel is past the coming-out age, and . . ." He looked at me. "We have another reason to celebrate." He raised his glass to me.

Charles's flirtatious glances always made me feel ill at ease and I found myself turning away from his eyes. I looked up to see Richard glancing at me speculatively.

"Perhaps you are right, Charles," Richard said. "It is well past time for Annabel's coming-out ball. Perhaps we shall make it a dual celebration. Emily *should* be introduced to society."

"Oh, dash it!" Annabel drew her napkin on the table.

"Does that mean I must take dancing lessons!"

"Definitely," said Charles.

"But I must speak with Uncle before any arrangements are made." Richard frowned in Annabel's direction. "And please watch your language, young lady."

And with that the table was awash with speculations about the ball and I found myself filled with excitement. To think that a short time ago I was alone in the world, in a boardinghouse in a poverty-stricken street in London. And now, I was one of the landed gentry, with a room in a mansion overlooking the sea. I was eating a seven-course meal with a family that I never knew I had and helping them plan a ball in my honor. It felt like a dream.

Dinner concluded and the family would be going into the drawing room. I was very tired and I begged to retire early.

"Oh, but I so hoped to hear you play the piano," Annabel pleaded.

"There will be countless nights for that, Annabel," Richard said.

I gave him a look of gratitude and I excused myself from the table. Before I reached the stairs, I heard a voice behind me.

"Have a good night, Emily." It was Richard. He was standing in the entrance hall, his jet black hair gleaming in the candlelight. "I hope that you had a pleasant day."

"That I did," I answered, smiling. "Thank you for taking me to see the farms."

"The pleasure," said Richard, "was mine."

I mounted the stairs to my room with a light heart, all the shadows of the early day forgotten. As I brushed out my hair, I found myself remembering with a smile the way Richard's eyes had met mine for just an instant when he said that Edgecliff needed a mistress. And the way his lingering stare had followed me up the staircase. Perhaps—

I shook myself from this momentary bright dream. For just a moment, I had seen myself as mistress of Edgecliff, married to Richard. How foolish. And how dangerous of me to let my feelings run away so with me, I told myself. It was because he was so handsome, with his black hair and green eyes. It was because I found his serious demeanor attractive, especially when the rare gleams of his humorous, teasing side showed through. Oh, at those moments, I thought he was much more charming than his brother, for all Charles's easy address and ready smiles.

But such dreams were dangerous. I must forget them, and try to snuff out the spark of attraction I felt for my cousin. I reminded myself that I did not know him yet.

Besides, the truth was I was a plain poor relation, a teacher, attractive maybe, but without even great beauty to catch a man's heart. When Richard married, he would marry a woman of his own standing, one who would bring him both beauty and wealth. And if I allowed this day-dreaming to continue, the day would come when I would stand at his wedding, watching with a broken heart as he married his lovely heiress.

My elation gone, I climbed into bed and snuffed the candle, determined to put such foolish notions completely out of my heart in the coming days. I was sure that I could. I had had many tests to my will in the past, and learned I could do what I set my mind to. And I had other things for my mind to be troubled with. The ring, my mother's ring, which seemed to burn my skin where it lay dangling from the locket chain. Had it been stolen? And would I ever know the truth? Yes, I would see the wise-woman, I reminded myself and settled into sleep.

But I was not to visit the wisewoman for three weeks. Constantly during those three weeks I looked for opportunities to be alone, so I could visit Malvina without anyone knowing. But I was swept into the life of the gentry, forever busy. I was happier than I had ever been; yet I felt the question of the ring like a shadow. And I had other things on my mind.

During the next few days, I saw little of Richard, and never again alone. I saw him only at meals, and he was absent from many of those. Sometimes I imagined he watched me, was aware of everything I said and did, and that special spark between us was still there.

And I was not able to visit my uncle for days after our first meeting, for his condition had worsened. Even then, I did not mention the things that were troubling me, for I did not want to excite him any further.

I remember knocking softly on my uncle's door, and as I entered, I was struck again by the gloom of the place. I wondered if it would not be healthier to open the curtains and perhaps even the window to let in the spring sunshine and some fresh air. But the doctor and the housekeeper had charge of such things; I must keep my opinions to myself at present, I remember thinking.

"Good morning, Uncle," I said, advancing to the bedside. I saw his color was better and his eyes were bright and alert as he greeted me.

"Emily. Pull up a chair, child. I am anxious to hear more about you."

I sat down in the red gloom and studied his face. He was obviously very ill. "What would you like to hear about, Uncle? There is so little to tell."

"I would like to hear about your life after your . . . father died. Tell me everything. How you managed, where you lived, about your pupils. Was it very hard, my dear?"

And so, for a half an hour, I told him details about my life as a music teacher. I tried to keep it pleasant—I made him smile several times with stories about the gay times I

97

had had, or with anecdotes about my pupils and their families. It all came vividly before my eyes, the narrow street with its smells and refuse, the pinched, hungry faces, and I looked around with wonder at my luxurious surroundings as I spoke.

"I want you to have a bit of gaiety now, Emily," he said when I'd finished. "Just because I am ill, it doesn't mean the house must go into mourning. Richard has spoken about a ball. It shall be arranged. And, of course, you must have clothes. I shall see to it that Annabel takes you into town to choose materials for a new wardrobe. Don't count the pennies," he said firmly, seeing that I was about to protest. "You must be properly outfitted for your station in life. You are one of the family now. Let Annabel guide you as to what is proper—she'll know." He smiled. "She's a bit wild, but she's got taste and she'll see to it you don't stint yourself."

I leaned over and kissed his sunken cheek, and felt my eyes mist when I saw the pleasure this brought to him. "Thank you," I said.

"I'll have no talk of thanks," he said gruffly. "It's only your due. You will come into everything that is yours, soon enough. Remember, Emily, as my niece and my closest relative, you are the mistress of Edgecliff now. I mean for you to take your place as such. Little enough to make up for—but there, it's only proper."

I looked up, distracted by a movement at the corner of my eye. There was a shadow at the door, and then it was gone.

I stared, trying to decide if I'd imagined it or not. Had it been a trick of the light, my eyes adjusting to the gloom . . . or was someone listening at the door as I talked to my uncle? Then I dismissed it with a shrug. If indeed someone was listening, I knew who it must be. Mrs. Kerrenslea, making sure there was no repeat of the past visit's disaster. I felt a slight flicker of resentment at the thought.

I looked back at my uncle, wanting to thank him for his generosity.

"Oh, Uncle . . ." I began, but he stopped me.

"I said, no thanks from you. Now ring for Kerrenslea, child, I'm tired." He smiled wearily at me, his pain-clouded eyes managing to twinkle, telling me quite clearly he would have none of my gratitude. I left the room before the housekeeper appeared.

When I reached my room, I went to the window and leaned there, my knees feeling weak. My uncle's words had moved me, I felt tears start down my cheeks. I was deeply happy as I looked out over the lawns to the sea beyond. "Mistress of Edgecliff." What strange words for him to utter. But they made my breast fill with joy. For I finally felt at home, at last.

Little did I realize what those words would mean to me in the future, what pain they would bring. For shortly after, things began to happen to me, strange things, confusing things, the answer to which I would not discover until long afterward.

One afternoon, Charles took me riding on the trails that ran through the woods near the cliffs, and we came across the old gazebo. I remembered seeing it once, from the distance on my first tour of the grounds with Richard.

But this day Charles and I rode more closely and I was drawn to the building with a strange fascination.

It was a folly, built in the style of an Oriental pagoda, and it hung almost precariously on the cliff's edge. It looked about to fall down, the paint was peeling, and there were weeds growing tall around it. Neglected though it was, there was something romantic about it. Once it must have been beautiful.

When I asked Charles about it, as happened so often, the conversation turned to Richard.

"That monstrosity?" He slowed his mount and gave the gazebo a look of contempt. "Spoils the view. It should be pulled down."

"I think it is rather pretty . . . but why isn't it in repair?" I asked. "Everything else on the estate is in such good condition."

"Yes—thanks to Richard's unceasing efforts." I studied his profile as he stared at the gazebo, and a hard look was in his eyes; the look his face always took when he spoke of Richard's achievements. "Everything must be in top repair now that he is the steward in Uncle's place. But even Richard's power doesn't extend to that thing. No one knows why, but Uncle Ralph almost seems to have purposely let it fall to rack and ruin, though he won't hear of it being leveled."

"Why?" I was intrigued. It looked even more romantic to me now. "Did he have it built? Or perhaps it is haunted?"

He laughed. "Everything in Cornwall is haunted, you'll find. I don't know when it was built, but I think it was before Uncle's time. Shall we dismount and explore it? I don't believe in ghosts myself, but lately I have found that your eyes are haunting me. I see them in my dreams." There was a gleam in his eyes that made me believe he spoke in jest, so I aswered him in kind.

"I must decline your offer, kind sir. I fear those thorns would tear Annabel's habit. Perhaps if Richard could persuade Uncle to have those cleared at least, he could then show me the gazebo."

"I see," Charles said and looked at me speculatively. I wondered then if I had betrayed thoughts about his brother that I had not even admitted to myself.

100

The next afternoon, Charles confirmed those suspicions.

I was in the front garden, cutting roses and placing them in a basket over my arm. They were in the fullest bloom, proliferative, their scent heady in the warm sun. I had been enjoying a few moments alone, and yet I was not sorry when I saw Charles walk down the path.

His face was alight as he joined me. It was clear he was glad to see me, and I smiled back at him. But that was all that passed between us. He was the model of propriety as we exchanged conventional greetings. He took my scissors so that he could cut the roses I might select. For a few moments our conversation was entirely unremarkable.

And then he said abruptly, as if troubled, "Emily, I must speak to you about something."

"Charles, I am not ready to listen to any more of your romantic declarations," I protested, trying to make my words sound light.

He smiled a trifle wistfully. "And I don't intend to make any . . . even though I find doing these small things with you—like cutting roses—frighteningly enchanting."

I laughed softly. He was incorrigible. "What did you wish to speak with me about?"

His blue eyes were suddenly serious. "I wanted to speak with you about Richard."

"Richard?" I asked, feeling a nervous shock all through me, but managing to make my voice sound cooly inquiring.

"Yes, I felt I should warn you, Emily, that Richard is very likely to marry soon. We've all known it for some time. He has been courting a woman who is very wealthy, and I might add, very beautiful. The whole village expects an announcement of their engagement any day now."

101

I turned away to hide my emotions, my hands icy on the basket handle. "And why do you feel you must tell me this?" I asked, in a voice that sounded too high, too insulted to my ears. I turned back to face him. "Why do you imagine it would matter to me?"

He looked at me seriously. "I hope it does not. But I have noticed that Richard pays you attention . . . I do not want you to believe he means anything by it." He saw my face, and rushed on. "I know it is not my place telling you any of this, Emily, but I—I don't want to see my brother hurt you."

I stared at him silently for a moment, many feelings battling in my breast.

"I have no interest in Richard except that of a cousin," I said at last, knowing that it was a lie. But a lie I was determined to make the truth.

Relief crossed Charles's face. "Then you forgive me for saying what I should not have? It was only my concern for you that led me to say what I did."

It was a hard question to answer. I was filled with shame that my feelings for Richard were obvious to Charles. Did everyone know, then? "It was not necessary for you to tell me, but I believe you did so on the best of motives," I said as evenly as I could.

His expression lightened into a smile that held that hint of devilry I knew so well. "Thank you, Emily. And of course I had another motive for speaking—one I am sure you are aware of. I have grown to hope that it is a different cousin who has attracted your interest."

"Charles—" I could not go on. I didn't know what to say. I only wanted this conversation to be at an end. "If you will excuse me, I must go in the house. I—I need to finish a letter." I gathered to courage to face him squarely. "I have been here too short a time to feel an interest in anyone. But I believe you to be my friend, Charles."

With that I fled. It is true my feet walked sedately down that gravel path ablaze with roses, but I was fleeing all the same.

I was relieved to reach the cool of the house. I set down the roses, and agitated, I tried to collect myself.

I must put Richard Woodstock out of my mind forever. I saw then clearly I had been spending too much time thinking of him.

As I stood in the chilly hallway, I decided the answer was to keep busy. Too busy to ever give him a thought. And to try harder to solve the mystery surrounding my mother's death and the ring. If I were thinking of such things, I would forget my cousin Richard Woodstock . . . forget him, before he married another.

Chapter Eight

From that day on, I was almost never alone. In the mornings, after breakfast, I would visit my uncle, but the visits were short. He was very weak, and I was saddened to see that he would not recover from this illness, for I had grown very fond of him. My presence at his side seemed to comfort him. I hoped he would speak of the past, but I dared not question him.

When my visit was ended, I would go down to lunch. As I left his room, Mrs. Kerrenslea would be there, like a shade, ready to slip in the door. Her eyes were always cold, and I was sure she listened to us.

The afternoons I spent with Annabel, shopping or receiving riding lessons. There was talk of holding Annabel's coming-out ball on her birthday, in August, but nothing was decided because of Uncle's illness. We spent much time being fitted for new wardrobes that would reflect our changed stations in life, and in receiving callers. It seemed every family in the district wanted to make my acquaintance.

But one afternoon I found myself quite alone. Richard and William were out on the farms, Charles was in town, and Annabel had gone on an outing with a friend. At last it was my chance to visit Malvina.

My excitement rose as I rode away from the stables toward the cliffs. Old John, the groom, had lifted his eyebrows at me when I asked the way to Malvina's cottage. I believe he thought I was going to have my fortune told. But I ignored him, elated that at last I could ask someone questions about my mother . . . about the past.

I entered the gloom of the forest path, and I could hear the roar of the sea. Malvina's cottage stood at the very end of the forest path, close to the cliffs. I thought that doubtless such a dramatic location must enhance her business. It was a snug enough gray stone cottage, but missing the roses most cottagers grew around their doors. Instead, an extensive herb garden fronted the house, though I looked in vain for the black iron cauldron every witch should have.

Instead, there was Malvina, suddenly at the door.

It was a good trick, for it startled me. Then I smiled inwardly. Of course, she'd heard my horse's hooves on the path and timed her appearance for maximum dramatic effect.

"Good morning. I have come to see you, Dame," I called as I dismounted and tied my horse.

"I knew this past week ye were coming," she said, staring at me with those wild black eyes. "And I am glad ye've come at last, so I can warn ye of the danger."

I stifled a sigh. Well, Richard had warned me that she was a fraud, but I had expected a better performance than this. "Warn me, Dame? Of what?"

"Of what ye are awakening. I see a night of dancing, and you in one brother's arms while the other feels murder in his heart."

I tried to appear suitably impressed by this, for I wanted her to tell me about my mother. A summing-up on her part now seemed to be completed. "Come inside and I'll read yer palm," she said abruptly, and disappeared inside the doorway.

I followed eagerly, resigned to the inevitable palm-reading. It might be a good way to get her talking, I reasoned.

Inside, it was neat, if dim. There was no sign of a cauldron, nor indeed any of the things I would have associated with a witch, other than a row of bottles on the mantel and bunches of drying herbs hanging from the rafters.

She laughed, a high-pitched laugh tinged with scorn. "No, I ain't no witch, child. My powers run to herbs, no more. That, and what I can see in the smoke—or in a body's hand."

I looked at her sharply, startled. But as I took the stool she indicated, I reasoned she must know very well what newcomers were thinking of her. Oh yes, she was very good.

"I wasn't thinking that you were a witch, Dame," I said, politely if untruthfully. "In fact, I came here because you said you knew my mother. I wish to ask you about the past."

"And don't you think I don't know why ye came here? And what ye were thinking just now?" There was a sharp amusement in her eyes that gave me the disconcerting feeling she knew very well that I had lied. "Give me your palm, child, and I will tell ye what ye should know."

I held out my hand, and she took it, examining it closely. Then she dropped it and looked at me a long time, until I began to be uncomfortable.

"What did you mean when I met you, about the hawk, and the eagle, and the dove?" I asked, hoping to prompt her.

"'Twas the brothers I spoke of. Yer father and yer uncle. Two Woodstock brothers, at each other's throats. And now, time comes a-circling, and it is happening again. Like an echo."

"Yes—I believe everyone knows my uncle and my

106

father quarreled. And now, that Richard and Charles compete. But it is exaggerating, surely, to say they are at each other's throats?"

"Not yet, mayhap. But now you have come. I tell ye, ye must beware of completing the circle, or surely tragedy will follow again."

"I cannot understand what you mean if you are not clearer. Of what are you warning me?"

She took my hand again and stared at the palm. "I see love for you, child. And I see danger surrounding you. Words any wisewoman would tell you, eh? Have a care who you marry. They have told you the brides are cursed? Then I say to you, heed them and do not become one."

"Become an Edgecliff bride, do you mean?" I was embarrassed, feeling she knew my secret thoughts. "I do not think there is much possibility of that."

"Ye do not know yer own possibilities, child. Neither did yer mother. Ye may set something in motion merely by being here."

I leaned forward. "Do you know something you are not telling me? Something about the past? Please, what do you know of my mother and father? Were you here when they lived here—when she died? For I must know—"

"Was I here when she married?" Again, that high-pitched laugh. "Aye, I was here. Call me Malvina, child. Yer mother did. When ye rode up here, ye were thinking about why my cottage was on the cliffs. I had it built here because I'd grown used to the sound of the sea beneath me. I'd lived on the cliffs before. In the big house. I came there with your mother." She grinned evilly at me. "I were her maid."

I stared at her. This mad old woman, my mother's maid?

Again she read my thoughts—or more likely, my

expression. "Ye're wondering how a mad old woman like me could ever have been a maid? I were her maid right enough, when she were engaged to become a bride up at the big house. She needed a maid then, but not always. Once she were just the doctor's daughter."

"I know," I whispered. "My father told me."

"In those days, I were her nurse. Doctor's wife died a-birthing Amelia, so I were called in to nurse her, for I'd just lost a babe of my own. My own husband, he were long gone, follerin' the sea." She grinned at me. "So I might be yer grandmother, in a manner of speakin'. I loved yer mother like she were my own."

I did not answer, not wanting her to stop.

"Doctor, he came to these parts when Amelia was just fourteen. Pretty she was, but a mirror'll tell you that. She caught his eye up at the big house. Yes, he loved her from the moment he saw her, no matter what her station was."

"My father loved my mother, as you say. But he never spoke of you."

"Much he never told ye, it seems. And why should he speak of me? Her was dead by then. And I was gone. I came to this cottage after she was married. I never knew your father well, nor he me."

"But you said you lived at Edgecliff."

"Aye. During the engagement she came, and so did Doctor, to live at the big house. There were to be lots of parties, so folk could meet her. Accept her, like. She hadn't a penny to bless herself with and she were marryin' above her station. But once folk saw her, holdin' herself like a queen and smilin' that pretty smile of hers, they came on her side. We stayed there, she and I, for five months afore the weddin'. Then she didn't need me no more, and I came here."

If her story was true, I was glad she hadn't been with my mother after her marriage. For that might have meant she'd have been my nurse! But I guarded my expression,

108

for I meant to find out about the ring, and my mother's death.

"The curse of the brides you mentioned. Was it not simply the ring that was cursed? And now that it has disappeared, perhaps it would be quite safe to marry a Woodstock—not that I intend to," I added hastily.

Her eyes suddenly pierced me, as if she knew very well where the ring was at that moment—around my neck. "Has it disappeared?"

"It's—it's common knowledge that it did," I faltered.

"But I have uncommon knowledge. And I tell ye, do not become an Edgecliff bride! I loved your mother and for her sake I warn ye. It's a black family, and they make their own tragedies. Don't 'ee make yours.

"But shouldn't you be going?" she asked suddenly. "Miss Annabel is back and is wondering where you are. It's common knowledge the two of you have become friends." She smiled ironically at me.

"But Miss Annabel is to be gone the entire day. I can stay longer without being missed. And I have more to ask you." I reached into my pocket.

"Keep your silver, child. 'Tis for the sake of your mother I warned ye. And I have no more to tell."

"Will you not tell me of the day my mother died?" I asked softly. "My father never told me any details."

"It were an accident. She went walking on the cliff paths, and they gave way. That is all I can tell ye."

"Then—she did not jump? For some have said she was believed to be mad."

"Mad? She were mad enough, marryin' a Woodstock. I can tell ye no more, child, though you stay here all day."

I rode away, pondering the strange "fortune," sure there was much she was not telling me. I must visit her again, I thought. Perhaps she would trust me more as time went by.

As I climbed the steps of the house, Annabel appeared

109

in the doorway. "Emily!" she cried. "Where have you been? I arrived home early, and I have been looking for you everywhere!"

With a chill, I realized that in this, at least, the wise-woman had seen clearly.

Two weeks later, Annabel and I took the pony trap down to the village in a state of great excitement. It had at last been decided that a ball was to be held. And soon, not waiting for her birthday. Though no one said it, we all knew we wished to hold it before Uncle died. We were going into town to choose the material for our ball dresses.

As she fearlessly piloted the trap down the narrow street into town, I must admit I clutched the side. The walls came so close to either side of the trap they almost brushed it. And the road was of almost vertical steepness. The ancient, gray stone cottages seemed built atop each other, cascading in a jumble down to the tiny, wall-enclosed harbor. I could see the sea at my feet, it seemed, the fishing boats, the turquoise water, and everywhere the cries of gulls resounded. The town smelled of flowers and pilchards, and more than once a tumbling brilliant tendril of fuscia or roses threatened to sweep my hat from my head. I was relieved when we pulled up in front of the dressmaker's shop.

Annabel and I were in the midst of an exhaustive debate over the merits of violet blue or midnight blue ribbons to trim a dress when the door bells jangled and a woman entered the shop. I was at once interested in her, for though she was dressed in the most costly fashion, we had not met her on any of our calls. And she was beautiful. Strikingly, arrestingly beautiful.

Her skin was a creamy white that never saw the sun, and her abundant shining hair was red-gold. She turned

110

wide, lazy cat's eyes on us, and her full red mouth smiled.

"Why, Annabel Woodstock. How nice. You must call on me at Woodmere." Her eyes turned to me questioningly.

"Mrs. DeVere." Annabel was at her most frigidly polite. "How lovely to see you. This is my third cousin, Emily Woodstock. Emily, may I present Mrs. Evonne DeVere?"

I resisted the urge to stare at Annabel. I hadn't known she had such formality in her! I exchanged a small polite nod with Mrs. DeVere, and she repeated her invitation to tea.

"And how is everyone at Edgecliff? Such a grand house, I always say. I have not called for some time, but I do try to keep up with the family. I understand your uncle does not improve?"

When Annabel shook her head mutely, she went on, not seeming to notice Annabel's coolness, "Yes. So sad. Richard was over at Woodmere just last night, and he told me. Only imagine, he is kind enough to help me with my accounts, and to advise me. I am a widow, Miss Woodstock," she said, meeting my eyes, "and running an estate is new to me. I don't know what I should do without Richard's kind help. Well, I shall let you get on with your shopping. So nice to meet you both. Do come to tea."

Richard had been absent last night. As he was many nights. As she turned away, her cloak gaped to reveal a truly voluptuous expanse of bosom. I did not have to wonder why Richard would want to assist the helpless widow.

So this was the woman Charles had warned me about. He'd said their engagement was expected any day. Probably it was put off only because of Uncle's illness. *"But not his only passion."* I felt sick as that sentence, spoken by Annabel on my first day, flashed through my

111

mind. Oh, I had been warned often enough.

So why did it hurt so much to see her?

I let Annabel choose the violet ribbons without a murmur, and I have no idea what else we bought in that shop. My eyes kept being drawn back to the lovely widow. I wondered how they amused themselves when the account books were closed. A clear picture of the widow bending over Richard's shoulder, dressed in sparkling jet, came to me—and they were laughing . . .

I bent my head and examined the lace on the counter with fierce intensity.

Mrs. DeVere left the shop at the same time we did. As I stood laden in the open doorway, waiting for Annabel to return with the trap, I could clearly hear voices behind me in the shop.

". . . cheeky, her saying that about the account books to Miss Annabel! But she's brazen, she is. Thinks she'll catch a husband, and that great estate of Edgecliff along with him. But Mr. Richard'll never marry her. Why should he, when he can get what he wants for the asking?"

I felt ill. It was clear enough they meant he shared her bed.

"Aye," said the other shop woman. "But she married old DeVere right smart enough, and him old enough to know better. No doubt she thinks she can do it again and marry above herself. Can't say as I blame Mr. Richard, though. Not many gentlemen could resist her flaunting ways. But they say he's not the only one who spends the night at Woodmere. Though if he ever finds out, I'd not answer for her chances. He's got a black temper, has Richard Woodstock . . ."

I turned away and deliberately walked out of earshot. I could hear no more.

In the trap, Annabel turned to me, fuming. "That woman!" she said sharply. "I cannot abide her. She has

112

no sense of propriety, and I for one wish my brother would cease 'helping' her with her estate!"

I silently agreed, but said aloud, "Who is she? One of the neighborhood gentry?"

"Hardly," Annabel said tartly. "In fact, we know precious little about her background. She came here for a visit—a most strange place for a lady of quality, though I will not admit she is one—and the next thing we knew, she'd married DeVere, who was old enough to be her grandfather! Oh, if Richard—" She stopped.

"If Richard?" I prompted.

"Well, if he marries her, it will be too bad! Though she does have extensive lands that adjoin Edgecliff, and Richard would probably marry the devil himself to advance the cause of the estate. It is such a shame that you have nothing, Emily, for I would far rather see Richard marry you, and he does seem to like you."

I did not trust my voice to ask her why she thought such a thing. But how true her words were. Even his sister saw that I was not a suitable match for him. And the lovely widow was very far from being the "devil himself!" Evidently Richard found she had abundant charms.

To my dismay, Richard was waiting for us on the front steps when we arrived at home. Annabel greeted him cheerily enough, I with more reserve. His eyes flew to mine inquiringly, as if he was surprised by my coolness. I averted my gaze and looked at the lawns. But I soon had reason to regret my hasty behavior. To my horror, Annabel was saying:

"And then we ran into Evonne DeVere at the shop. She said you were at Woodmere last night. I think it's dreadful, Richard, the way you carry on!"

At the mention of Evonne's name, his eyes flew to mine, and to my astonishment, he colored deeply. Embarrassed, I said, "Excuse me, I must go in and—"

113

"Wait." Richard's tone shocked me. "I insist you hear my answer, Emily. I will not be lectured to by you, Annabel. How dare you imply I am 'carrying on'! I was merely helping her to sort out her accounts. They were left in a terrible mess. And who is to help her, if not her neighbors?"

He was nearly shouting. This must be Richard's famous temper. I was seeing it for the first time. But Annabel was not cowed. "Hasn't she any family?" retorted Annabel. "Besides, her husband died over a year ago. That redheaded baggage just wants to be mistress of Edgecliff. I tell you, I won't stand for it, Richard. She's as common as she can be. But I expect you are thinking of it, just because the DeVere lands adjoin Edgecliff!"

His face was black with anger. "Insolent chit! So you believe I would marry simply for advantage! I hardly think that when I marry, I shall consult you on my choice. And as for being common, what are you being by repeating village gossip? There are far too many ready to believe the worst of me because of my acquaintance with the widow."

"Then you deny it is true you have been linked with her? If not, where have you been so many nights, riding home at dawn? Your mines, I suppose?" she inquired sarcastically.

I was mortified, and made a move to go. His hand shot out and grasped my wrist in a vise of iron, staying me. "Yes, at the mines," he ground out. I thought if he looked at me the way he was looking at Annabel, I might faint. "Not, as you imply, in the bed of the widow DeVere." I blushed. Was there no lengths these two would not go to?

His words seemed to recall him to coolness. Icily, he said, "Set your mind at rest, Annabel. Her estate seems to be in fine order." His eyes sought mine for a moment,

114

and he dropped my wrist. "I shall not be visiting Woodmere any longer."

"Good," said Annabel, not in the least discomfitted. "I am glad to hear it, Richard."

He turned to me, then. "Emily, I am sorry you had to witness this incredibly rude display on both our parts. But I wanted to be sure that my name was not blackened unnecessarily. There are too many true sins that can be laid at my door."

I did not answer, and followed Annabel inside, much confused. She bounced at my side, unaffected by the passionate scene she'd just participated in.

"You see what a beast he can be at times," she said. "I hope you didn't mind our fight, but really, someone must stand up to him sometimes! Heavens! We must rush if we are to change for dinner!"

I went to my own room, thoughtfully. Though Richard disclaimed any current involvement with the widow, he had been involved with her once. And I was determined on one thing. I must put any thought of my cousin Richard out of my heart. I saw clearly I had been allowing myself to indulge in foolish fancies.

But Richard himself was soon to make this resolution a difficult one to live with.

I looked at myself in the mirror. I wore a new dinner dress, one of palest green changeable silk that was turquoise in some lights. It shimmered like the sea, and was caught up at the shoulders with velvet violets and green leaves.

To my surprise, I saw a different woman looking back at me from the mirror. The thin teacher who had arrived here was gone. I had filled out from the rich meals. The neckline of the dress was cut rather low, and I now had a bosom to show. I was prettier, too, I saw.

And wiser? It seemed I was learning some difficult lessons about life.

I descended the stairs a bit early, and found Richard standing before the fire in the drawing room. Alone. My heart beat a bit faster, and I almost turned and slipped away unseen. Since our tour together, we had never been alone for more than a moment. Huge though Edgecliff was, every room seemed filled with cousins or servants. But I was too late. He saw me in the doorway.

"Emily," he said.

When I hesitated, he added, "Come in."

I walked into the room, running my fingers along the gleaming top of the pianoforte.

"You have not played for us yet," he said.

"I have played for the others. You are rarely home in the evenings."

I heard him crossing the room and turned. He stopped before me. He looked magnificent in his black evening clothes, and I was afraid. Afraid to be alone with him, afraid of the way my heart was beating.

"So you are holding that against me. I thought so. You have been avoiding me. But I want to tell you that it is work alone that has been keeping me away of late."

I could not meet his eyes, but I felt my heart speed up even more. He spoke in such a low and serious tone.

"I have not been avoiding you."

"You have. You will not even look at me."

I looked at him then, and I was lost.

"What a very beautiful dress," he said softly. "Something a mermaid might wear. Perhaps that is what you are, and not a dryad after all?"

There was a spark deep in the green of his eyes, but his voice was still serious. I knew he must be able to see the pulse at my throat.

116

"Where are the others?" I said desperately, dropping my eyes again.

"Are you so afraid to be alone with me? You were not afraid, that first morning. I have often wondered where that girl went . . . the barefoot girl with flowers in her hair, the mischievous smile. She has been replaced by a proper lady whose hair is never out of place, who is so reserved I cannot believe she would ever take off her shoes, a lady who avoids me . . ."

"Oh, Richard." I laughed, in spite of myself, at his faintly teasing tone. "I told you, I do not avoid you. And you will never let me forget that I was so improper at our first meeting, will you?"

"No," he answered. "Because I shall never forget it."

Just then the door banged and we were awash with cousins. They were all there, laughing and boisterous, quarreling and bickering. I stood rooted for a moment, looking into those green, green eyes, before I was swept away to dinner.

Chapter Nine

"I cannot believe I will be going to a ball! I feel like I am in a fairy story!"

I laughed as Annabel held out her arms and pretended she was dancing with someone. She whirled about my room, waltzing, then came to a halt. Her face was sparkling.

"Get up, Emily, and practice with me! It is only two weeks until the ball!"

"But we have both spent hours practicing. I feel I can waltz quite competently now."

She pouted at me, and flopped in an armchair. "Always so practical. And I thought being here had changed you. You have been so much gayer."

Could it be love that had changed me? I left the thought unspoken, though I had been able to think of little else since the night Richard and I had been alone in the drawing room. I feared I was in love with Richard Woodstock. It was a feeling that I had no power to change in my heart, no matter what my sensible side told me. And a foolish hope was inside me—a hope that he felt more than cousinly affection for me.

And at the ball—it was another unspoken hope. On that night, there might be chances to dance with Richard.

To be alone with him again. To better judge, perhaps, what he really felt about me.

Oh yes, I was mastered by these new feelings. They left room for little else. The mysteries that had seemed to surround me had vanished like clouds in the sun, no longer important. All that was important—

Was Richard.

Yet I was not completely lost in my feelings. I knew that I did not really understand him. Cold and hard he seemed at times, withdrawn. But when he smiled, his smile seemed more brilliant than anyone else's, and that in a family endowed with brilliant smiles. He remained an enigma to me.

I continued to pin my hopes about Richard on the ball, for we were not alone again. Yet I believed our feelings were growing for one another. He seemed to enjoy speaking to me at the dinner table, and one night he and Annabel had a rather spirited argument about it. He had been telling me about mining in Cornwall when suddenly Annabel piped up:

"Oh, Richard, you must be boring Emily to tears! Haven't you anything more interesting to talk about than dirty old mines?"

"Dirty old mines, as you call them, are the foundation of many fortunes in Cornwall . . . including ours," he retorted. "And it may come as a shock to you, Annabel, but some women are interested in more than horses."

"Interested!" she sniffed. "Polite is more the ticket! You monopolize poor Emily at dinner every night, until I am sure she must wish herself back in London!"

"No," I protested, feeling this was going too far. "I really am interested, Annabel. I have only to change the subject, were I not. The history of this area is most fascinating."

"Changing the subject with Richard is like trying to stop a charging horse with the bit between its teeth, when

119

he gets started on one of his pet subjects. Well, suit yourself! But I won't be surprised if you fall asleep in your plate one of these nights!"

That was an end to it, for Charles was laughing amusedly, and Richard was giving him and Annabel black scowls. Later that night, Richard hung back a moment as the others went into the drawing room, and asked, "Is it true? Do I bore you, Emily?"

I smiled. "No Richard, you do not. I am afraid Annabel does not understand my interest in such subjects, though. And I am sure she would think me a dreadful bluestocking if she did. I confess what does bore me is nothing but talk of gossip, gowns, and horses."

He was looking at me with not a little admiration, and though it was only a moment's interlude, it made me very happy.

The morning of the ball came at long last, and I awoke to find my room was light. Dawn was just breaking, and the first startling burst of bird song shattered the gray stillness. I was up in a moment, throwing the covers back. I had awakened several times during the night, too excited to sleep, always disappointed that the sky was still black. I was like a child on Christmas.

I unfastened the window and leaned out. The world was still colorless, but the sea was very still and only a gentle breeze was blowing warmly over my shoulders. There was not a single cloud in the sky. It was going to be a glorious day. The perfect day was like a gift, a sign that the ball would also be perfect. I dressed hastily, anxious to go for an early morning walk.

On the lawns behind the house, I turned back to look at it. It was like a castle in a fairy story, tinged pink by the rising dawn. Tonight how it would sparkle, every floor alight with a thousand candles! And the glamorous people who would alight from the carriages crowding the drive, each girl in a ball dress she hoped would be the prettiest there, each man with his eyes bright at the sight of the lovely women around him. Romance! It would fairly crackle in the air tonight, as meetings were made, love stories begun, some ended perhaps. The Edgecliff ball would be a magical night for everyone, I felt.

The rising sun felt so warm on my face as I walked to the cliffs. I thought of the way, such a few short months ago, my hands had been reddened with cold, my frame thin, my pride daunted by scraping for a living. Never again. I was Miss Woodstock of Edgecliff now, and my uncle had said I would live here for the rest of my life.

I was overcome with happiness. I was so glad I had come to Edgecliff. I realized that I loved it with the fierceness of possession, the woods, the sea, the green hills, the sprawling gray house. I had never dreamed I could have such a sense of belonging, be so conscious that here was where my ancestors had been born, fought, loved, and died. I was glad I'd been born here. Yes, I belonged to Edgecliff as I had never belonged anywhere on earth before.

At length I turned back to the house, hungry for break-fast. How slowly that day passed! Annabel and I were underfoot everywhere we went. Mrs. Kerrenslea and Penwillen were in their element, directing the staff and the hired help. Penwillen was constantly down to the cellar and back, selecting the wines and champagnes that would flow like water that night. Mrs. Kerrenslea over-saw the laying of the linens and silver, the transforma-tion of the ballroom with plunder from the gardens and the greenhouse.

It seemed endless before it was time for Annabel and me to retire to our rooms and transform ourselves. Anna-bel looked almost sick with excitement, but though the ball was in her honor, I think I was as excited as she. It

121

would be the first ball for both of us, and we could hardly wait to wear the dresses that had been made for us.

My dress lay across my bed, and I touched its shimmering folds reverently. It might not be a Worth creation from Paris, but to me it was the most beautiful gown on earth. It was of rich cream-colored silk with wide insets of Irish lace. The neckline was low and round, and the skirt fell in simple, lovely lines. Palest green ribbons were laced through the openwork, and hemmed every tier of the skirt. It seemed to take forever for Nan to help me into it, she was so careful not to mar it as she maneuvered it over the petticoats and corset I wore.

"Oh, miss," she breathed when she was done with my hair. I believe Nan was as elated as I. She had worked wonders on my hair, piling it on top of my head, pinning a single cream rosebud behind one ear. We both held our breath as she clasped the single, long strand of pearls around my neck. Two days before, my uncle had presented them to me to wear at the ball. When I'd tried to protest at the costliness of the gift, he'd smiled and told me they were from the vault. Family jewels. I'd been deeply touched by the gift, which represented to me that I belonged to this family.

There was a knock on my door and Annabel burst into my room. "Oh, Emily, you look so beautiful!" she gasped. "Like a young queen! How I envy you your willowy figure."

"Willowy figure! And what do you call your own?" I laughed. "You, too, look beautiful, Annabel."

For a few moments, we admired each other, and were cooed over by Nan. Though at times Annabel was still a child inside, tonight all traces of the wild tomboy had been smoothed away. Her pale green dress deepened her eyes to emerald, and her smooth black hair shone like satin. "Oh, isn't it marvelous?" she cried, almost dancing with excitement. "And don't I look smashing?"

122

She pirouetted on her toes, her dress belling out around her ankles in an unladylike way.

"But come on. We must go and show ourselves to Uncle before the ball starts!" she reminded us, and the two of us left my room and walked down the hall to his door.

Mrs. Kerrenslea was there, and tonight she had traded her inevitable black for gray. But she still looked like a gore crow. I gave her a bright smile, for tonight no one could spoil my mood.

"Hello, Kerry, we've come to show ourselves to Uncle. Is he awake?" questioned Annabel breezily, in a tone I would never dare to adopt with the housekeeper.

Mrs. Kerrenslea's eyes softened as they looked at Annabel, and she smiled. "Indeed, Miss Annabel, he is waiting anxiously to see you. You look lovely tonight. Allow me to congratulate you on the occasion of your coming-out ball."

"Thanks ever so, Kerry. Though it's more fuss than I like, it's also much more fun than I expected!" Annabel knocked softly and led the way into Uncle's room.

Mrs. Kerrenslea's brief smile faded as she nodded to me as I passed. So she could be warm to others, I thought. No wonder the family put up with her. It was only me she acted so coldly to.

I will always remember that brief time Annabel and I stood next to Uncle's bed. We were so young, so high-spirited, so happy. In the years that have passed since that day, I have learned that such moments are to be treasured in the heart, for they are regrettably all too rare.

"You both look so lovely," my uncle said, looking from one of us to the other. "Emily, I see our local bachelors must beware tonight, lest they lose their hearts." Then his eyes came to rest on Annabel with pride. "And so you've grown up. And now you'll be marrying."

123

She stooped to kiss his cheek. "Maybe I will," she said impishly. "But don't get your hopes up, Uncle. I'll probably shock you all by marrying a stableboy."

"Minx!" He pinched her cheek, but I could see she did him good. It was a poignant moment, for he was looking weaker this week, grayer. And he had begun to lose flesh. But his illness had not affected his mind, or his spirits.

"Emily, darling," he said as I leaned to kiss his cheek. I could see he was filled with emotion. "You have become like a daughter to me."

"And you have given me a home, Uncle. Thank you," I murmured, touched deeply by his words.

"Don't take him too seriously, Emily . . . he's always telling us we're like children to him. But I imagine I've been a big enough disappointment that now he needs a new daughter to take my place!" said Annabel.

We all laughed, lightening the emotion of the moment. "I have been fortunate to find my house full of my children, though I never married. . . . Now run along, all of you, and have a wonderful time for me. I shall expect a full report tomorrow," he said, and watched us as we walked out the door.

It was time to go downstairs. My heart began to beat so hard beneath my stays that I felt I must sit down, or faint. But I held my head high and tried to adopt a cool insouciance I did not feel. I was nervous about the numbers of people I should have to meet shortly, about appearing at ease with my new social status. We reached the top of the stair, and paused. How glad I was to have Annabel at my side!

Charles, Richard, and William were standing at the bottom of the stair, looking up at us. For a moment we all formed a motionless tableau. Then Annabel picked up her skirts and started down the stairs. I don't know if I should have had the courage to move without her. How startlingly handsome Richard was in his formal dress. I was so nervous I had to hold hard to the banister. I could not look away from him, and his eyes never left mine as I descended.

Charles, of course, came forward first. He took my hand and kissed it, saying, "My God, Emily, you look ravishing." He turned to Annabel. "I can see the time has come to stop teasing our tomboy. Annabel, you look like a princess."

Richard, too, kissed my hand, an ironic smile on his lips. His eyes met mine again. "I meant to compliment you also, but my brother seems to have said it all—how can I possibly compete?" He turned to Annabel and kissed her cheek, and the two of them smiled at each other for a moment, their fondness for each other evident. "So you've grown up into a beauty, brat. Lord help the man who marries you!"

"Congratulations on your ball, Annabel," said William, kissing her cheek. "You do look nice. And he'll be a lucky man, as long as he rides." He looked at me, too shy to follow his brothers' example of hand-kissing, but managed, "Both of you look lovely. Shall we all go into the ballroom and toast Annabel's come-out, before the hordes arrive?"

William's suggestion was enthusiastically received, and we all went into the ballroom, talking and laughing. Penwillen was there, looking lordly.

"Oh, Penwillen," I exclaimed impulsively. "It looks wonderful!"

He beamed, letting his dignity slip for once. "Thank you, Miss Emily. Everything has gone most satisfactorily."

It did look beautiful. The ballroom floors shone, reflecting the candles in the chandeliers up above, and in the sconces along the walls. The French doors were open, and warm summer air carrying the scent of flowers came in. Chairs had been placed all along the walls, and potted palms and banks of flowers softened the baronial air of the ballroom. A huge table stood ready at one end for its burden of food and drink.

"It looks a fit setting for the twelve princesses to dance 'til dawn!" said Annabel.

Charles laughed gaily. "I propose a toast to dancing 'til dawn—in the finest house in Cornwall." He led the way to the table, where the champagne and wines were already set in ice, and an array of crystal goblets sparkled. Charles let the cork out with a pop, and poured.

"Ah! The first bottle of the night," said Richard. "I can't imagine a better way to begin a ball."

"And to give us courage to face the masses!" I said, holding my sparkling glass aloft for the toast. "Give us the toast, Richard—it is only fitting for the heir to the kingdom to open the ball for us!"

He held up his glass. "Then, to Annabel—and to a beautiful kingdom. May it always retain the happiness of this night."

We drank, but had barely time to finish our glasses before it was time to receive the first guests.

It was something of an ordeal for me. They had asked me to act as hostess for the ball, as Annabel had no other female relative. So I stood beside Richard in the entrance hall. Charles, Annabel, and William stayed in the ballroom. Many of the faces I greeted were familiar to me from calls, but many others were not. An endless period ensued, of watching the new arrivals hand their wraps to Penwillen and his minions, then bowing and exchanging pleasantries. They spoke of the perfect weather for the ball; how glad they were to meet me; did I miss London; and so on, until I could have turned and fled. But then Richard's hand covered mine for just a moment, and he gave me a reassuring squeeze, smiling down at me as if to tell me I was doing fine.

My heart sang, and I thought wistfully that this was

what it would be like if we were ever married.

He was amazing. He smiled, laughed, and talked, as if hosting balls was something he did every day of his life, and I thought how gracious he was when he wanted to be.

Then Evonne DeVere came in. I saw her sweep in, handing her lace wrap to Penwillen with a theatrical gesture. She wore an emerald green gown, cut very low, and an emerald-and-diamond necklace that drew the eyes to her bosom. She looked very beautiful.

Richard was talking to a friend of his. Sir Neville Trewithyian caught me staring toward the door and followed my gaze. He gave a low whistle, and said under his breath:

"Well, well. If it isn't the lovely widow. I'll just make myself scarce, old boy. Miss Woodstock, I know you won't want for dancing partners tonight, but all the same I'd be rather pleased if you'd have a hop with me later. Old Richard here'll tell you I'm safe enough—though I can't say the same for him." He grinned, with another impudent glance at the impatient Mrs. DeVere. He bade us farewell jauntily, and I saw her come forward.

She held out her hand for Richard to kiss, not even glancing at me. He bent briefly over her hand, his kiss the merest brush. "Hello, Richard," she said with an intimacy in her tone that rankled me. They might have been alone in the world. "It has been so long since I've seen you. Too long. You must not become a stranger at Woodmere."

I dared not glance at Richard's face, but his voice was expressionless as he replied, "Good evening, Mrs. DeVere. I have been busy of late. I find matters at home most absorbing." He paused. "You have met my cousin, Miss Woodstock, I believe?"

Her eyes sparkled angrily for an instant, then she turned to me with a sugary smile. "Oh yes, we have met. It is a pleasure to see you again, my dear. Such a sweet gown! So very correct for a young lady your age. You are a very correct young lady, I would guess, and I envy you for that quality. I am afraid I have the fault of liking to be daring sometimes . . . just a little bit naughty. But that can get me into trouble sometimes!"

I could not deny that she had charm. She gave these words a lilting tone, laughing at herself, and I knew she spoke for Richard's benefit. She made me feel too young, too prim, too plain. Her words held a double meaning, I believed. She was asking Richard what he could see in a proper young girl like myself when there was an exciting woman to be had.

"Such fun to be at a ball!" she exclaimed, and before I had a chance to answer her, she cast a final simmering glance at Richard and swept off.

I looked at Richard, but his face betrayed nothing. He was already turning to greet the next arrival. Not long after she left us, we all left Penwillen to greet the remainder of the guests, and walked into the ballroom to open the dancing. Richard was to take Annabel out for the first dance; I was to dance with Charles. William was partnering a girl named Hetty Lerryn, and as the first strains of a sweet Strauss waltz began, Richard turned to me. "Will you save me the next waltz, Emily?"

I promised him that I would, and then was whirled out onto the dance floor in Charles's arms, alight with happiness. My dreams of a magic evening were coming true, and I recklessly decided Evonne DeVere did not matter. She was in Richard's past.

It was tonight that mattered.

I laughed with Charles as we waltzed, hardly hearing what he was saying.

And then our dance had ended, and I was taking the floor with Richard.

Oh, to be held in his arms! I felt that my veins were filled with champagne. I was heedlessly, foolishly in love as I gazed up at his face and thrilled to feel his hand at my waist, his other hand clasping mine. To me it seemed we danced together as if we were made for each other.

"Your eyes are sparkling like stars. It must be the flower behind your ear," Richard said.

We laughed, and I knew he was referring to the first morning we'd met. "It's because I'm happy," I answered, and wondered if he knew it was because we were dancing together.

"I am glad you are happy. And glad that you are avoiding me no longer. How your gown becomes you. In a dress like that, the proper teacher has vanished. Is it possible you are barefoot under the dress?"

I laughed. "No, though—I feel as though I am."

"So, Emily . . . this ball is as much for you as for Annabel. To welcome you to Edgecliff. You love it here, do you not?" He was looking at me with a strange mixture of intensity and what seemed to be tenderness.

"I do."

"It seems . . . right, to have you here."

After that, we spoke no more. But I was powerfully conscious of the strength of the arms that held me, of the scent of bay rum and the faint aroma of a cigar, of the feel of his hand clasping mine.

That dance ended far too soon.

I remember only fragmented scenes from the ball after that. Standing with Annabel, Sir Neville, and Charles when William joined us, Hetty Lerryn on his arm. She was a sweet girl, with direct brown eyes, and William had been courting her steadily for some time. William had taken much teasing from Charles and Annabel at how slow he was being about asking her to marry him. We all greeted them merrily, and as I spoke to them, I heard snatches from Charles and Sir Neville's conversation.

"By jove, Annie Ilmenath is here—did you see her? She's grown from the little carrot-topped girl I remember! And Charles, I saw Helena Herringdale."

"Oh yes?" said Charles with eager interest, and I wondered if Helena Herringdale was a beauty, or an heiress, then laughed at myself at the tiny dart of jealousy I felt. What a dog in the manger I was becoming!

But I did not forget Richard. Far from it. I could not help glancing his way often that evening. But we were both caught up in the crush. Many of the young men and not a few of the old asked me to dance, and I sat down for supper with Neville Trewithyian.

I wondered what effect my popularity was having on Richard—if any. Sometimes we would dance past each other in someone else's arms, and our eyes would meet. Then I saw him dancing with Evonne DeVere, and I looked away, giving Charles, who was my partner at the time, a brilliant smile.

"Emily, I don't know what's come over you tonight," he laughed. "But I must say I find the change most enchanting. Where is the prim girl I've come to know so well?"

"She has vanished for this night. Charles—I am a bit warm from all this dancing. Would you mind if we joined the people in the garden? It's a lovely night." I wanted to get away from the sight of Richard and Evonne dancing. She was laughing up into his face, and he was smiling.

Charles led me from the crowded dance floor and out into the garden. Colored lanterns shielded candles against the breeze and lit the brightly dressed throngs. It looked glamorous.

"It's so crowded here. I propose a walk in the rose garden. It's lovely in the moonlight, and less stifling than this press," Charles said, surveying the terrace.

I agreed to go. I was reckless that night. I didn't stop to decide if it was the champagne I had drunk, or the sight of Richard and Evonne.

The rose garden was deserted and hauntingly lovely in

130

the moonlight. The scent of the roses was vivid, and music and laughter drifted to us from the terrace. We walked in silence for a short time, and I heard the faint sound of the sea.

Charles stopped at a stone bench that was set before a trellis, laden with blossom. We sat down, and I smiled at him.

"You look like a flower in the moonlight, Emily," he said, reaching out to touch my hair. Then he leaned toward me, as if to kiss me.

I got up and walked a few paces away. "Charles, please. I would not have come here alone with you if I thought—"

He was behind me, his hands on my shoulders, turning me around, and his next words stopped my protests.

"Emily—I love you. I have tried my best not to love you, but it seems that I have failed. I want you for my wife. Emily—will you marry me?"

I stared at him, speechless. I had not expected this! I had always taken Charles's flirting lightly, and believed he meant it so.

"Charles, I—I do not know what to say," I began. "This comes as a complete surprise to me." I was struggling for words, not wanting to hurt him, not knowing how to tell him I could not love him . . . nor marry him.

"It comes as a surprise to me, too. But do not answer me yet. First, may I not kiss you, lovely Emily?"

And without waiting for an answer, he did.

For a moment I did not resist, fearing to hurt him. But then I pulled back from his embrace and said seriously:

"Charles, please—I cannot answer you as you would like. For I do not love you, except as a cousin."

He smiled, and pushed back a strand of my hair. "Then I must be content with that for now. But I hope you will at least think about my offer of marriage. God help me,

131

Emily, but I mean it as I have meant nothing else."

"I—I will think about it." How could I tell him I loved his brother, when nothing had been spoken between Richard and I? Promising to think about it seemed the least I could say to him. I disengaged myself gently from his arms and smiled up at him. "Please, let's go in now, Charles. I fear we will be missed."

"And I hope it," he said, sounding perfectly easy, the old Charles I knew. "To have absented myself with the belle of the ball would surely be a feather in my cap."

We walked through the rose garden together, laughing, friendly together once more. Yet inside I was agitated, wondering if I had done the right thing, feeling I should have turned him down more firmly.

We stopped at a side door that led into the rose garden. "You go back to the ball, Charles. I'll go in this way, for I want to go upstairs and freshen up a bit."

"Oh! So you are afraid of what the gossips will say if we walk in together?" he teased me.

I was afraid of what his brother might think. But I merely smiled, and left him. Inside, I made my way up the stairs. I wanted to be alone for a few moments at least to think about Charles's proposal, collect my emotions. My slippers were noiseless on the thick carpet. The door to the upstairs library was open, and as I passed it, I glanced in. And then I halted.

Richard was standing there with his back to me, staring out the window. I was about to say something, when a clammy chill overtook me. I hurried noiselessly on. I had suddenly realized that the window of the upstairs library overlooked the rose garden!

I ran to my room and, shutting my door, sat down at my dressing table. Where was the bench in relation to the library window? Could he have seen us? I closed my eyes and pictured the view, then felt sick at heart. He would have had a clear view of that part of the rose garden from where he stood.

But had he seen us—heard us? I thought frantically. Even if he saw us, he couldn't have heard us. The library window was on the second floor. And then I realized it. That was much worse!

What a misleading little tableau it must have been if he could not hear what we were saying! Myself, obviously walking willingly with Charles alone into the rose garden, sitting down with him . . . and then, when he had kissed me, I had not resisted, nor seemed insulted, merely drawn back and talked for a few moments while he held me in his arms! And afterward, we had laughed together as we sauntered back to the house.

In that moment, I wished more than anything else that Richard had not seen us from the library. If he had, I knew well it would be the end of whatever was growing between us.

And then I wondered what he was doing in the library, away from the ball. Had he seen me leave with Charles, and gone there to spy on us? I felt hot and cold as I walked to the mirror, knowing that I dreaded going downstairs, knowing that I must stay away from the ball no longer . . .

I went back down to the lights and music and laughter. At first I didn't see Richard, and I did my best to pretend nothing was wrong with me as I stood and talked to Roger St. Hilary and Hetty Lerryn. Charles was dancing with a pretty blonde whom I guessed to be Helena Herringdale. I was glad he was occupied. I did not want to meet Richard with Charles at my side. My eyes kept combing the ballroom as I spoke to my companions. And then I saw Richard.

He had come in by a side door, and stood in its entrance. Our eyes met across the room. And at once I knew, I knew, that he had seen Charles and me. There was a coldness in his eyes, a dangerous glitter. He turned away and began to talk to someone else.

I was both dismayed and relieved. I could not face him yet, and yet—I had to talk to him. Tell him the truth of what had happened. Surely he could not ignore me the rest of the evening? I felt slightly ill. I accepted a dance with William, trying to put it all from my mind.

Later, Charles asked me to dance, but I refused, pleading fatigue. He looked at me curiously. "I'll bring you a glass of champagne. Cures everything!" he said, and was off before I could protest. I watched as he made his way to the table, filled with apprehension, for Richard was there. Charles walked up to him, all unsuspecting, and greeted him cordially. I saw Richard's black look, saw how savage his face was as he spoke, before he turned and made off, glass in hand. Charles looked after him, bewildered, and turned and made his way back to me.

He handed me the glass, saying, "I wonder what the devil's gotten into Richard? He looked like he had murder on his mind just now. Drink up, Emily—something seems to have gotten into you, too. All your sparkle's gone. What's the matter?"

"Oh, Charles," I said, feeling I must tell someone, "Richard saw us in the garden—I am certain of it! He was in the upstairs library, looking out the window, and—"

But he didn't let me finish. His eyes were cool, appraising me. "So that's the way of it? His seeing us in the garden worries you, does it?"

"Charles," I said miserably. "I'm sorry." There didn't seem to be anything else to say.

His eyes were hard. "Has he asked you to marry him?" he said brutally.

"No." I looked at my hands, which were tightly laced in my lap.

"And he won't. Forget about him, Emily—he seems to have found comfort elsewhere."

I raised my head and followed Charles's angry gaze

across the ballroom. Richard, glass in hand, was talking to Evonne DeVere.

"Emily, let me warn you about Richard," Charles said in a stony voice. "He is a hard man, and very ambitious. His only love is for Edgecliff. He wants to raise the fortunes of this family to a point no other Woodstock has ever managed. He will probably sit for Parliament one day. Only an heiress—someone who has lands to bring him, like Mrs. DeVere—will do for him. I know you thought the same was true of me . . . and once it was. Once I would have married for my gain. Then you came here and proved to me that some things matter more than money. But do not deceive yourself that Richard would let love stand in the way of advantage . . . if he can even feel such an emotion."

I was silent. What could I say? I feared he was right about Richard . . . and I feared that if Richard had begun to feel love for me, he felt it no more. How ironic it seemed that one of the brothers, at least, was willing to marry me just for love . . . but not the brother I wanted.

I thought of the old wisewoman's warning about marrying any Woodstock and felt cold.

The evening that had begun with so many hopes had ended dismally. Richard did not speak to me the rest of the evening, nor meet my eyes. At last the late-stayers departed. I felt bedraggled, like a flower that had wilted, as I made my way to my room.

I could barely wait for Nan to help me out of my dress and into my nightgown. It had been too many hours of pretending, hiding what I felt so that no one would see . . . not even Annabel. I pulled up the covers, wondering if I would be able to sleep. But I was so exhausted I must have fallen asleep almost at once, for I did not even blow out the candle.

I awoke with a start. The candle had almost guttered, and I had the feeling that a noise had awakened me. I turned, then sat up. A shock of terror jolted through me. My door was open, and outlined in the doorway was the black shape of a man.

Before I could scream, he stepped forward a few paces, and I almost fainted with relief.

"Richard!" I gasped. "Oh, you gave me such a scare! What are you doing here? Is anything wrong?"

He walked around the end of the bed and stood near me. My hand crept back to my throat. The look in his eyes stopped all further utterance. Suddenly I was conscious of how I was dressed, the thin white nightgown, my hair falling unbound around my shoulders—and as suddenly, I realized he had been drinking. His jacket was off, his shirt loosened, and there was a glitter in his eyes that made me afraid.

"What are you doing here, Richard?" I repeated. "What do you want?"

At this he smiled. "What do I want? Only what you see fit to give others."

And so saying, he bent and, pulling me to him, kissed me roughly.

I struggled wildly, frightened of his strength, of his anger. But his arms were like iron, holding me easily, hard against him, his lips burning mine in the most insulting of kisses, opening my mouth under his.

I felt a shameful fire start in my veins, an answering response to his passion, and just for a moment, I was kissing him back.

And I felt his breath draw in, his arms tightening around me, and his kiss softening for an instant. With a gasp, I turned my face away.

Then he released me, and flung me back on the bed. His eyes raked me, and my cheeks burned at the way he was looking at me. His eyes were so very angry.

"Thank you for a most . . . enjoyable kiss," he said sardonically. "Your lips are sweet—not less so because

136

many others must know it."

And then he left me. The door closed behind him, and for a moment, I lay there, stunned. Then I ran to the door and bolted it. I sank to the floor, trembling. With rage, fear, insult. Oh! Why hadn't I slapped him? Screamed at him to leave my room? Told him exactly what I thought of such behavior?

But I didn't know what I *did* think of such behavior, that was the problem.

I burst into tears. The first gray light of dawn was coming through my window. The long-awaited night of the ball was over at last.

Chapter Ten

I could not sleep.

At length, I dressed and slipped downstairs. I wanted to be alone to think, and I was afraid Annabel might want to talk over the night's events. But it was still early, and not even John, the head groom, was about. I saddled my mare and rode away from the house.

I barely saw where I was going, and so found myself at the cliff's edge, near the ruined gazebo. Though the dilapidated structure looked gloomy, this morning it suited my mood. I climbed the creaky steps and went inside the octagonal folly just as a light rain started to fall.

I could barely discern the sea through the gray mist that hung like a curtain in the sky, but I could hear the waves as they slapped against the rocks below.

Sitting on one of the dirty wooden benches that lined the inside of the gazebo, careless of my skirts, I closed my eyes. My thoughts were in turmoil.

If it had been anyone but Richard who had come into my room and subjected me to such treatment . . . I would have been angry and insulted. I would have screamed, brought the household running, demanding atonement. But because it had been Richard . . .

I was completely absorbed, I realized, in wondering what it meant that he'd done such a thing, on how I should act when I saw him next. And how he would act. And there was another, more disturbing, turn to my thoughts. I could not stop remembering how it had felt to be held in his arms, to have his lips on mine in an impassioned kiss. I saw him above me, his eyes dark with desire, felt myself being jerked tightly against his chest and crushed to him in a savage kiss.

The truth was, I had felt a wild thrill at his touch.

Emily, the ever reasonable and calm, had lost her head. Or was it her heart?

Oh, this was not how I had imagined it would be when I fell in love. I had pictured a gently growing feeling, based on respect and admiration, warming slowly like the sun as it climbs toward its zenith. Never this sudden passion, a passion that seemed to have burst into hot flames all at once, and was based on neither reason nor respect.

I had been swept away by my handsome cousin, by the long glinting green eyes, the black hair brushing the shoulders and the barely leashed aura of savagery . . .

I brought myself up with a start. This was not the way I should be thinking of him! Instead, I should be thinking of the words of those who knew my cousin better than I did myself. "He's got a black temper, has Richard Woodstock . . ." "A hard man, and very ambitious. Richard would never let love stand in the way of advantage . . ."

And why should I hope he would ever marry me? When he had not married Evonne DeVere, who was so much more beautiful than I, and who had money and lands to boot? I was only his penniless cousin, plain and with nothing to bring him . . . except my heart.

Yet I could not stop speculating. Why had he kissed me so passionately? Perhaps he did feel something for me, enough to cause jealousy. But he would never let such feelings stand in the way of advantage. Everyone told me so. I must forget such fantasies or I was courting disaster.

And what would I say to him when I saw him again? I did not know.

The rain clouds gathered deep in the sky, the wind picked up, threatening storm, and I rode back to the house, but I did not avoid a soaking. Once I had gained my room, I stripped off my wet things and climbed into the bed, pulling the covers over my head, shutting out the world. The fire crackled in the grate, and the rain beat against the windows. I was exhausted and soon slept, though my dreams were troubled by a tall, black-haired man who stood above my bed . . . or was it above me on the cliff's top, and was he laughing as I fell?

I was awakened by a knock. Confused, I sat up, seeing that the room was dim. What time could it be? It was dusk outside my windows. I had slept the entire day.

I opened the door and Mrs. Kerrenslea stood there, her black eyes cold.

"I have waited the entire day for you to stir so that I might deliver this note," she said. "Finally I was told to knock on your door and awaken you."

"Who told you to—" But she had thrust the envelope in my hand and walked away.

I recognized the strong script from the hours we had spent addressing invitations for the ball. It was from Richard.

> Dear Emily,
> Please grant me an interview alone, tonight after dinner. I must talk to you about last night. I will wait in the rose garden and I promise no repetition of last night's unforgivable behavior.
>
> Richard.

I took a deep breath. At least he regretted his actions. I

140

realized that it must be after the dinner hour, and he might be waiting for me at this moment.

I dressed plainly, in a dark blue gown with a high neck and long sleeves. I had no wish to appear alluring now. I grabbed my black cloak and hastened down the stairs.

The evening was gray and close. The wind that had threatened so early this morning had disappeared, not a breath stirring the air. As I entered the garden the scent of roses seemed heavy, almost intoxicating.

Richard stood with his back to me, gazing at the evening sky, and the sight of him made the breath catch in my throat. I walked slowly toward him, uncertain yet what I would say, what I felt.

The sound of my footsteps made him turn. "Emily," he said in a low tone. I could barely make out his features in the dusk. "Thank God you've come." There was emotion in his voice. He led me to a low bench next to the path, hemmed in by rose bushes.

The moon broke through a rent in the clouds and lit his face clearly then. My heart seemed to contract at how handsome he was. Suddenly the situation seemed false, strained—even ridiculous. I had always been one to speak my mind, and unbidden, words sprang to my lips.

"Richard. I know that I should be insulted and outraged at your behavior last night. But somehow, I don't feel that way. It isn't sensible for us to behave as if a tragedy has occurred. I hope we shall go on being friends, and forget all about this—unfortunate incident."

"I cannot forget," he said. "Nor can I forgive myself. But you astonish me, Emily. This proves to me what I already believed—that you are the most honest woman I have ever known."

I hesitated, then dared to speak my mind once more. "I should like to know, Richard, what could have prompted such an action?"

He was silent for a long time, and when he spoke, it was

141

slowly and carefully, as if he were weighing every word. "I shall do you the honor of being as honest with you as you were with me. I was jealous, jealous because I saw you kissing Charles in the garden." He stopped and looked at me seriously. "Do you love him, Emily?"

I was suddenly angry at the question. "It is hardly any of your concern. You are not my guardian."

"But why did you kiss him?" he demanded roughly.

I stood abruptly. He should be asking for my forgiveness, not asking me questions.

"I am not in love with Charles, if you must know. And I did not kiss him, he kissed me. If you believe your brother could be alone with a woman in the moonlight and not kiss her then you do not know him. I let him know gently that such advances were not welcome."

"If you admit you know my brother Charles could not be alone with a woman in the moonlight and not kiss her, then why did you go alone into the garden with him?" he said angrily.

"Perhaps it is because I was not the only one flirting last night! It seems to me that certain people could not resist dalliance with an old flame! And when you get your papers of guardianship over me, you may show them to me." I almost shouted the last words and turned to walk away.

Richard was beside me in a moment, pulling me tightly to him. "So you were jealous, too—as jealous as I was," he murmured in my ear.

"I thought there was to be no repetition of last night!" I cried, struggling. "Let me go!"

"I have not finished explaining," he said, and there was something in his voice that stilled my struggles. I looked up at him and saw his eyes glinting in a frightening way. And then he bent his head to mine and kissed me.

All the world vanished in that kiss. I clung to him,

dizzy with the sweetness of it. It held tenderness, yes; but there was a tightly leashed fire burning just beneath the tenderness.

He broke the kiss, for I must admit I would have permitted him to kiss me all night. "I have something to ask you when I am done explaining, my Emily. You see, I am jealous because I have come to—"

There were footsteps, hasty footsteps, on the path. Richard released me. Someone was calling our names.

It was William. "Thank God I've found you!" His face was white in the dusk, shocked. "Uncle has taken a terrible turn for the worse and he has asked to see you both. Charles has ridden for the doctor. I'm afraid it looks very bad," he said gravely, in answer to the questions on our faces.

Richard grabbed me roughly under the elbow and the three of us hastened toward the house. My heart was beating much too rapidly; first, the thrill of Richard's words, what I had seen in his eyes—followed by the frightening news. We hurried to Uncle's room. The entire staff of house servants were gathered outside the door, and I saw a maid touching her apron corner to her eyes. I stepped inside the room. I could not see my uncle for the crowd. But the dark shadow of Mrs. Kerrenslea stood in the corner.

Her face was whiter than ever before, stricken. And there was something in her eyes, an expression I had never seen there before. And then I understood.

I turned from her with pity and went to kneel beside Annabel at my uncle's bedside.

"Emily, Richard." His voice was weak, barely a ragged whisper. I could see by his pallid skin that he was not much longer for this world.

"I am here, Uncle," I said, taking his hand. "Rest now and be still—"

"And I am here also, Uncle." Richard was kneeling

143

beside me, his face drawn and white.

"You will always stay here, Emily," the dying man murmured.

"Yes, Uncle—please don't try to talk."

But he had turned his head and was staring at Richard with burning, hollow eyes. "Richard. Forgive me if I have done wrong. You can make it right together. You'd both be happy—it is what I want." He looked at me then with great love. "My child," he whispered.

He gasped, and stared at my face, eyes unfocused, then cried, "Amelia!" And died.

Everyone was staring at me. I bent my head, and my tears fell on his hand.

"He is dead then." Richard's eyes were wet as he reached out and gently closed my uncle's eyes. "So passes a great man."

Unrelenting sobbing broke out behind us and I turned to see who was so grief-stricken. It was Mrs. Kerrenslea. She had backed into a corner of the room, and I shall never forget her paper-white face, her fists pressed to her mouth, her eyes holding a naked misery in the first living emotion I had ever seen in them.

I knew then that she was in love with my uncle, and probably had been for many years. I felt a sudden sympathy for this woman who'd been forced to live in the same household for so many years for the man she felt an unrequited love for, and shuddered to think that I might very well be forced to share the same fate. For the king was dead, long live the king. Richard the heir was about to take his place on the throne and would no doubt be ready to claim a queen.

At length, someone pried my fingers from their tight grip and I kissed my dear uncle's cheek for the last time.

It was a dismal time until the funeral. The house soon

filled with guests, and everywhere I went there was the scent of funeral flowers and the sight of ominous black crepe hangings. Black, black, black. We all wore it, and it depressed me. How swiftly the gaiety of the ball had passed. "In the midst of life we are in death." The phrase occurred in my head monotonously.

How I missed my uncle. Though I had not known him long, he had become dear to me. I cried often as I thought of his kindnesses to me, the welcome he had given me. He'd offered me a family where I had none. "You will always stay here, Emily," he'd said on his deathbed. Everyone had heard it. It comforted me not a little to think that the home I had so lately found should not be taken from me because my uncle was dead. But I missed him as more than provider, rescuer from poverty. I had grown to like my uncle, nay, to love him. I only wished we had had more time together—and yet, I was grateful that they had not found me too late, that I'd had the chance to know him.

I had no chance to see Richard alone. He was busy with the funeral arrangements, writing letters, greeting mourners. Would I ever learn what he had meant to say in the garden? I had believed that he was about to say, "I have come to love you." And what had he meant to ask me? To marry him?

Now he was pale, withdrawn. He seemed to be truly grieving for Uncle. And it was all his now, the whole kingdom. He hardly noticed me. I could see that his responsibilities weighed heavily on him. No more dalliance with a poor relation, a cipher who would bring him nothing.

It rained on the day of the funeral. The air was warm, but the skies were gray and lowering. The church was filled, and the farmers stood hatless in the rain outside to show their respect for Squire. My heart was heavy as we followed the funeral coach to the churchyard.

145

So short a time I had known my uncle. Now I would never be able to ask him any of the questions that had plagued me. The quarrel with my father. Now I would never learn what its roots were.

And what had Richard to forgive him for? Uncle's last words seemed little more than gibberish to me. I thought of my father's last words, realizing how significant they had been, not the feverish ravings I had mistaken them for. And—it was disturbing. Sir Ralph had died calling my mother's name. My mother's name. Why had his thoughts turned to her last of all, when he stood at death's portal?

The thought of my uncle's cryptic words and of Richard brought my mind naturally to the scene in the garden. In the days to come, how I was to wish I knew what Richard had been about to say to me. Too many mysteries would surround me.

I followed the procession, lost in my thoughts, and I hardly felt the soft rain as it fell on my cheeks dripping from my black lace veil and mingling with my tears. The pall bearers lowered the casket into the ground and I bent to pick up some moist black earth. I let it slip through my fingers and the sound of it landing on the carved wood coffin would be in my memory for a very long time.

At last it was over, and the house was empty save for the family. Most kept to their rooms. That afternoon the will was to be read in the library.

I wished I did not have to be there. But everyone was sure Uncle had left me something, enough to leave me comfortable. Not enough for Richard to want to marry me—of that I was certain. Suddenly I was fiercely glad of that. At least he would never marry me for my money!

The library looked a solemn place when I entered. Everyone, still dressed in black, was seated, facing the man who had been the first to change the course of my life, the solicitor, Mr. Carrington. He cleared his throat into the silence, and looked most grave.

There were many bequests. A large one for Mrs. Kerrenslea, including a cottage on the estate, along with a provision for her continued employment as housekeeper until such time as she wished to retire. A sizable sum for Penwillen. A dowry for Annabel, legacies for Charles and William, personal belongings.

And then: "With the exception of the appended bequests, the bulk of my estate and all of my fortune, I bequeath to my nearest relative, Emily Woodstock."

I sat as if thunderstruck. Later, Annabel told me I had turned as white as the pages the solicitor was reading from. His voice droned on, mentioning Richard, but I did not hear. Everyone's eyes were riveted to me.

At last I looked at Richard. He was deadly pale, staring at me as if he would never stop. I couldn't bear it. I got up and rushed from the room before the reading was over. I could not hear any more.

"No, no!" I moaned in the hall, tears on my face. "No, Uncle, it is all wrong! Edgecliff is his—it belongs to Richard!" I reached my room and sank into a chair, sobbing.

It was a terrible mistake. How could I, who knew nothing of running an estate, be expected to accept such an inheritance? I did not understand.

But one thing I understood all too well. Now I knew why my uncle had apologized to Richard on his deathbed.

I was sitting with my head in my hands when there was a knock at the door. I did not wish to be disturbed, to answer the family's questions, indeed, even to face them, so great was the shame I felt. The stranger, who had so lately come, inveigling the inheritance away from them!

"Miss Woodstock—it is Mr. Carrington. May I see you?"

I rose and opened the door. If there was one person

147

who could help me in my plight, it was Mr. Carrington.

I thought he looked at me with some pity as he took a chair. I am sure he could see how distraught I was.

"This has been a great shock to you, no doubt, Miss Woodstock," he began. "But I must assure you that I myself saw to the changing of the will, and your uncle was in sound mind when he changed it. It was his dearest wish that the estate should go to you—to 'right past wrongs,' he said."

"But Mr. Carrington," I said quickly, "All past wrongs were righted when my uncle took me in and gave me a home. I do not know the nature of the quarrel—and what is more, I have no wish to know." Though this was untrue, at the moment it seemed true to me. At the moment, I almost wished that I had never heard of Edgecliff, or relatives, that I was safe back in my lodgings in London. "Mr. Carrington, you must help me. You must help me to undo this great wrong."

He raised his eyebrows at me.

I leaned forward, clasping my hands in my eagerness. "The estate must go to Richard, do you not see? You must help me sign it over to him. You must draw up the necessary papers, at once."

"I am afraid, Miss Woodstock, that even if I did not believe that to be a very misguided course, it is also an impossible one."

"What do you mean!" I cried, distressed.

"Under the terms of your uncle's will, the estate—which was never entailed—remains yours for life. But unless there is bankruptcy, you may not sell nor transfer ownership of the estate. If you are worried about your cousin Richard, which is admirable of you, let me say that your uncle was most generous with Richard in terms of money. He will be what amounts to a rich man."

"Do you think Richard cares for money when he has spent his whole life caring only for Edgecliff—yes, and

148

slaving for it?" My voice rose. "You know what shape the estate would be in were it not for Richard, since my uncle fell ill. Then you mean to tell me I cannot—cannot sign it all over to him?"

"You cannot. And it would be against your uncle's dying wishes, in any case."

"Then—then, I shall give away all the money until we are bankrupt, and sell it to Richard!" I said wildly. "I tell you, I cannot accept it."

He looked at me as one might look at a small child. "My dear Miss Woodstock, even Richard's fortune would hardly be adequate to purchase Edgecliff. And the terms of the will specify that it be sold for the best prevailing price, perhaps to prevent such a giveaway. I am afraid that, little as you may like it now, your uncle wished you to be mistress of Edgecliff. In time, I think you will see he did it out of great love for you."

Mistress of Edgecliff. My heart turned to ice.

"Th—Thank you, Mr. Carrington. I—I am sure I will wish to speak to you later, to discuss many details. I—" I was crushed that there seemed to be no way I could give the estate back to Richard. I felt dull, broken.

"There is one more small matter. Your uncle left an envelope for you in my care." He reached into a pocket and handed it to me. It felt heavy.

"Thank you, Mr. Carrington," I repeated, rising. "I appreciate all your help."

"I am always here, and remember, all that is said between us will remain in confidence. Good night, Miss Woodstock. Try to rest with an easy mind."

As he turned for the door, I saw his eyes rest on the envelope clutched in my hand, and I was surprised to see a speculative look in them.

Chapter Eleven

I had no heart to open the envelope that night. I took to my bed, and I fell into a deep dreamless sleep. In the morning I sent a message down with Nan that I was indisposed and would be unable to breakfast with the family. I could not bear to go down and see them, see their speculative glances, and most of all, I could not yet face Richard. I needed time to think, time to decide what could be done. I would be unable to do anything to remedy the wrong that was done, save taking to my deathbed, if there was any truth to Mr. Carrington's words. I only knew the truth of how I felt, that Edgecliff was not mine, it was Richard's. Maybe I should stay in my bed, I thought, because sleep seemed the only comfort for me now.

I requested a tray brought to my room and Nan served breakfast with much formality. Her manner toward me had changed overnight and for a moment I wondered why and then chastised myself. Of course. I was the mistress of Edgecliff now, no longer a poor relation that she could feel comfortable gossiping with.

I wondered, too, how differently the family would treat me, now that they would be living under my good graces. I shuddered at the thought, not wanting such power, such responsibility. And Richard, what of Richard? How must he be feeling? My heart ached.

How could my uncle have believed this bequest would be a good thing? I wondered miserably. I was so new to Edgecliff—though I loved it, I was not prepared to be its mistress, with all the responsibility that entailed. I knew nothing of running farms, or mines, or even a great house. All I had hoped for was an independence, nothing more, so that I would not have to go back to a life of poverty. Enough to leave Edgecliff when Richard married another.

After I had dressed, with a heavy heart, I picked up the envelope and fingered it, almost dreading the thought of opening it. Would it contain yet another trouble for me? With a sigh, I tore it open.

It contained a key, and a short note in my uncle's handwriting.

My dearest Emily,

I think of you as a daughter. By now you will have learned of my wishes, my wish that you should take your rightful place as mistress of Edge-cliff and everything in it. The past reaches out long shadows that fall on the sunshine of today. May the shadows of the past not trouble you as they have me. With what I have done, I feel at peace at last, the old hurts healed in the only way they can be.

This key is to the locked room in the West wing. The room and everything in it is yours now, as it should be. With much love and a wish that sunshine will always follow you,

Your loving Uncle,
Ralph Woodstock

Tears were falling as I finished the letter. So leaving Edgecliff to me had brought my uncle peace. But why?

And a locked room. I suppressed an urge to laugh wildly. It was all so melodramatic. It hardly seemed as if it could be happening to me. And, I thought, I knew which room he meant. The only one in all of Edgecliff that was locked.

I opened my door and looked both ways down the hallway. No one was in sight. I knew I was behaving like a coward, but I simply could not face anyone yet. I set off toward the West wing, carrying a lit candelabra, and met no one on the way there.

Locked room . . . I thought I knew which door it was, a door to a small tower that I had never been shown. Mrs. Kerrenslea had said that the stairs were unsafe. Were they—or was it just another lie to keep me from asking questions?

I was apprehensive as I turned the key to the door. It fit. Apprehension about the stairs, and about what I would find in the room, I climbed the dark stone staircase slowly, but the stairs, though worn in the middle, were strong enough. At the top was another door, shut but not locked.

I carefully stepped into the dim room and it took more than a moment for my eyes to become accustomed. The windows, on three sides, were covered with thick velvet draperies so no sunlight could enter. But soon enough the splendor revealed itself.

It was the most feminine room I had ever seen. All white and lavender, from the four-poster bed awash with lace and ruffles, the delicate vanity with its gilded mirror, the armoire that dominated the far side of the room. It, too, was painted white and the intricately carved flowers were done in the palest lavender with light green leaves and stems.

I felt as if I had stepped back into the eighteenth century. On the floor by the fireplace was a white fur rug. I looked up at the white marble mantel and my eyes widened in wonder.

There was a portrait there, and with a dizzy sense of unreality, I stared up at it. Faintly smiling gray eyes met mine. Eyes almost exactly like mine. In fact, I might have been looking at a portrait of myself, had not the different style of clothing betrayed its age.

Beneath the painting, a small gold plate proclaimed *Amelia Trevant*.

My mother had been beautiful, more so than I. Her expression was sweet, and slightly sad. She was dressed in deep red, her hair dark in a cascade of ringlets that fell on her white shoulders. I felt a surge of deep love and longing as I looked at her portrait.

"Oh, Mother," I whispered. "What does this mean?"

And then I saw, and I believed I knew.

On her finger was the ring. The ring of the Edgecliff brides. I touched the ring where it hung on the chain around my neck.

The ring that was given by the eldest son, the heir, to his betrothed. Not stolen, no. You did not have a portrait painted of a thief wearing the stolen goods. This room was a shrine, a shrine to a lost love. It must be the answer.

Was my mother once engaged to marry Sir Ralph?

And now it was all too clear what the brothers may have quarreled about.

And so . . . and so my uncle had left Edgecliff and everything in it to me, to me, the daughter of his rival, the daughter of his lost love. He'd said he thought of me as his daughter. I was his closest blood relation, and not only that, borne by the woman he'd loved.

Had I solved the mystery at last?

In time, I turned from the portrait to explore the rest of the room. The armoire held old clothes, carefully preserved with lavender sachets in the folds. I touched the velvets and silks with a reverent hand, then closed the door. I opened drawers, hoping perhaps to find letters or diaries, but the drawers were all empty. Except for

153

one, in which there was a jewel box.

I opened the lid, and color winked at me like a dream from Aladdin's cave. One by one I drew out the pieces.

There was a great strand of moonlit pearls with an elaborate sapphire and diamond clasp. There was a breathtaking emerald set that included a necklace, bracelet, earrings, and a hair clip. There was a sapphire set of equal magnitude. And then there were the diamonds. In every shape imaginable, I marveled at their magnificence, struck almost dumb.

And all to belong to me? No. I should give the emeralds to Annabel, I resolved, for they would match her eyes. The sapphires to Richard, and diamonds to Charles and William. For their brides.

I moved aside the lesser jewelry, amethysts, carnelians, opals, and topaz, for at the bottom was a heavy black velvet box, quite large. I gasped when I opened it.

It was the rest of the set. Those heavy, old-fashioned settings could not be mistaken. Rubies and diamonds flashed savagely at me from a necklace, two bracelets, a brooch, and two hair clips.

"The blood and the tears," I whispered, and drew the ring on its fine chain out of my collar. Oh yes, it matched.

The ring would have to take its rightful place, I resolved. I saw that the lining of the case was old and worn thin, and it was the work of a moment to make a small tear in the corner. I would tell them I had found the ring in the lining when looking at the jewels. I picked up the jewelry box and took a last look at the portrait of my mother. I would bring it downstairs when I dined with the family—perhaps tomorrow. Then I could give them the jewels and—

"Guilt gifts, Emily?" a mocking voice in my mind asked me.

I squared my shoulders. Yes, and why not? Why should I not be guilty?

154

For I had stolen Edgecliff from them, and everything in it.

Had I not?

The next day, I awoke at dawn. Today would be the day I faced the family. All the day before, I had stayed in my room, but I could not stay there forever. Somehow, some way, there must be a solution.

I dressed and went to the stables. It was a beautiful, mournful morning. The clouds were so low that the mist crept in streamers over the tops of the hills and steamed in the valleys, so that the delineation between cloud and fog was impossible to make. Near at hand, the grass was long and an unearthly brilliant green, heavy and bent with dew. Each blade sparkled with silver drops that caught the growing light and made it seem as if I rode over a carpet of diamonds.

I was reminded of my first morning at Edgecliff, when I walked barefoot along this thick grass. That day when I had first met Richard, and tears came to my eyes.

At last I reached the cliffs and sat on my motionless horse, looking down at the angry gray sea crashing below. Spray with a tang of salt blew in my face, and the wind had a raw, cutting edge, blowing apart the rags of mist. This was where my mother had come, perhaps, and fallen from the cliffs. Beloved by two men, she had set brothers at each other's throats.

I turned my mare toward the little copse that grew in the shelter of a small valley between the great shoulders of the cliff and the old gazebo at its edge.

I dismounted and tied the mare to a sapling, then sat upon a great hoary log, green and soft with moss. Primroses made a mist about my feet, and iris stood in tall ranks. A brake of fern spangled with dew-hung spiderwebs flashed red in the growing sunlight.

Crackling and snapping in the underbrush broke my reverie. I turned, and presently a horse and rider loomed out of the mists. The mare's ears were pricked alertly, her head turned to watch them. The figure on horseback resolved itself. It seemed inevitable. I would have known that great rangy black stallion anywhere.

It was Richard.

Chapter Twelve

He reined in his horse when he saw me. "Emily," was all he said, no note of feigned surprise in his voice.

"How did you find me?" I asked wearily. He was the last person on earth I wanted to see at the moment.

He dismounted and tethered his mount next to mine, and the animals were at once occupied in nuzzling each other. Richard came and stood closer, but made no move to sit down.

"Dryads tend to haunt the same places . . . and I saw you leave the house," he finally answered, looking down upon me.

"But it must have taken you some time to mount and follow me here. How did you know where to find me?"

"It was quite clear which way you'd ridden." He indicated the dark green track over the fields, where my mare had brushed away the morning's dew.

"What have you come for?" I asked when he did not volunteer any more.

"I wanted to speak to you alone." He laughed shortly. "It is amazing that in a house the size of Edgecliff, opportunities to be alone should be so few. But so I have found it. Every room has a brother or sister and you have been keeping to your room."

157

"And why is it important that you speak to me alone? I, too, have things to say, but I have come here to decide just what those things are to be. I am sorry, Richard."

"Do not be. It is a grand joke that Uncle Ralph played on us all at the last, isn't it? But that is not what I wished to speak of."

"But now that it has been brought up, I would like to say something," I said, suddenly coming upon the solution that I had been searching for these past days. "I ascertained from the solicitor that I may not sell Edgecliff, not even to you. But I am willing to leave and let you run the estate as if it were yours, Richard. It is not right that he left it to me, regardless of his reasons. I do not wish it so. If you will trade bequests with me, I will be happy."

He was watching me with a strange gleam in his eye, then his breath heaved, almost a convulsive sob or sigh.

"Of course that is out of the question. My pride forbids it, and that is not what Uncle's dying wish was in any case. But thank you, Emily. No, one of the things I had wanted to speak to you about was the Woodstocks. My brothers and sister certainly expected to remain here in the event that I inherited, at least until they marry. I hope that you will ask them to stay still, for I am afraid they have nowhere else to go."

"Oh, of course!" I cried, marveling at the unselfishness that must have prompted this request, a request wounding to his great pride, I had no doubt. "You must all stay, for the rest of your lives if you care to! In any case, Richard, how shall I run this great estate without you?"

"No, Emily. I spoke for my brothers and sister only. I plan to go away."

I blinked my eyes and clutched tightly to the moss-covered log. "Go away?" My voice broke, wild.

"It would be best for me to leave. Perhaps America. I

hear that a man can make much of himself there if he is willing to work."

"But you cannot! You must not!" I leapt to my feet and looked into his eyes pleadingly. "I—did not jest when I said I could not run this estate, and think how much you love it! It is your home and besides—"

"Besides?" he said, looking into my face with quickening interest. "It would matter so much to you if I went away?"

"Yes, it would matter," I cried, throwing caution to the winds. Now was not the time to be coy. It had suddenly struck me with force how bleak and weary my world would be if Richard went away, to America of all places! I would never see him again.

"It would matter very much to me," I continued in a low voice, averting my eyes from his. Even if he did not love me, I would be happy to have him near.

"And I would hate to leave," he said. "To leave everything that I ever loved, and everything I have grown to love."

I dared not look at him. I was silent.

"I would hate to lose what I have so lately found," he continued, and his voice was husky.

"What have you found?" I almost whispered, my voice shaky.

"Emily!" He was beside me, pulling me close. "I have found you. I love you, Emily," and he turned my chin up to look at him. His green eyes were like burning coals.

"Love me?" I tried to laugh. "What nonsense is this, Richard? I—"

"Ah, you do not believe me. I have waited too long to speak. That night in the garden when we were interrupted—I was going to ask you to marry me then. How I wish I had! Before this damned will was read."

I was breathless.

He went on, "I think I have loved you since that first

159

morning, when you seemed like a dryad to me. And how changeable you were! I loved to watch you ever since, so prim and quiet, knowing that a wild girl lurked somewhere behind those downcast eyes! And . . . and I love you the most, I think, because you are sensible. I have never found a woman whose mind I could respect before, who I could talk to. How can I convince you that I love you?"

And then his lips were on mine, gentle at first, then demanding. The world vanished for me and I was swept away into a realm I had never known existed.

"Do you love me, Emily, my darling?" he was murmuring against my lips. "I love you—say you love me."

"I love you." It seemed inevitable.

"Then marry me, Emily," he said.

It brought me to my senses like a cold slap. I struggled with him, pushing him from me.

"Richard, I must—I must think!"

The thing that I had dreamed about, wished for, had seemed forever out of reach, was being offered to me and I was filled with a panic. So much had happened, changed. The words of Malvina burned in my memory. *"The Edgecliff brides are cursed . . . heed my words and do not become one."* How much more filled with meaning they were now. I could not say yes without visiting Malvina first. For this and so many other questions.

Richard's lips closed on mine again, stilling my protests.

"I love you, Emily," he was saying again. "I love you and cannot live without you. If you do not say yes this moment, I shall leave for America tomorrow. I could never be on the same continent as you—the temptation to come back would eat at me all the time. I love you! Do not say that you will not be mine. Marry me, Emily."

Leave tomorrow! I could not bear to have him go away. I loved him. I wanted him to be with me, to live with me at

160

MORE PASSION AND ADVENTURE AWAIT... YOUR TRIP TO A BIG ADVENTUROUS WORLD BEGINS WHEN YOU ACCEPT YOUR FIRST 4 NOVELS ABSOLUTELY *FREE* (AN $18.00 VALUE)

Accept your Free gift and start to experience more of the passion and adventure you like in a historical romance novel. Each Zebra novel is filled with proud men, spirited women and tempestuous love that you'll remember long after you turn the last page.

Zebra Historical Romances are the finest novels of their kind. They are written by authors who really know how to weave tales of romance and adventure in the historical settings you love. You'll feel like you've actually gone back in time with the thrilling stories that each Zebra novel offers.

GET YOUR FREE GIFT WITH THE START OF YOUR HOME SUBSCRIPTION

Our readers tell us that these books sell out very fast in book stores and often they miss the newest titles. So Zebra has made arrangements for you to receive the four newest novels published each month.

You'll be guaranteed that you'll never miss a title, and home delivery is so convenient. And to show you just how easy it is to get Zebra Historical Romances, we'll send you your first 4 books absolutely FREE! Our gift to you just for trying our home subscription service.

BIG SAVINGS AND FREE HOME DELIVERY

Each month, you'll receive the four newest titles as soon as they are published. You'll probably receive them even before the bookstores do. What's more, you may preview these exciting novels free for 10 days. If you like them as much as we think you will, just pay the low preferred subscriber's price of just $3.75 each. *You'll save $3.00 each month off the publisher's price.* AND, your savings are even greater because there are never any shipping, handling or other hidden charges—FREE Home Delivery. Of course you can return any shipment within 10 days for full credit, no questions asked. There is no minimum number of books you must buy.

4 FREE BOOKS

Edgecliff Manor. I wanted to be his wife.

"Yes," I breathed. Why had I resisted?

He kissed me then with a passion that I had never known. He lifted me with his strong hands and twirled me around in the air, my skirts billowing in the breeze and we laughed together. And then he kissed me again.

Much later he released me and helped me, shaken, onto my horse's back. He smiled up at me, beautiful in the morning sunlight. A dream come true.

"I will make you happy, Emily," he promised. "You will never regret this. And you have made me the happiest man alive!"

How could I not believe him? We rode off, my heart singing, sure in newfound love. I had made him the happiest man alive. Then a thought struck me, which I banished almost as quickly as it had come. I had made him the happiest man alive—for had I not given him Edgecliff?

"I am so happy Richard is marrying you, Emily," said Annabel. "Thank God he has shown some sense at last. You know that I was terribly afraid for some time that he might marry that awful DeVere woman. Woodmere does adjoin Edgecliff, and I thought he might overlook her crassness for the sake of her lands. But then you came along and Richard seemed to forget all about her! I'll be happy to have you as a sister," she finished. I smiled but sighed inwardly. Would people never tire of reminding me about Richard's fling with Evonne DeVere?

Then she slanted a look at me with her green eyes. "But . . . isn't this decision just a bit hasty? It's not like you not to be more . . . sensible."

This was not the reaction I had hoped to hear. I was still shaking from the excitement of his kiss, and I had drawn Annabel into my room to tell her that we would be

161

married. I had expected her to be overjoyed. But instead, she seemed reserved at my news, as if she wanted to say more.

"Oh, Annabel, so much has happened to change me! I know that it must seem sudden to you, but really it is not. I have felt this way since I first saw Richard. I tried to suppress it, I tried to change my feelings, but I couldn't. I am in love, you see. I have never known it before, but I am certain that is what I feel for him. I was certain on the night of the ball when he took me into his arms for our first waltz."

"Are you sure it is love, and not passion?" she asked me with a smile. "He is very handsome, and has swept a number of girls off their feet. Do not construe me wrong, I am happy for the family that Richard is going to marry you, but I have grown fond of you, Emily."

"Richard is not a rake," I said, somewhat indignantly. "Besides, can you name a man who works harder, or is more dedicated? He is always either at the mines, or overseeing Edgecliff. Now, I can understand your doubts if it were Charles I was thinking of marrying, someone whose only asset is his charm, and who has never done a day's work in his life. But Richard is different! He lives for Edgecliff."

"Well, you said it before I could. He lives for Edgecliff. And now you are Edgecliff. If he loves you, why didn't he ask you to marry him before, when you had nothing? Are you sure he is marrying you—or marrying Edgecliff?"

I jumped up, grabbing the shutters and throwing them open. I needed air. It hurt to hear her put into words all the secret doubts I had felt. I had hoped for reassurance from her. But they say that love is blind . . . and I say that it is blind and stubborn. Since she would not say what I wanted to hear, I would say it myself. My heart felt so strongly that it was true.

"He is marrying *me*, Annabel," I said coldly. "He told me he has loved me since he first saw me . . . that he loves me for my mind and heart. He was in anguish because he had not proposed sooner. But Uncle died so suddenly. In fact the night he died, Richard and I were in the garden. From what he said, I am certain he was about to propose. But then William came running with the news that Uncle was dying. So you see, he never had the chance. He wanted to leave for America . . . I even offered to give him Edgecliff, but he refused!" I finished angrily, angry because even to my own ears, my explanations sounded weak.

Annabel looked at me and shut her lips, as if over words that wanted to spring out. There was so much I could not tell her. I had never told her about how Richard had come to my room the night of the ball . . . but would even that convince her? She would blame it on the drink . . . or on lust. Her next words confirmed this.

"Then marry my brother, Emily, and make the family happy. Give Richard back the kingdom. I am sure he will make you a good enough husband. I have seen the way he looks at you . . . I have seen him look at other women like that before. I am sure you will please him in the marriage bed. It is just that I know my brother, and I fear the wife for him should be a woman who is as hard as he is in every way. In any case, I have said more than I meant to—and more than enough." She rose, and looked at me as if regretting my foolishness.

"I am sorry you cannot approve of my marriage, Annabel," I said coldly, very angry now. I saw the hurt in her face at my tone, but I went on. "I would think that you would support me, and want my happiness, even if no one else would. I believe I have proved that I am your friend . . . and my home is still open to you, even if you cannot be as loyal to me as I am to you."

She gasped, then turned red. I saw tears start in her

163

eyes. "I am sorry," was all she said before she left the room.

I was a frozen icicle, clutching the desk for support. I was alone in my room, in my house, on my estate. I studied my face in the mirror. Was this a madwoman inside me, taking control? Where had Emily gone? Cool and practical Emily who looked toward the future and studied it carefully not to make the wrong decision. Could love change one so? How could I have said such cruel things to my dear friend? When she was only speaking the truth out of love for me? I bowed my head and cried, deeply ashamed and deeply confused.

That afternoon there was a knock at my door and I was surprised to see Richard standing there.

"You look sad," he said to me as I opened the door. "Are you not happy with our engagement?"

"Oh, yes! That is the one thing that I am happy about. Do not worry, Richard, I am well." I stood at the doorway, reluctant to invite him in. Even though we were bespoken, it would still be improper.

"Then you will be able to come down to dinner, to finally dine with the family again." I felt suddenly ashamed for hiding in my room.

"Of course," I said and smiled.

"Because I would like to announce our engagement at dinner."

I took a deep breath, wondering what the family might think, then pushed those thoughts from my mind. Nothing mattered except that Richard and I loved each other.

"There is something I must show you first," I said. No servants lurked in the hall. "Come in and sit down."

I could feel Richard watching me as I went to my bureau and removed the black velvet box. I turned, and explained to him that I had already opened Uncle's secret room and that soon I would take him there.

"In the room, there was a portrait . . . a portrait of my mother," I said, watching his face.

"I know—I have seen it," he said.

"You have seen it?" I was startled.

"Yes. Do you not remember how once I said you were too thin? Now that you have put on flesh, you are more like her than ever."

"Then—has everyone seen it?"

"Yes, at one time or another."

"And have you seen what she wears on her finger?"

"The ring of the brides. Yes," he said.

I had to sit down. "Richard, I—"

"Do you have it?" he asked softly, his eyes glinting at me like a panther's in the grass.

For an answer, I pulled the ring on its chain out of my dress.

"I thought so. I always wondered if your mother took the ring."

"Does—does anyone else suspect?" I said weakly.

"I doubt it. They were not in the room more than once. But I went there more than they did. And I noticed, though I never dared to ask Uncle about it."

"The portrait . . . and the ring, does this mean that my mother was engaged to Sir Ralph?"

"Oh, yes. That, at least, is common knowledge in these parts."

I rose, agitated. "Then why did no one ever tell me?"

He shrugged. "Ancient history, no doubt. Besides—I simply presumed you knew. May I see the ring?"

He stood and waited while I unclasped the chain. I handed him the ring and then he startled me, going down on one knee.

"Will you wear the ring? The ring of the Edgecliff brides? For I must ask you again, when I am not kissing you senseless—will you marry me?"

"Yes." I was breathless at this romantic gesture. "No

165

matter how many times you ask me, I shall say yes."

My eyes were brimming with tears of joy when he slipped the ring on my finger. As if fate had ordained it, the ring was a perfect fit.

When he had risen, he kissed me, and again, my head spun. His lips on mine were enough to make me forget the world and everything except the feel of his arms around me. At last he released me.

"Richard—the ring. I'd rather not have it all raked up again. I had thought to tell everyone else that I found it in a tear in the lining of the box."

For a moment he frowned. "But Emily, why?"

"It—it still seems to me as if my mother should have returned the ring, since she did not marry Sir Ralph. It is too like thievery in a way. And besides, what does it all matter now?"

"Very well. You will find, my darling, that your lightest wish is my command."

I left the room a happy woman, once again sure—as I always was when I was with him—of his love.

That evening at dinner, Annabel was polite to me, but avoided my gaze. I longed to draw her aside and apologize for what I had said. It had been so wrong of me to remind her that I had asked her to live here, as though it were a favor that made her owe me her unqualified support.

Richard noticed my preoccupation. He seemed puzzled that I didn't look happy, and several times gave me an inquiring look. But of course, with all the cousins at the table, I could say nothing to either of the two most dear to me.

After dinner, we all retired to the drawing room. I knew that Richard meant to announce our engagement now, and I was suddenly nervous. Would they all think what Annabel had thought?

"I have an announcement to make," Richard said, raising his glass. How tall and handsome he looked in the lamplight. Everyone looked up, curious. Richard continued, smiling at me.

"I believe that congratulations are in order. Today, Emily has agreed to become my wife, and the ring of the Edgecliff brides has been found."

I raised my left hand and there were gasps from around the room. With every eye on me, I told them my lie of how the ring was discovered.

There was silence for a moment. Charles's eyes opened wide in shock. I saw him start. Then he smirked, and I felt cold. Annabel was staring at Richard. It seemed like an eternity before William raised his glass and said heartily:

"Congratulations! This is wonderful news! Richard, I think you could not have chosen a better bride!" That seemed to unfreeze everyone. All at once they were congratulating us, and laughing, and demanding when the wedding would be. It was as if the short shocked silence had never happened.

William called for champagne, and in the confusion, Charles came up to me. He maneuvered his way to my side, champagne glass in hand. "Congratulations, Emily," he said quietly, with a mocking smile on his face. "Of course, Richard is even more to be congratulated on his luck . . . or should I say perception. It is not often a man is fortunate enough to obtain his heart's desire . . . all by merely marrying a beautiful bride. But Richard has always known what he wanted, and how to go after it. Didn't I tell you that he is a hard man, and ambitious, that his only love is Edgecliff?"

"Richard and I love each other, Charles," I said hotly, stung by his cynical words.

"On one side maybe," he said. "I do not think Richard is above feigning love if that is what would get him what he wanted. It is unfortunate you could not have loved me, Emily. Remember that my proposal came long before the will was read." He placed his nearly full champagne

167

glass on the table loudly. "I cannot drink anymore, for some reason this champagne tastes flat to me."

I turned away from him as quickly as possible, unable to hear any more of his cynical words. I was downcast. I wanted this to be a happy occasion . . . but no one seemed to believe that Richard was marrying me for love.

But I had to. I had to believe it, for the thought of it brought me such great joy.

That evening I went to Annabel's room and knocked on the door. When she opened it, I started before she even had a chance to speak.

"Annabel, can you ever forgive me for the hard words I spoke to you today? I have been so ashamed of myself. You are my dearest friend, and I realize you spoke your doubts out of love for me. It made me angry because I believe in Richard. I love him so much, Annabel, and I so wanted you to be happy for me. I was disappointed, and I am sorry it made me act so foolishly."

She saw the tears in my eyes, and I saw her eyes soften. "Emily, we have both been foolish," she cried, throwing her arms around me. "If you must have Richard to be happy, then I am truly glad you will be married." And then we were both sobbing and vying with each other in protest that the other had been right.

But somehow, when I went back to my room, my joy was still dimmed. The seeds of doubt had been planted, by looks and words, and I wondered perhaps if they all saw something that I refused to.

And the nagging shrill voice of Malvina still echoed in the back of my mind: "Have a care who you marry . . . the brides are cursed . . . do not become one . . . do not become one."

I could not ignore it. I must see Malvina before I married Richard.

*   *   *

The next morning, I took my mare and rode to her cottage alone.

It seemed as if she was expecting me. She stood out in the yard, watching me with her bright eyes as I dismounted and tied up the horse.

"So." Her voice held a jeering note. "You are going to marry Richard Woodstock, and become one of the Edgecliff brides, though I warned ye not to."

I dropped the reins, startled. "How did you know?" I began, almost ready to believe in her foresight. But then I remembered. We had announced it to the family. Servants spread news such as this very fast. Of course, she had heard.

"Yes—I am going to marry him," I said, advancing on her.

"Ah, yer as mad as yer mother was!" she sneered, and stooped and went inside her cottage.

I swallowed my indignation, for this was one of the things I had come to ask her about, and followed her inside.

With a contemptuous sweep of the hand, she indicated a chair for me, and sat opposite me.

"Malvina—was my mother truly mad? For now that I am to be married, perhaps have children, I should know if she was."

"Mad?" She laughed scornfully, witch eyes bright. "No more mad than you are right now. Mad with love is what she was. Ready to throw all away for it. But as right in her head as anyone."

I let out a breath of relief. If anyone would know, it was surely the woman who had been my mother's maid. "Mad with love?" I questioned. "I have seen my uncle's room, where he kept her portrait. In the portrait, she wore the ring of the brides. Was she once engaged to him—to my uncle?"

"Aye, the ring of the brides. And now you wear it."

She looked at my finger, where the rubies sparkled like blood. "And it will curse you, yet you will not heed me. Curse you as it did her. All those who wear it will die."

I shifted my shoulders, impatient with this well-worn legend. "Malvina—"

"And the one who marries you. Richard Woodstock. Is he marrying you, or marrying Edgecliff, child?"

I stared stonily at her, refusing to answer.

"Eeh, yer young. Ye'll live to see the truth in my words—perhaps. Yes, yer mother were once engaged to Sir Ralph. Mad with love for her he was. He saw her and he had to have her, though she were but the doctor's daughter. And she, poor sweet child, she had her head turned with it all. Came to the big house with me as her maid. What girl could resist betterin' herself so? And he were handsome, was Ralph. But it weren't love. I could see in her eyes she never loved him, even when he set that accursed ring upon her finger."

She paused, seemingly lost in the past, and I waited, breath caught in my throat. I could see it all, the doctor's daughter and the Squire, she so dazzled as she came to that magnificent house on the coast, to be Mistress of it all . . .

Malvina shot me a sharp glance. "And then he came home. Thomas Woodstock, the younger brother, and twice as handsome as his brother. But it were more than his looks. He were gentle enough for Amelia, ye see. They were alike that way. And the moment they saw each other, they were in love. It were at a ball to celebrate her engagement, and she come down that stair on Ralph's arm. And at the foot of the stairs she meets the eyes of the man she falls in love with—his brother. And he loved her too."

"What happened?" I asked, fearfully.

"My miss was beside herself. 'I can never marry Thomas, Malvina,' she'd say with one breath, and then, 'I

170

cannot live without him!' And 'How can I hurt Sir Ralph so?' I think she'd never have left with Thomas at all, for she were a soft-hearted girl with a sense of honor and a horror of scandal—if 'tweren't for Sir Ralph himself. One evening, he comes on Thomas, a-kissing of Miss Amelia's hand in the rose garden. He don't show himself, but he were in a jealous rage. Later that evening he were well in his cups, and he comes on Miss Amelia walking near the gazebo. He dragged her inside.''

She stopped, ominously. ''She come to me, a-sobbing, her gown all torn. 'I will make you mine—you shall have to marry me!' he'd cried. And he forced her. The wedding was only a week away. 'Pack for me, Malvina,' she told me, a-trembling and pale. 'For I shall never see that monster again.' We left that night, and she married Thomas right off. So ye see, child, why Sir Ralph left it all to ye?''

I was shaken. ''Yes. How horrible. And tragic. He must have felt so guilty. I imagine he wanted to atone for such a terrible act.''

''Atone?'' She cackled. ''Nay. He left it to ye, ninny, 'cause ye might be his daughter! Ye were born just nine months later, and either one of the brothers could lay claim to ye.''

The world spun. I hadn't thought—hadn't realized. Sir Ralph's daughter—or Thomas's?

''Dear God,'' I whispered.

''Yes, dear God,'' she said sarcastically.

''But Malvina—why did they come back? Surely I was born here at Edgecliff? And the ring? Why did my mother never return it?''

''As to the ring, she run off with it on that night, never thinking. She meant to give it back, but Sir Ralph would never hear of it. So she kept it in a drawer, like, to give to ye one day.''

''But why did they come back?''

171

"Money, child. They had almost none. Sir Ralph implored them to come back, begged their forgiveness. Said the child, hateful as it might be, could be his and he had the right to provide for it. So in the end they came back, to live in the Dower House. It's since burned down, but it were a fine, spacious house in its day."

"Then—then that was not the reason for the quarrel between them?" I asked, puzzled. "What Sir Ralph did to my mother?"

"Nay. It were after ye were born. Ye see, Sir Ralph still loved Amelia. And I think he believed that if he only hadn't forced himself on her, she would have married him. So one night—it were a foggy night, so thick a body couldn't see—he asked her to meet him at the summer-house. He wanted to talk about yer future, he said, without Thomas there. Settlin' money on you, he said, makin' you his heir. Well, she were a proper mother, and she went. To her sorrow, she went."

Something in Malvina's face chilled me. "What happened?" I whispered.

"I don't know the whole of it. I follered her without her knowin', for I had one of my feelin's. He talked love to her. He begged her to leave Thomas, and marry him, and he'd treat ye as his daughter and leave Edgecliff to ye, he said. And then yer father came."

"He came?" I could see them all, so fatefully linked, in the gazebo, not a ruin, but beautiful. Could almost feel their passions as the three of them stood face to face— the two brothers and the woman they loved.

"There was a mort of shoutin'. Thomas was like a madman. He accused yer mother of meeting Ralph as a lover. And then I heard her break into sobs, and she ran away. Down the cliff path, through the fog. I ran after, but I weren't fast enough. I heard a her sayin' 'No, no— please!' and a struggle. And then a scream. And when I reached the cliff, they were both standin' at the edge,

172

starin' down into the sea, and she was gone."

"My God!" I stood. "You don't mean to say that one of them—pushed her!"

"I do mean to say it," she said grimly. "She never jumped, not my Amelia."

"But she could have lost her way—fallen—"

"Or she could have been pushed in a passion. I tell ye, I heard her pleadin for her life! But they both turned on each other, and each swore the other had done it. They were like to kill each other. At last I separated them, and made them see reason. She were gone, and neither would say which done it. I told them they must say it were an accident—and I would back them up."

"But Malvina, why?"

She shrugged. "There was ye to think of, as I made them see. Having perhaps yer father on trial for murder and hung would leave you an orphan. And there was no tellin' which would be believed. It was the fog, you see. None had seen him who pushed her over. And all I heard were her cries—not the voice of the one who done it."

I sat, stunned. "So she was never mad," I said at last.

"Never. Yet she set passions in motion that led to her death. As ye are doing, child. I tell ye, don't marry Richard Woodstock. Throw the ring into the sea. Or perhaps there will be two more Woodstock brothers with blood on their hands."

A long time later, I rode home. As I rode, I looked down at the ring on my finger. So I knew the truth now. The whole tragic story.

But the past was the past. There were no such things as curses. Only tragedies made by human beings. I would take care to make no tragedies of my own.

For I was in love and I knew that nothing on earth would stop me from marrying Richard Woodstock.

Chapter Thirteen

"Pull in as far as you can, miss, and hold it!" With that injunction, my maid Nan pulled mightily on my stays until the corset felt like an iron vise.

"Nan, I won't be able to breathe! And we've such a long day ahead. Need they be this tight?"

"It's how you were fitted for the dress, miss—you should have spoken up then, for there's naught that can be done about it now."

Perhaps the breathless feeling was from the excitement. The stays had certainly seemed snug during the fittings, but not this binding. I tried to steady myself with a deep breath as Nan carefully maneuvered the elaborate, voluminous wedding gown over my head.

It was a lovely gown, but I felt fresh dismay at how uncomfortable it was going to be. The ivory satin was stiff with seed pearls, layered over with lace; I would be afraid to move for marring its creamy, rustling perfection.

"Now, miss, if you'll bend at your knees just a little?" Nan asked as she prepared to set the heavy headress on my head. I bent slightly with my back straight to accommodate Nan's small stature. She placed the headdress of satin and pearls to the crown of my head and pinned it securely. Yards of frothy veil streamed down my back, mingling with the unwieldy train. All this for what I'd hoped to be a small and quiet wedding!

How I wished for a simpler gown. The village seamstress had been scandalized when I had suggested one. The mistress of Edgecliff, marrying the "Squire" in a simple gown? It was too much for her imagination. The wedding had taken on almost fuedal proportions in this tiny town in Cornwall. It seemed to possess the villagers' minds like a fever. Richard was extremely popular because of his concern for the farmers and miners, and his involvement with village affairs.

And I had captured their imaginations. From the seamstress I discovered that many of them remembered my father. It had pleased their hearts that Sir Ralph had summoned me and made me part of the family, that it was "right and fitting" that I should have come to Cornwall, "where the Woodstocks belong." It seemed a romantic fairytale to them that Richard and I should wed, for they were a close-knit group who did not accept outsiders easily. And after the shock of my inheritance, it seemed doubly right to them that the "Squire," as they called Richard, should keep control of the estate.

So although the wedding was to be small in deference to Sir Ralph's death, I knew the church would be crowded with villagers. And they would be expecting grandeur. Annabel had been firm on the matter of the dress. It must be exquisite, something suitable for an Edgecliff bride.

I looked down at my left hand, where I now wore the ruby ring openly, as my betrothal ring. Everything was coming in full circle. The ring that had wrongly left the family had returned, to be worn as tradition demanded, on the left hand of the bride of Edgecliff. Yes, times were going to get better, and this marriage was a symbol of that in everyone's mind.

A symbol. I felt like a symbol as I stared in the mirror

at the unfamiliar ivory-clad reflection. If only Richard and I could have eloped, run off in the night to some far-away place, away from the staring eyes, the questions, the curiosity, the doubts. I knew there were some who were cynical, who believed that Richard proposed to me for reasons that had nothing to do with love, that this was a marriage of convenience for him. But I could not let their negative thoughts put a shadow on my wedding day. I knew that Richard loved me. And oh, how I loved him.

Nan pressed the bouquet into my nerveless fingers. "Miss, you look lovely! A proper vision! If you'd smile just a bit," she added, looking startled at her forwardness.

"I expect I'm just a bit nervous, Nan." I smiled weakly. "It will be much better when we get safely to the church, and the ceremony has begun."

It was time to go. Nan wrapped me very carefully in a white cloak that was designed to keep the dress from harm on the trip to the church.

"I'll just go and see if Mister William is ready, miss," she said and left me alone.

It was decided that William would give the bride away. So he would escort me to the church and walk with me up the aisle. I was glad that Charles was acting as best man, and that it had fallen to William to give me away. I could use his steady arm to lean on, and find support in his calm, kind eyes.

Nan came back shortly, and told me Annabel had left in the first carriage, and that so had Richard and Charles. In fact, everyone was on their way to the church. It only remained for William and me to follow. I looked down at the orange blossoms I carried, once more at the ring, and a last time at my reflection. I was ready.

The rest of the day remains unclear in my memory, with events jumbled and juxtaposed, in no clear order. The church was decked with a wealth of flowers, and I remember the warm gray stone walls, so ancient, glowing against the green grass. The stained glass lit here a hat, there a cheek, with beams of red and gold. The vestibule was crowded, Annabel in her pale blush-colored gown kissing me, William steadying me when I wavered a moment, quite faint. The strains of organ music, then I walked as if in a dream down the aisle, clutching tightly to William's arm, with eyes for no one but Richard. He stood haloed at the flowery altar in the soft bright light; he turned to look at me, his shoulders so square in his dark coat. I ventured just a glance into his green eyes, so solemn, when I joined him at the altar. And I remember how steadily he looked at me, as if impressing on me his eternal promise.

He turned to me and took my hands in his, looking down at me as we spoke the vows.

"'Til death do us part," he said solemnly.

The organ surged and he leaned down and kissed me, quickly but passionately, and at last I smiled, as if the whole world had just lit up. I turned to face the church then, my hand proudly on his arm, and I think I have never felt happier than I did at that moment, when Mr. and Mrs. Richard Woodstock walked down the aisle.

The church was packed with people, many standing in the back. I saw family friends in the first pews and the villagers all in the back. Nan was touching a handkerchief to her cheek, Sir Neville Trewithyian beamed proudly at us. I missed seeing Mrs. Kerrenslea; to this day I don't know if she was there.

As we were almost down the aisle, a bright green hat caught my eye, and under it a mass of auburn curls. It was Evonne DeVere. I had not known that she was invited, but there was nothing to stop her from attending. She smiled at me, her eyes like a cat's, and it was an unpleasant smile. It seemed to mock my happiness. I tightened my grip on Richard's arm and turned my head away, giving a startled villager the most brilliant smile I could muster.

The sun had broken through the scattered clouds just as we left the church. I was glad of the sunshine, for it was some time before we could leave, finding ourselves pressed on every side by well-wishers. Our hands were wrung, Charles demanded to be first to kiss the bride, there was a veritable circus of gaiety.

"My sister!" exclaimed Annabel in her impetuous way, flinging her arms around my neck and hugging me tightly. She stepped back her eyes sparkling. "Now you are stuck with me—with all of us! Perhaps you can keep us in line when we behave outrageously. We needed someone steady in our family!"

"What about William?" I asked and then laughed.

"Pooh! He's too quiet to ever intimidate us! No, the job falls to you, sister Emily. At least now you shan't turn us out."

"Turn you out? And sister Emily? You make me sound like a nun!"

"With the ceremony we just witnessed, it's the last thing we should call her," smirked Charles, coming up to stand with us.

The look in his eyes was disquieting. His advances toward me still hung like a curtain between us which he would not let me forget. Even now, as I stood there, his brother's wife, there was something beneath his lowered lashes that made me quite uncomfortable.

"Emily, you have not yet thanked me for my contribution to your wedding," he said.

"And what was that?"

"Why, Richard's being suitably dressed for the occasion, of course. While you and Annabel thought of nothing except that beautiful dress which you look so very exquisite in, I was at pains to take Richard to the tailor and see he was fitted for something decent. Along with his best man, of course. For otherwise, the groom would probably have showed up in his farm clothes. Tell me if you approve—or have even noticed."

For the first time I saw that Richard's splendid dress clothes—a dark gray coat with tails, over lighter gray pants, a white waistcoat and a burgundy cravat—were the same as Charles's. And they both looked wonderful. I doubted if there were two handsomer men in Cornwall, for with Charles's golden glory and Richard's dark magnificence, they were a contrast indeed.

"You did a wonderful job, Charles. Thank you, for I confess I had not thought of what Richard was to wear."

"I had them made the same, in case, at the last moment, you came to your senses and changed your mind about which Woodstock brother you should be marrying," he replied.

I blushed and turned to the vicar with relief, thanking him for the lovely ceremony. He smiled and complimented me on my dress, and chatted pleasantly to me for some moments. At last Richard came up and took my arm, and in time maneuvered me through the crowd to the waiting carriage.

There was a shower of rice and laughing calls as we settled in breathlessly and Polker started the horses for Edgecliff. There was to be a small wedding breakfast before we changed for our journey and left that afternoon. Richard was smiling down at me, and suddenly bent to kiss me, in full view of the cheering onlookers.

"My wife, at last! No more stolen kisses!" he said, holding me closely. "Are you happy, my darling?" he whispered to me quietly.

"Oh Richard, so very happy." I managed to smile before he kissed me again.

The trip to Edgecliff seemed short, over in a moment. I remember how my heart lifted as we turned onto the drive and saw the great stone walls set against the deep

179

blue sky. The clouds had completely broken and looked like white cotton surrounding the jutting towers and the green hills in the distance.

"Our home!" I exclaimed.

"Yes, Edgecliff belongs to both of us now. This was meant to be, Emily," Richard said. "Uncle Ralph would be very happy if he could be here today."

I agreed, gazing happily on our home.

When I turned back toward Richard, I found his expression had changed. It had turned suddenly thoughtful, serious. I pondered his words, "Edgecliff belongs to both of us now," and saw again Charles's accusing looks. Then I laughed at my fancies. It was my wedding day!

It wasn't until much later, when events forced me to remember, that I knew that this had been a premonition of the turn that our marriage would take. And I would regret not paying more careful attention to my instincts.

Richard and I slowly climbed the steps of Edgecliff for the first time as man and wife. When we reached the door, he suddenly swept me up into his arms. "The threshold to our new life together," Richard whispered huskily in my ear as we stepped through the doorway.

I was laughing up into his face as he set me down in a swirl of white. My face crimsoned. Just inside the hall, every servant was lined up to greet us, dressed in their best. Penwillen stood, stiff and formal, all in shining black at their front, and Mrs. Kerrenslea was a gaunt raven in black at his elbow. They were a dour pair compared to the smiling, gay group all in brighter colors. I caught sight of Nan, neat and pretty in dove gray and a white lace cap, and I smiled at her, cheered by the sight.

"The staff would like to extend our heartfelt best wishes and congratulations, and a pledge that we hope to serve our new master and mistress as well as we served the late master."

"Thank you, Penwillen," Richard said, and bowed slightly.

I glanced up at him, my fingers laced through his arm. Though his voice held a seriousness, a firm air of command, he looked unaccustomedly gay, with a bright, almost boyish, smile on his face. Looking at him now, I thought, who could doubt that he was happy?

"We must all have a glass to celebrate, and to drink to our health," he declared. "Champagne, Penwillen, the best for this happiest occasion of the estate!"

Within moments, Penwillen and two young footmen dressed in dark suits returned with the champagne and glasses.

"Congratulations, master!" "Best wishes, miss— mistress!" were the happy murmurs as we toasted, Richard shaking hands on all sides.

"Ooh—she's madam now," giggled one of the maids reprovingly.

How bright and kind the servants all looked. All except Mrs. Kerrenslea, of course. "My best wishes, Mr. Richard, and to you," she said, looking at me coldly as I passed her.

"Thank you, Mrs. Kerrenslea," I murmured, avoiding her eyes.

How I wished Richard would hear of replacing her with someone more friendly to me. But although I was mistress now, he had objected strongly when I had once hinted my distaste of her.

"She has been with the Woodstocks since she was a girl, and served us faithfully all these years. It would be unjust to dismiss her," he had said. "Perhaps you will grow to appreciate her in time. She runs the house quite efficiently, and have you forgotten? Uncle stated in his will that she was to stay as long as she wished as house-keeper."

I remember feeling pained that Richard had not understood that it was Mrs. Kerrenslea's coldness to me and not my dislike for her that had prompted my objections to her presence. But I ignored the fleeting thought and kissed him happily, ready to give in to any demand he might make.

He had always been master of my heart and now he was master of Edgecliff as well. I paused in the great hall, and took a deep breath, thinking how right it seemed that the prince had at last come into possession of his kingdom. By marrying the princess too, I thought, then laughed at myself for my fancifulness. "Love does make you romantic and mad," I thought, listening with half an ear as Richard instructed Penwillen to prepare for the arrival of the guests invited to the wedding breakfast. I stole a glance at Nan as she sipped delicately at the effervescent drink and smiled. Champagne for the servants! Evidently I was not the only one who was made romantically mad by love and happiness.

All at once Richard took me by the arm and led me into the drawing room.

"Champagne for the servants, Richard," I teased as he closed the door behind us. "We shan't have any discipline anymore, and I'm sure the breakfast will be burnt!"

"And we shall have a glass ourselves, all alone, at least for a few moments, until the guests begin to arrive." He poured two sparkling glasses, then shot me a look. "Happy?"

I sent him an equally sparkling look from the couch, where I had collapsed amid a swirl of ivory satin and lace. "Do you have to ask? Oh, but Richard, how I wish there were no guests coming. Dreadful of me, I suppose. One should want to spend such a moment with one's family and friends. I can't help wishing we could just rush off to the continent now, so we can be alone. But I suppose we shall be alone soon enough and for long enough while we

182

are there."

He sat beside me and held the crystal champagne glass to my lips. "Soon enough? And long enough? I don't agree, Madam, I am counting the minutes."

Then he set the glasses down on the marble and mahogany table and took me into his arms. The passion of his kiss took my breath away. All trepidations about my wedding night ahead burned away with its fire and tenderness.

A discreet tap on the door made us jump and parted us, as if we were caught in some guilty secret. We were laughing like two children when Penwillen and a footman came into the room and announced that carriages were approaching the drive, signaling that the guests would be arriving presently.

The wedding breakfast was to be held in the great ballroom. Richard took my arm and led me, walking down the long hall, to its massive oak doors, where we would receive our guests. Penwillen pulled the doors open and I gasped at the splendor in front of me. I had been much impressed by the ballroom unadorned, but now it appeared as a vision from the imagination.

The parqueted wood floor gleamed with fresh polish, reflecting the sparkling chandeliers. It looked as if a thousand and one diamonds covered the floor and I was afraid to step on its smooth surface as we came in through the doorway. There were flowers everywhere; fresh-picked poppies, pimpernels, and hydrangea hung from baskets that were suspended from the wood beams. Purple heather and bearded iris rose from the tall porcelain vases that graced the long tables on the far end of the ballroom. The banquet tables, draped in white linen, were laden with a feast. It took my breath away. All this for a simple wedding breakfast!

When the last of the fine coaches had turned out of the drive and their guests greeted and inside the ballroom, the party began. Toasts were drunk, champagne and ale flowed freely, and the servants buzzed in and out like bees near a hive, bearing trays and covered dishes.

Annabel whispered to me, "Perhaps I shall be next!" She barely left Timothy Odgers's side all through the meal, which set me to wondering about those two.

Hilary St. Clair rose and gave a rather funny muddled toast, welcoming me to the family, but Charles shouted him down with, "But Hilary, she was already a member of the family!" Charles kissed me on the cheek and murmured, "A new sister! How touching and rather quaint, isn't it, Emily?"

I ignored his remark and turned away toward Richard. But he wasn't paying attention to the conversation at the wedding table. His eyes were in the corner of the ballroom at a table in the back. I saw the flash of a green plume and upon careful inspection realized it was Evonne DeVere who was receiving Richard's rapt attention. I frowned and felt a flash of uncharacteristic anger surge inside me. Why was *she* invited? Evonne DeVere was no friend of mine. Obviously she was still one of Richard's.

I placed my hand on his arm possessively and whispered, "This is so lovely, Richard. I'm glad now that we didn't elope together without celebration."

"Yes, Emily," he replied, but his eyes seemed blank as if his thoughts were somewhere else and I felt a stab of jealousy. Soon, I thought, we would be far away from that woman, alone together for weeks in the continent with nothing else to do but enjoy each other's company.

After what seemed an eternity, I rose, announcing that I must go and change. It was a struggle to get through the well-wishers to the door, but at last I managed, feeling as though I had just kissed half of Cornwall.

Nan was waiting in my room, my traveling suit laid out on the bed. Her eyes were enormous, and she looked almost sick with excitement. She and Tall, Richard's valet, would be accompanying us on the honeymoon. Nan had never before left Cornwall. Looking at her, I felt almost overwhelmed with my good fortune. A few short months ago, I had been, like her, a poor servant to the rich, and I had been as excited on the eve of my journey to Cornwall as she was in leaving for Paris. How close I felt to her at that moment, and how well I could remember the emotions I had felt. But there would be no rich, dying uncle for Nan, no handsome cousin to marry. I startled Nan by hugging her suddenly.

"Oh miss—madam—there is no time for that now! We've got to get dressed in a blink, or we'll be missing the train. The breakfast lasted ever so long." Her eyes were bright with tears and I had to smile at her sentimentality.

"I would not miss that train for anything!" I said excitedly.

We would be taking the train to Dover and from here a ferry across the channel to Calais, where we would spend our wedding night before boarding another train to Paris. Excitement almost choked me. A train to Paris! To me it seemed the height of romance.

Nan helped me quickly into my traveling suit. It was an exquisite creation of pale sea-green silk, with apricot-edged sleeves, a lace jabot, and apricot bands about the hem. My hat was a slightly darker green, lined with deep apricot satin and trimmed with matching plumes that danced gaily near my ear. I wore a jade and coral necklace with earrings to match and a deep green pelisse over the whole to complete my dress.

"Madam, you look like a vision," Nan whispered with undisguised awe.

My eyes sparkled as I looked at the picture of a rich man's wife that stared back at me from the mirror. I gave Nan my biggest smile through the glass. Then, snatching my reticule, I rushed to the stairs.

About to scurry down, I was stopped at the first step by the sound of urgent voices in the vestibule. I could not distinguish who was speaking at first until the voices became louder, with clipped words and heated tones.

"Din' want to disturb yer wedding, master. But the accident, 'tis mighty bad, sir. A shaft broke at the hundred and fifty fathom level in the Wheal Lass copper mine in Penryn. They need help in the rescuin', men, food, an' a doctor." I heard Polker's voice above the others. "The workers are complaining of a riot in two days' time, lest something be done by then. And if you ask me, sir, I daren't blame 'em."

"None of this insolence!" Charles shouted. "Just report to us the facts."

"It's all right, Charles, I shall take care of this." Richard's voice sounded not shy of irritation.

"But Richard, this is your wedding day. Surely I can be of help in this matter while—"

"Charles," Richard interrupted. "As master of the house and owner of the mine, this is my duty regardless of what day it is. This is too serious a matter to dismiss lightly."

I could almost feel the tension between the brothers from where I stood. I knew then why Charles always acted like the carefree outsider, unconcerned with the estate affairs. It was because Richard did not allow him to be of any help with them.

"But Richard—"

"Silence," Richard snapped.

I could hear the hurt in Charles's voice and the firmness in Richard's and I felt a wave of compassion for the younger brother.

How I wished at that moment that Richard could have relinquished some of his control. For Charles's sake and for mine. For I knew that whatever had happened would affect me as well.

186

I took the stairs slowly, knowing that events had turned to put a dark cloud over our wedding day. But I did not realize the magnitude until later, when the voices died down and Richard finally noticed me standing alone in the corner, a silent witness to all that had transpired.

"Oh, Emily." He rushed toward me. "Something dreadful has happened."

"Yes," I murmured. "I have heard a good deal of it." I could not disguise my disappointment and I felt a twinge of guilt.

"Then you know that our honeymoon plans must be postponed."

"Or canceled," I interjected, remembering the words I had heard him use.

"I am so sorry, Emily." Richard pulled me into his arms as if oblivious to the eyes of those who stood near us.

"Don't be." I leaned away, keeping my composure, even though at any moment I felt I might cry. "I feel sorry for the families of those hurt in the accident. Our honeymoon can wait. We have the rest of our lives together. This matter must be attended to straight away."

"Emily, you are the most understanding wife in all of England."

"Not in all of the world?" I teased, feeling more like the most foolish woman in the world. I was agreeing to the postponement of our honeymoon. "You must travel to Penryn this very evening." I smiled to hide my disappointment.

"What is this?" I heard Charles from behind us. "Richard, nothing can be done in the darkness. Surely you shan't run away and leave your new wife without a wedding night?"

I blushed at Charles's boldness until Richard softly touched my cheek.

"No, of course not," my husband whispered and I felt

the blush rise again, much hotter, a different feeling entirely. "Nothing can be done until morning."

"Aye!" Polker chimed in. "And I know the perfect spot for a wedding night. Down near the cove at Falmouth is an old inn, The Swan. Got a touch of romance and genteel enough for a lady. Ye both can ride in the carriage and I can pull an extra mount for the master so's he can continue on to Penryn."

"Splendid idea, Polker," Richard said and smiled truly for the first time since hearing the news of the accident. "And the supplies we need for the miners can be gotten at Falmouth Harbor."

Polker left for the stables to ready the horses and Penwillen to inform Tall and Nan that they wouldn't be traveling to Paris. Indeed their services would not even be needed for one night's stay. I suddenly felt more sorry for Nan than myself. For though I would not be going to Paris, I would have Richard for the rest of my life. There would be plenty of time for seeing the continent.

Richard left to give orders to the men gathered in the front of the house. I was left alone in the vestibule with Charles and I felt uncomfortable, at a loss for what to say.

"I am glad that your wedding night is not ruined, Madam Woodstock. It is most good of your husband to make time for you when the mine needs him." Charles's tone betrayed a bitterness. Although I knew I was not the cause for his distress, I was hurt deeply by his implication.

"Charles, please—"

He suddenly took me by the shoulders. "I have already kissed the bride, have I not? Too bad. Emily, if I were your husband, I would never have let you miss our honeymoon. No mine could tear me from your side . . . especially not when there are others as competent to take care of the problem. No, it would be you I would take care of—I'd take care to see you knew just how much I loved

188

you . . ." He paused. "If I were your husband. I still think you would have been a happier bride if it were me you'd married."

I stepped away from his grasp, and decided to ignore his words about my relationship with Richard, and with him. "It would have pleased me more if Richard had accepted your kind offer of assistance."

"I thank you for that, at least. It seems all of my offers receive nothing but rejection of late. If you'll excuse me, there is much more champagne to be drunk," Charles replied sullenly and turned away from me.

The wedding breakfast was still in progress and I thought briefly of returning to the ballroom myself. But I promised Richard that I would wait in the vestibule. And Charles's words had stung me. His jealousy of Richard seemed to spill into every area, including me. I could not understand this. I had never given him hope. How I wished he would treat me more like a sister. Perhaps this would come in time, I thought, as I went to the mirror to adjust my hat.

All at once I felt a strange sensation. It seemed as if someone was standing behind me, taking careful inspection of my every gesture. I turned to look over my shoulder and saw a shadow move in the doorway. Mrs. Kerrenslea? Perhaps. But why would she eavesdrop, hiding in the doorway as an outsider? I stepped closer and saw that no one was there. But there had been. I wondered who it was and how much they heard and if they could read what I had read in the words that Charles had said to me. I prayed that it had not been Richard.

Chapter Fourteen

By the time the carriage reached Falmouth, the sun had already disappeared into the sea, leaving a brilliant wash of color. Sky and sea reflected orange and red, separated by the lavender horizon. The waves crashed a brilliant pink against the cliffs, jagged black and purple granite that sliced through the darkening sky.

As I looked out from the carriage window, I felt a momentary twinge of fear. The Swan Inn was perched so close to the edge that it looked apt to go tumbling down the cliffs and onto the sharp rocks below. I hadn't been this close to the cliffs' edge since Malvina told me the story of my mother's death.

Now, even the unfamiliar shoreline filled me with fear. The sound of the sea crashing against the rocks held an entirely new meaning for me and I felt great pain in its sounding. The roaring ocean and howling wind were suddenly enemies. I felt my heart start to beat faster. I couldn't tell if it was caused by my fears or the anticipation of my wedding night. Or something else. Perhaps the sensation I could almost feel as tangible was my mother's spirit, still lost at sea, waiting to tell someone of her secret. For only she would know which one of the brothers, Sir Ralph or my father Thomas, had thrown her from the cliff in a jealous rage.

I shivered and took a deep breath to steady myself. Polker had already been inside the inn to announce us and had returned for the baggage before I could open the carriage door.

Richard came around from the other side and took my arm, helping me out onto the soft grass. "Your eyes look so brilliant. Could it be that you are as anxious as I, my darling?"

"Richard!" I felt myself blushing. "My eyes are bright with fear. The inn seems hardly able to stand the force of the wind. What if we are swept away at sea while we sleep?"

"Then I will be happy to be locked in your embrace for all eternity." He put his arm around my shoulder and pulled me close.

We paused for a moment, facing the sea. A smell of tidal water mingled with the sweet scent of rhododendrons growing wild and the fresh tufted grass.

I could see Falmouth Harbor just below, a wide curve of cliffs and high scrubby hillsides separated by a few rolling fields.

"I would much rather be embraced on the soft sand in the coves of St. Just than these ominous cliffsides," I said.

"Ah, but we might be carted away by a smuggler running his cargo to those secluded coves." Richard laughed and it filled me with good humor.

He turned and we walked arm and arm toward the inn. I was happy that he could laugh. I had feared that this night would be troubled and not the joyous occasion that it was meant to be. Richard was always so serious and concerned with business affairs that I had thought his mind would be too clouded with thoughts of the disaster to be attentive to the moment and to me.

The Swan, though run by a Cornish proprietor, was

191

very much like a seventeenth-century French country inn. The stone, whitewashed, two-story structure was crossed with heavy wooden beams. All of the windows had strong wooden shutters that were locked tight this windy evening.

Through the doorway was a small dark reception room and a long oak table. Some of the long tapers guttered when we stepped through the door and I felt an unexplainable apprehension in entering.

A short, round man greeted us effusively. "My name is Tilberry and I am honored to have a gentleman and lady such as yourself spend this momentous night at The Swan. Would you mind signing the guest book, sir?"

"Will it be long before our room is ready, Tilberry?" Richard asked as he bent over the register.

"Nay sir, a matter of minutes. My wife Fanny is attending to it now."

I sat in the settee by the window and folded my hands on my lap. I could wait. Although I was filled with love for Richard, I could not control my uneasiness of what lay in store for me. I felt ill prepared for my wedding night. Mrs. Hall's quick explanations of married life offered me little clue. I had heard that there were women who loved the marriage bed and others who did not. And those who did not made life difficult, caused themselves and their husbands great pain and disappointment.

I wondered for a moment which of these types of women I might be. For surely there was no way of knowing, at least not now. But shortly it would be revealed to me and I feared that revelation.

"Glory be, 'tis an exciting occasion. Good evening, Mister and Missus Woodstock." A buxom woman with round rosy cheeks and brown hair came down the stairs rubbing her hands together. "The room is ready for ye." She winked at Richard and I felt a blush go to my cheeks.

"Shall I help settle Madam, sir?"

I felt her kind eyes on me and felt a wave of relief.

Richard hesitated in his answer and I looked at him searchingly.

"You can take a pint of ale in the great room while yer wait, Mr. Woodstock," Tilberry said.

Just then Polker came through the door with our baggage, one small trunk and a saddle that Richard would need for his ride to Penryn. "'Tis the best ale in southern Cornwall I'm told," Polker said. "And I be game to try some soon as this baggage is safely set and the horses housed for the night."

"Very well then, Fanny," Richard said. "But don't dally. One short pint and I shall be upstairs."

"Ready, madam?" Fanny asked and I nodded, rising slowly on shaky legs.

I followed her up the narrow creaky steps.

"Watch your step, madam," Fanny said. "'Tis a hard stone floor below, and with no hand railings, 'tis a dangerous staircase."

And much too dark as well, I thought, and looked down to watch carefully my footing.

At the top of the stairs was a long hallway. We walked down to the very end and here Fanny paused and opened a large oak door with a flourish. For a small country inn, the room was remarkably beautiful. A four-poster bed dominated the space, its deep mahogany arms lifting almost to the ceiling. The bedding was awash with white lace and ruffles and a bright red rose lay on each of the overstuffed feather pillows. The room was warm from a small fireplace in the corner. I looked at the flames as they danced from behind the grate and they calmed me.

I smiled at Fanny meekly, sensing that she could see my uneasiness.

"Shall I heat some water for Madam?" Fanny asked. "There is a small hip bath behind the screen. I have some rose water to add to it if you wish."

Still unaccustomed to such treatment, I simply nodded my agreement.

Fanny stepped behind the screen and produced a large cast iron pail filled with water. She barely managed to carry it to the fire, huffing with each step. I had the urge to help her, but I quickly remembered my place. I was mistress of Edgecliff now, not a simple music teacher.

"'Tis a special night, madam," Fanny said again as she hung the pail above the fire. "But if ye don't mind me sayin' so, ye look as white as the cliffs at Dover! There be nothin' to fear if you are in love with 'im."

"Oh, I do love my husband, very much." I sat heavily on the window seat.

"Then there is naught a thing to worry of." Fanny's kind voice reassured me. "Ye should take a leisurely bath, madam. Let the warmth soothe you. Think of the love that he makes you feel and of his kisses and everything will be beautiful. But ye shan't let him hurry you. If he comes a-pounding, I'll keep 'im out until you feel ready."

"Ready, I don't know how long that shall take!" I said and laughed at the thought of Richard pounding impatiently on the door for hours with Fanny arguing all the while.

"I understand ye, madam. I remember my wedding night . . ." Her eyes turned misty with reverie and I could tell by her expression that it was a happy one. "I locked the door and sat by the fire for near two hours, afeared of him at first. And so . . ." She let out a cackle that nearly made me jump. ". . . he busted clear through the door, lifted me into his arms, and straight onto the bed."

"And then . . ." I asked, my eyes wide with interest.

"And then, well . . ." She cackled again and the sound of it made me feel gay.

"Well!" I let out an uncontrollable laughter.

194

"Ye shall find out fer yourself," Fanny said firmly and went to the fireplace. I could hear that the water was starting to bubble in its pail. "But I can say that if you love 'im, this will be the most beautiful night of your life so far and ye shall have a lifetime of them ahead of you."

By the time Fanny was gone and I had climbed into the bath, I felt much less nervous. How kind she had been! I decided to take her advice, and thought of Richard's kisses. And I knew, remembering the feelings he had made me feel, that it was unlikely I should be one of those women who does not like the marriage bed.

Moments later, I was dressed in a long white gown of satin and lace. It was the finest thing that I had ever worn, soft and silky against my skin. I undid the pins in my hair and it tumbled onto my shoulders. I was sitting before the vanity, brushing the tangled strands to a shiny luster when Richard stepped into the room. I could see his eyes in the mirror and I caught my breath at their intensity.

"Oh Emily, you are the most beautiful woman in the world." Richard knelt down beside me and took my face in his hands. "I shall love you always."

He lifted me in his arms and slowly, lovingly, laid me down onto the soft sheets. Suddenly I thought of Fanny's cackling laughter and couldn't stifle my own.

"I amuse you then?" Richard asked as he removed his top coat and started to untie the burgundy ascot he wore around his neck.

"I am happy, Richard. Happier than I have ever been."

"Don't tell me that now," he said mischieviously.

"What do you mean?" I questioned and looked away as he started to undo the buttons on his suit pants.

"I hope you will save those words until the morning, when you wake up in my embrace." The tenderness in his voice forced me to look at him, shyly, and I marveled at his magnificence. I had never seen a man unclothed before, and I thought that Richard was beautiful. My mind went back to that first morning when I had mistaken him for a gypsy farmhand, and I saw that his hours of manual labor had given him the most impressive muscles.

He kissed me then, so deep and so long that I felt my consciousness slipping away. All fears, everything vanished in that kiss and I was no longer myself but an extension of him and I wanted to be a part of him forever.

That night, Richard showed me a new world that I had not suspected. He was a tender lover, and I could tell he was holding a great passion in check, being gentle with my inexperienced newness at love. As we completed our union, it seemed to me that we became one person.

Afterward, he looked down at me, brushing a strand of hair from my face. "Did I hurt you?"

"Oh, Richard—it was wonderful," I said shyly. "Is it—that way for everyone?"

"Indeed, it was wonderful," he said gravely, and I saw the laugh in his eyes at my innocence. "But I don't believe it is that way unless you are in love."

Smiling, I laid my head on my husband's shoulder, and listening to his breathing, feeling his arms around me, I fell asleep.

Something awakened me in the middle of the night, the sound of a night owl or perhaps the beating of the sea against the jagged rocks below our window. Whatever it was faded in and out of my consciousness almost instantaneously.

I felt a warmth in my body, a deep satisfaction. So this was love. I reached over to Richard, only to discover that next to me the bed was empty. The sheets still felt warm and I realized that Richard must have left the bed only moments before. Perhaps his movement had stirred me from my deep sleep. Where could he have gone?

I opened my eyes and slowly they grew accustomed to

the darkened bedchamber. The moonlight created an eerie effect in the room and I thought I saw a shadow pass. All at once something came crashing through the windowpanes and I sat up in the bed with a start. Smoke assaulted my nostrils and I saw that the white curtains were being eaten up by flames. There, on the floor below them, I could see a torch spreading its fire into the room.

I threw the coverlets from me and leapt from the bed, stumbling against a chair as I made my way through the dark toward the window. The wind howling through the break in the window chilled my skin. I leaned out, and there below in the darkness, I saw the tall shape of a man, running away down the narrow alleyway behind the inn. He was tall, with wide shoulders, and there was something horrifyingly familiar about him. But his hair? He wore a hat, and I could not see what color his hair was.

But I had no time to waste. My lungs felt about to burst from the smoke as I ran to the door. I pulled against the doorknob in vain.

It was locked! How could the door have been locked? I heard movements downstairs, the shuffling of feet and the loud clanging of a bell. So quickly did the room become engulfed with flames that I panicked, feeling that I would never leave this room alive.

Coughing, barely able to breathe, I screamed, "Richard!" through the locked door. "Help me, I'm trapped inside!"

All manner of disturbing thoughts whirled through my imagination. What if it was Richard who had locked me in this room? What if that was he running away? He must still be in love with Evonne DeVere. Charles's bitter words rang out in my ears. "It is Edgecliff he wants, not you, Emily."

But I would not let myself give in to these terrors, these wild thoughts. Throwing myself angrily against the door, I pounded and kicked until finally, somehow, the hinges came loose. I escaped from the room just as the flames reached the doorway. I paused for just a moment outside the door to catch a breath of air before making for the stairwell. I felt so dizzy, my mind was so clouded from the smoke and the heat.

My hand rested against the wall and I had barely taken two stairs when I felt something against my ankles, tight and sharp. I lost my balance and time seemed to stop. I felt myself falling into a cavernous pit. My imagination flashed an image. I saw the roaring sea below me, the sharp rocks and foaming waves. Two brothers stood at the top of the stairs and they were both laughing. One had coal-black hair and sharp green eyes, and the other was sunny blond with the eyes of the summer sky.

In reality, I felt myself tumble down the narrow wooden steps to the stone floor below.

The next thing I knew it was morning. I opened my eyes to the simple furniture of a small unfamiliar room. I could smell the faint odor of charred wood mixed with the scent of hay and horses. My head pounded so horribly that I found I had to shut my eyes against the bright sun that streamed through the window. Around the back of my head and continuing around to my forehead was a thick cotton bandage. Even though I was bundled up securely in between two woolen blankets, my entire body felt stiff and tense and cold. But then, I suddenly realized, all that I wore was a thin satin nightdress.

"Richard." His name came croaking from my dry throat.

"I am here, my darling."

I squinted through the brightness to see him kneeling at my side, looking anxiously into my face. He at once took my hand, and pressed it to his lips. "Thank God you are awake," he said, and there was emotion in his voice.

"I—what happened, Richard? I was—I was locked in! The flames—" Suddenly the memory of the events of last night came back with horrifying clarity.

"So you remember? We found you in a heap at the foot of the stairs, unconscious, with a great bruise on your forehead. And flames shooting out from the bedroom above, ready to sweep down the stairs. I was nearly mad, I tell you. And then I rode for the doctor when it looked as if you wouldn't wake up. He has just left. Oh, Emily . . ."

He gathered me into his arms as if I were a fragile and precious bit of porcelain, but I could feel how his heart beat as he held me against him. His face was white and strained and his green eyes burned like coals. I melted happily into his arms, so glad to be safe, so happy that Richard loved me so—

And then in horror, I stiffened, remembering the figure I had seen, running away down the dark narrow alleyway.

"Richard—Richard, where were you last night?"

He put me away from him, his brows knit. "There was a disturbance in the town. Some miners shouting and throwing rocks. I heard it and rose—though even my leaving the bed didn't wake you." He gave me a brief, tender smile, then his face became thunderous. "I got up to see if I could do anything to calm matters. I am much afraid—nay, certain—that one of the rabble threw a torch through our window last night. Doubtless I was their target. But to involve my wife, by God! It was damnable! When I think of what may have happened . . ." Richard looked as if he would murder them all.

"Oh—a torch—the miners," I said, relieved. Of course! And the man running away? Not Richard. Just a tall man, near to him in build. For a moment I was so happy I forgot everything else. And then sinister memory, insistent, intruded itself.

"But Richard—the door was locked from the outside,"

199

I whispered. "That would mean more than unrest—more than a bid to frighten us. It would mean murder was meant."

"Locked?" He looked at me strangely. "Darling, I am sure you must have believed so in your excitement, but it is quite impossible. The door doesn't lock from the outside. And besides, darling, if it were locked, how on earth would you have opened it in the end? Perhaps it was jammed for a moment. But there. Rest now. The doctor says you have sustained a bad blow to the head, and it may be some time before you are again your normal self."

I sank back slowly, biting my lip. He didn't believe me! But it was true. Even if the door did not lock from the outside, it had been jammed shut somehow. Not meant to be opened. And what about the tight band at my ankles, the one that had tripped me on the steep stairs? Meant, no doubt, to finish me off if the fire did not?

But should I tell Richard? He would probably think I was raving from the blow to my head. Instead, I asked a question.

"Richard—did the whole inn burn down?"

"No, thank God. The town was full of men to haul buckets from the ocean. Only the upper bedrooms were lost. The rest still stands and can be rebuilt. But darling, really, the doctor said you must rest. I shall take you back to Edgecliff tomorrow if you are strong enough to travel. Right now I will leave you so you can sleep." He was suddenly grim. "And I shall go and find these murderers and see that they meet justice."

He rose, with a last touch to my face, and left the room. For the moment, I was alone.

It had been an attempt at murder. Murder of both of us—or of me alone? But Richard would never believe me unless I had some proof. I sat up, and at once put a hand to my head, wincing. The pain was excruciating.

I was determined, though. I threw back the covers and

stood unsteadily. It was only a short walk from the stables where I lay to the inn.

In the doorway of the stables, I paused. A few folk were gathered near the front of the inn, poking about in the still-smoking ruins. I could hear Fanny weeping. But the back of the inn was deserted. It was there that the stair was that I had come down last night.

The inn was a blackened ruin on the second story, and much stained with smoke and water below. Yet I could see that the structure of the building was still solid, and the back door stood open. I crossed the yard and slipped inside the doorway. Ahead of me stretched the steep stair where they had found me, crumpled in a heap at the bottom. I could almost see the scene—the red light of the flames roaring above, Richard's frantic cries as he knelt near my body—

I began to climb the stairs. Cautiously, in case they had been damaged by fire. Ahead of me loomed a blackened ruin of twisted timbers, a mere shell.

Near the top of the stairs I found it, untouched by the fire. A piece of cloth tied tightly across two risers, at the height where it would surely trip anyone running down the stairs. With shaking hands I untied it, and then drew it through my fingers.

It was Richard's burgundy cravat.

I stood, and the world began to whirl.

"Emily! What the devil are you doing here?" demanded a familiar voice behind me.

I turned, holding the damning evidence in my hands, and went slowly down the stairs toward him. I reached the bottom and stood staring up into his face.

"Charles," I said at last. "So you were here last night too?"

"I was," he said, and came toward me.

Chapter Fifteen

"Emily! Thank God you are all right! What are you doing in this ruin? Polker is awaiting you." For a moment, Charles's face was deadly white, and he looked almost sick with relief to see me.

I clutched Richard's burgundy cravat tightly in my fingers. "I had to come back, to see what had caused my fall." I answered. My eyes flew to Charles's neck, and his cravat, an exact duplicate of Richard's, was missing.

"What do you mean?" Charles asked. "They told me of your fall down the stairs. Surely it was an accident." His gaze moved from my face to my hand.

"No." I moved for the door, unable to bear any longer the smell of smoldering wood and the nearness of Charles. Inside I trembled. I had not dared to voice the terrible suspicions that were beginning to form in my mind. The cravat, Richard's—or Charles's? For Charles had the same type of cravat. Either one was too dreadful to contemplate.

I stepped outside and Charles followed me. I spun around to face him and held the cravat high. "I found *this* tied across the stairs purposefully."

"Why, it looks like mine." Charles's hand reached up to and he lightly touched his collar. "It was lost last night at the mines. Or perhaps the cravat is Richard's. You have had a very dreadful experience, dear 'sister.' Surely you are mistaken about it being tied across the stairs. Mayhap Richard dropped it."

"Mayhap," I answered him.

Just then Polker interrupted. "Oh, there ye are. T'master sent me to find you. If ye are well enough, he wants you back home and t'see the doctor there. Are ye ready for the trip back to Edgecliff?"

"Yes, Polker. Are you riding with us?" I asked Charles, hoping with all my heart that he was not.

"No," he answered. "I am going back to Penryn, to help with the unrest. That is why I came here last night. To see if there was anything I could do while Richard was . . . otherwise occupied."

"I see," I said coldly. I turned my back on him, not bidding him farewell. My mind was confused, and I knew I needed time to think before I was ready to confront anyone. Polker helped me into the carriage and we set off for Edgecliff.

Polker quietly maneuvered the coach along the steep, green coast roads while I rocked inside the carriage, alone with my troubled thoughts. How I wished that Richard were here with me now. I needed so much to hear him say, "I love you, Emily," and put my mind at ease. But he had remained behind to deal with the miners—and to find those who had thrown the torch. Or perhaps to avoid me.

Had my husband left the room, jammed the door, and hoped to rid himself of a wife he'd married for no more than her inheritance?

The torch would be blamed on the miners. The fact that Richard might have been in the room too would absolve him of suspicion.

But, oh, dear God, how could I be suspecting the man I loved and had just married? It was so much easier to blame it all on Charles. But what would *he* gain from killing *me?*

One nagging fear kept recurring in my mind. When I'd told Richard I had been locked in, he had refused to believe me. Had blamed it on panic and the blow to my head. Natural—or the actions of a guilty man trying to divert suspicion?

I resolved on one thing. When I reached Edgecliff I would keep my fears to myself, and do my best to find out the truth. I would show no one the cravat for a time, until I knew more. I looked down at the ring on my finger with a kind of horror. It was no longer a beautiful heirloom but something I regarded with a kind of superstitious dread. I'd worn it for such a short time and already I had almost died.

It was so ironic that just a short time ago, when I'd visited Malvina, I'd believed the mystery solved. Yes, the past was solved, but the present was closing around me with cold and implacable hands.

And my head was aching so. I still felt a dizziness, a disorientation from the fall.

We turned into the long and winding gravel drive. Malvina was probably the only one to whom I could confide my fears and yet I knew that I would never seek her out for such a purpose. She frightened me still with her mad ravings and I wanted no gossip about the new mistress of Edgecliff burning through the village.

As we drew up to the house, the doors were swinging open. Early as it was, someone was aware of our arrival. I climbed down, wishing I could run up the steps, to embrace whoever it was waiting for me, overjoyed at the thought of seeing Annabel or William, I was so glad to be home. But as I began to step down, a rush of dizziness overtook me and I had to grip the carriage door for support.

"Here, let Polker help you." Polker leaped from his

seat and took my arm, slowly helping me to step from the coach. I looked up, hoping to see Annabel's cheerful smile. Suddenly, some of the brightness went out of the morning, and I was no longer glad to be home.

It was Mrs. Kerrenslea. Her spare black figure stood motionless in the doorway.

"Send someone to ready the bedchamber. The mistress took a fall, she must rest." Polker helped me up the stone steps.

"Madam is ill?" Mrs. Kerrenslea looked searchingly into my face and at the bandage on my head. To my surprise, she sounded truly concerned.

"It is nothing, really," I protested. "There was a fire at the inn. I took a fall down the stairs escaping the flames and hit my head. The doctor says I shall be fine if I just rest."

"Aye, and t'master said to send for the doctor straight on my return," growled Polker. "I'll be off t'fetch him, then."

I didn't object, though I was sure the visit was useless. The evidence of Richard's concern warmed me.

Mrs. Kerrenslea took my arm. "But madam, how terrible," she said. "Come now and lie down in your room. I shall brew some special tea that is good for headaches. You look most pale."

Meekly, I allowed Mrs. Kerrenslea to lead me away to my room. How strange. Now that I was a member of the family on a more official basis, and mistress of the house, she seemed much warmer. I could see why the family were so devoted to her.

I took to my bed gratefully, and drank my tea obediently. When the doctor came, I was grateful, for really my head ached so, though the tea did seem to help.

"Now then. You must stay in bed for a few days, and I shall come to see you every day," said the doctor firmly. "These head injuries can be tricky. You must tell me at

205

once if you are dizzy or see double, or feel nauseated."

The prospect of a few days in bed didn't seem such a bad one, for I felt rather ill in truth. But it wouldn't help me solve the mystery. I hoped to be up and about sooner.

Annabel came to see me, full of excitement at the tales of the fire and my fall.

"Imagine! What a way to start a honeymoon!" she piped. "One could almost believe that the brides are truly cursed!"

I suppressed a shudder.

Though Richard sent messages every day, he did not return, and neither did Charles. After three days, I was up and about again, though still subject to headaches. On the fourth day, I had an unexpected caller.

"Mrs. Evonne DeVere to see you, madam." Penwillen bowed as he made his announcement.

"Evonne DeVere?" I nearly choked on my tea and I had to lay down my cup carefully for fear that I would spill it.

"Show her in," I said cautiously, wondering what possible business Evonne DeVere, my husband's former mistress, could have with me.

Evonne DeVere flounced into the room as if she owned it. Her dress, much too formal for an afternoon call, was of pastel apricot silk, cut low in the bosom. The top part of the dress was so tightly formed, it almost seemed poured on her body. But the full skirts flowed about her with each step and I could see French lace petticoats peeking out from under the hemline. Her matching hat had a wide brim and white ostrich feathers. It complimented her red hair, which framed her face like flames. How voluptuous she looked, and how graceful. I looked down at my pale blue muslin and frowned.

I, not used to unexpected afternoon calls, would have to take special care from now on.

"Good afternoon, Mrs. DeVere. To what do I attribute

206

this unexpected visit?" I asked guardedly.

She sat across from me and smiled as she removed her white gloves.

"I am sure you know that our properties adjoin, Emily." Her tone was too familiar and her addressing me by my Christian name offended me but I chose to ignore it, waiting for her to complete her thought.

"And being that you are now mistress of the household with many duties that I am sure are unfamiliar to you," Evonne continued, "I thought that I would offer any assistance that you might need in that regard. Although Woodmere is not quite as grand as Edgecliff, I am very well acquainted with the duties, as mistress of a manor house myself."

"There are no immediate questions that come to mind," I answered. "But I thank you for your kind offer." What was she really here for? I wondered.

Penwillen set the silver teapot onto the small table between us and looked at Evonne DeVere from under hooded eyes. I could tell that he, too, was suspicious of her presence.

"Shall there be anything else, then, madam?" Penwillen asked.

"That will be all, Penwillen," I replied, loath to dismiss him. I didn't know how I would take to being alone with the worldly DeVere.

"And so—you are back early from your honeymoon," she said. "And alone."

She seemed to imply that something had gone wrong with my marriage already.

"Yes. But I am sure you heard of the fire, and my fall. I have been indisposed. And naturally Richard must be with the miners at such a time."

"Naturally." But her lifted brows expressed her doubt. Her eyes went over my dowdy dress, my figure that was so inadequate compared to hers, as if to say a husband just married to her would never have left her side.

"Richard plans to take me to the continent as soon as the trouble subsides," I said, a trifle sharply.

"Oh? Well, at least you had your wedding night in a romantic setting. The Swan. How often I myself have stayed there. I have happy memories of that inn. Would I shock you if I told you I had stayed there with a lover?"

My heart burned. Oh, this was too much! She was telling me she had stayed there with my husband! Was it true? Would Richard actually take me to a place—for our wedding night—that he had taken her? Or was it just her malice?

"It would not shock me," I said, meaning it cattily. "Mrs. DeVere, thank you for calling but I am afraid you have caught me at a busy time." I indicated my dress. "This is my day for household duties. And I expect my husband back tomorrow. I am at home on Tuesdays and Thursdays for callers. I hope you will call again then." I rose, feeling I had had enough of her insinuations.

But she was not to be so easily dismissed. "I'd like to present to you a gift on the occasion of your marriage," she said, taking a prettily wrapped package out of her reticule.

"But you have already sent one, that lovely crystal vase," I protested.

"This is something special, something personal, just for you. I want you to have it as a token of our newfound friendship."

I hesitated.

"Please open it now, Emily," she instructed. "I must show you how it is to be worn."

The emerald green foil wrapper fell on my lap to expose a small white jewelry box. I opened it carefully. Inside, surrounded by white satin, was a small round watch.

"This is much too dear, I cannot accept this!" I

exclaimed, marveling at the fine gold casing and the delicately painted, ivory face.

"I won't take it back!" She took the watch from the box. On the back of the watch was a pin and she opened it adeptly and pinned it upside down to the collar of my dress.

"It isn't on correctly," I protested.

"Yes, it is." She smiled and turned the collar up to my eyes and I could clearly and correctly see the time. "You must wear this so every day." She walked to the door and nodded to me before she stepped through it. "As mistress of a great house such as this, it is important to know the time of day so that you may perform your duties on schedule."

I thought it odd that Evonne left through the back of the house. I knew because I saw her as she walked through the kitchen garden. She stopped and talked for more than a moment to Mrs. Kerrenslea, who was coming toward the house carrying a basket of herbs. The herb garden was her special provence and nary a cook or servant was allowed to go near it.

Their heads came together and they spoke familiarly. It seemed odd to me at first, but I dismissed it. Of course Mrs. Kerrenslea and Evonne DeVere would have cause to know each other. The properties did adjoin after all.

The next day, I began a solitary tour of Edgecliff for the first time with an open eye toward redecoration, changes that I could now make to suit my taste. Richard was to return in the afternoon, and despite my continuing headache, I wished to keep busy.

I discovered that many of the rooms, especially in the West wing, had had little use in many years. The furnishings and decorations were out of date, dark and quite unappealing. The rooms looked almost as if they belonged in the Middle Ages instead of a Victorian manor house.

I spent the morning happily engaged in going from room to room, making notes, and considering which furniture should stay, which should go to the attics, and which pieces should be covered with different fabrics.

At the far end of the West wing, behind the still locked door, was my mother's bedchamber. Uncle Ralph's shrine to her memory. I had not been inside since after the will was read.

I opened the door slowly and the mustiness of the room was almost enough to send me away.

I remembered that the armoire was filled with clothing and I opened it with excitement. Hung neatly in a row were six dresses, each one more elaborate than the next. So, these were my mother's gowns, I thought. A deep maroon velvet caught my eye and I removed it gingerly. Stepping up to the mirror, I held the dress against my chin and was amazed at how it transformed me. The deep color of the dress made my skin look as translucent as a pearl, soft, smooth, and glowing. The entire neckline was trimmed with sparkling silver beads. The bodice was a deeply cut V, and in the center was a delicate rose made out of silver filigree. My gray eyes seemed brighter, shining metallic, reflecting the silver brilliance. Although it must have been over twenty years of age, the dress was in perfect condition. And so classic was the cut that it could be worn today and look as if it had just been fashioned in Paris the week before.

On an impulse, I shed my own gown, and then dropped the velvet folds over my head. I struggled to button the gown in the back, not getting all of the buttons, and walked to the mirror. I looked for a time at myself, and then up at the portrait of my mother over the mantel.

The dress I had on was the one she had been captured in for eternity. The ring of the Edgecliff brides glistened blood red on her pale white hand and I held my hand up to the portrait to compare. Not even a master artist such as Reynolds could capture the shocking brilliance of the ring that I now wore openly.

I glanced into the mirror again, and loosened one chestnut curl to fall on my shoulder. Ah, now that I wore the dress, it might have been a portrait of me that hung over the mantel, so close was the resemblance.

A noise behind me made me spin around in fear, convinced that I would see my mother standing there. And there she was! Her gray eyes stared back at me. My hand went to my throat, my scream stifled into a whimper, and I almost felt about to faint. It was only a moment of fright for when I looked closer, I realized that I was staring into a mirror. It was no wonder that everyone had said how much I looked like my mother. For it was true. I had not realized just how close the resemblance was until now, when looking into a mirror led me to believe that I was staring at her ghost.

Then I heard a noise again, the definite sound of a step. "Who is there?" I cried, my voice sounding hollow in the musty room.

Mrs. Kerrenslea appeared in the doorway, and when she saw me, she went absolutely white. She took a step backward, her hand going out in a warding-off gesture.

"My God—Amelia—you have come back to haunt me?" she gasped.

"Mrs. Kerrenslea—it is I, Emily," I said.

For a moment, she still recoiled from me in horror.

"I have put on my mother's dress," I said gently. I knew well how superstitious the Cornish were. And had I not, only a moment before, taken my own reflection for my mother's ghost?

"I—Emily?" she said chokingly, then groped for a chair, sitting down abruptly, not even noticing her own familiarity.

"I am sorry to have given you a turn. I know what you experienced—I caught sight of my own reflection and, for a moment, thought I was seeing my mother's ghost."

"You look so much like her." The words were low, and she was still staring at me as if she could not believe her eyes.

Then she gathered her composure with a visible effort. "I am sorry, madam. You gave me a turn."

It was then I wondered what she was doing there at all. Had she been following me around the house all morning? Or had she come to this room for some other purpose, thinking that no one else would be here?

"I am sorry for that," I said, picking up my everyday dress and going behind the screen in one corner of the room. As I changed, it would give her time to recover from her shock. And besides, suddenly I did not want to have that dress on. From behind the screen, I called, "Mrs. Kerrenslea, I have been making notes this morning on certain changes I intend to make in the decoration of the house, and the furnishings. We shall be very busy in the future, for I'd like to change quite a bit about the house. I shall need your help. I'd like you to find me a reputable firm of painters and workman to start with."

"Very good. But is Madam recovered yet from your injury for such a great undertaking? You don't seem quite . . . strong enough."

"I feel fine. I should like to start with the West wing. This room in particular." I came out from behind the screen, smoothing my hair. "Now, the first thing I would like done is to have this portrait of my mother removed. It is not suitable for a guest bedroom."

"Very well, Madam, I will send one of the footmen up.

Would Madam like it wrapped and put into the attic?"

"In the attic! Certainly not. It is a beautiful portrait. No, I would like it rehung, in the minstrels' gallery with the other portraits."

She was silent a moment and her face seemed to whiten. Her eyes were fixed on the collar where I wore my gold watch, Evonne's gift. "In the minstrels' gallery?" she said at last in a disbelieving tone. "But I am afraid that would not be suitable, madam. The minstrels' gallery is where all of the family portraits hang."

"My mother was a Woodstock, and as such, family," I rejoined.

"I beg your pardon, madam," she went on relentlessly, "for speaking out of turn, but I feel it is my place to warn you that such an act would not be . . . well considered."

"What on earth do you mean?" I cried, irritated at her presumption.

"The Cornish servants are a superstitious lot, madam, and might think it was bad luck to hang the portrait there due to the circumstances of its history."

"I don't care what the servants think, Mrs. Kerrenslea." I said frigidly. "And what do you mean by history?"

She had the grace to hesitate. "It is what the servants would say. That your mother was mad . . . and died a suicide, leaping from the cliffs."

"She was not mad." How glad I was that I now knew this to be true. "Send a footman and have him hang the portrait in the gallery at once. I shall deal with the servants."

"Forgive me, madam, but it is I who will have to deal with their superstitious fears. The Cornish servants are so afraid of ghosts and legends. We shall lose several of them over this, no doubt, but I shall make do." She rose, and again, I saw her eyes go to the watch on my collar.

"I see you looking at my watch. I wear it upside down

213

so I can see the time when I look down."

"I see, madam. I shall send for the footman at once. But if I may say, you should go and lie down. You are looking pale."

I wondered, as she left me, if she thought I was strange for wearing the watch reversed.

But as I came out into the hall a few moments later and went down the stairs, I overheard her speaking aloud, in a very low tone. She was standing alone in the window embrasure.

"Ralph was mine before he was yours—yes, and after," she murmured. She then left the window and went down the stairs.

If she thought me strange, how much stranger did I think her! But her words were revealing. It was as I'd suspected. She had been Sir Ralph's mistress! No wonder she'd hated my mother—and me—at first. And to think she was tormented by guilt all these years over her "sin" with Sir Ralph.

Well, I reflected, it seemed everyone in this house had a secret. But at least she was being nicer to me now that I was the mistress of Edgecliff. Her eccentricities I could tolerate . . . as long as she treated me with respect.

That afternoon Richard came home. I was so impatient that I stood in the open doorway awaiting his arrival. And like a girl, I could not restrain myself when I saw him, but flew down the gravel drive and flung myself in his arms. All my suspicions of him seemed baseless when I saw his handsome, beloved face.

"Darling," he said, kissing me. "Now our honeymoon can begin in earnest. Not the continent yet—the miners are still upset—but it seems right to start our marriage here, does it not?"

"Oh, yes, Richard. I missed you so."

"And I you. Are you feeling better? How is your head?" He gently kissed the bruise that still stood out on my forehead.

"Fine. Mrs. Kerrenslea has been making me a special tea that helps greatly."

"Good. For I plan to subject my wife to some late nights, now that I have her to myself."

I blushed with pleasure, so glad he was home. "Richard—did you find the ones who threw the torch?"

From the way his face darkened, I wished I had not brought up the subject. "No," he said shortly. "But we will."

"Well—if it isn't the happy bride and bridegroom."

I turned, to find Charles regarding us cynically. He had just come out of the coach, having returned with Richard.

"Good afternoon, Charles," I said, watching the way Richard was scowling at him.

"Emily. You look blooming. Not as if you'd survived a brush with death. And I am not referring to spending the night with my brother."

"Damn it, Charles, you will address my wife with more respect!" Richard thundered.

Charles gave him a challenging look. "So you've remembered you have a wife—after four days? Bravo, Richard. But then, nothing keeps you away from Edge-cliff long in any case."

Charles took himself off, Richard staring after him with such venom that I was frightened. I remembered Malvina's words: *"Take care that you are not the cause of blood—and murder—on two more Woodstock brothers' hands."*

Chapter Sixteen

After tea, Richard left Annabel and I alone.

"I intend to dine at Polkerris House this evening," she announced.

"Would Timothy Odgers have anything to do with that?" I asked lightly, smiling at her. Ever since her coming-out ball, Annabel had set her cap at Timothy, whose father was a neighboring squire. He was a handsome and devilish young man with as much fire and mischief as Annabel herself. I thought they were perfectly suited, especially since they were both horse-mad.

"Yes—for Timothy has just acquired a new stallion I wish to see."

"Oh. A stallion. And last week it was a matched pair. You are there often. Isn't it absence that makes the heart grow fonder?" I teased.

"I hope I've already got Timothy's heart," Annabel laughed. "It's his name that I'm after."

"You'll have it soon enough." Then Annabel's face became suddenly serious.

"Emily—was it Evonne DeVere whom I saw leaving your morning room?"

"Yes, why?"

"I don't wish to meddle into your affairs. But tell me that you are not befriending her. I do not trust her."

"Neither do I. I was quite surprised when she called."

"I was too. She had just returned."

Something in her look unnerved me. "Returned? From where?"

"I wasn't going to mention this to you, to worry you unnecessarily . . ." She stopped and looked into the distance, biting back her words.

"Is there something I should know?" I asked.

"She has just returned from Falmouth."

I paled. "Do you mean she was there while we were?"

"Yes. And after you had gone, as well."

What was Annabel hinting? That my husband had spent my honeymoon with another woman?

She rushed on, not looking at me. "I saw Evonne DeVere in a shop yesterday. She was ordering perfumes, and as much as I dislike her, I found myself obligated to speak to her. I remarked that the scents she was buying were very costly, and she replied, 'Oh, but well worth it. An absent admirer of mine will be back tomorrow, and I am buying these scents against his return. I find these little investments in keeping a gentleman attentive'—she gestured towards the perfume—'and are well worth the return. Why this very gentleman gave me this.' And then Evonne held out a bracelet that was simply dripping with amethysts. 'He said they matched my eyes.' she said. And then she mentioned that she had just returned from Falmouth, where there had been a fire at the inn. When I said you had been there, she raised her brows and said, 'Imagine!' Oh, I tell you I wanted to scratch her eyes out!"

I felt sick. "And you presume the absent admirer is Richard?" I asked angrily, but my heart was pounding.

"I don't know. I can't think Richard would do such a dreadful thing, but I thought I should warn you to be on

217

your guard against that woman. Do not receive her again, for she is up to no good. She means to hurt your marriage by fair means or foul, I believe."

"Thank you, Annabel. I shall keep away from her in the future."

But I was heartsick. Did he still love her? Was that why he was anxious to be rid of me—if he was? And to marry the woman he'd always loved, one so much more beautiful than I?

I needed to be alone. I did not even want to see Richard, so I went out for a walk in the evening air.

I found my way to the gazebo.

It disturbed me greatly, the dilapidation of this once grand gazebo near the cliff's edge. At one time it must have been a magnificent sight. Now, it looked overgrown by a virtual jungle. The gazebo was surrounded by rhododendrons that stood twenty feet high, twisted and entwined with malevolent ivy that climbed even higher, covering the roof. Nettles were everywhere, choking the path that led to the entrance. Another ugly plant, some half-breed of nature, crept up the rotting stairs into the center of the structure, also entwined with wild ivy that seemed spread through the building like flames.

I knew now why my uncle had let it fall to ruin. The place where he had forced my mother, the last place on earth he'd seen her alive. It seemed eerie, haunted by an echo of strong passions.

I paused by the entrance and closed my eyes, taking a deep breath to compose myself. I could almost see my parents here that night so long ago. Even though there was nothing truly to fear, I took the steps with trepidation. They creaked beneath my feet and I felt a stillness in the air. Was it my parents' spirits that I felt, joined together again at this place of tragedy?

I made my way slowly, but soon I was seated along one of the rotting benches that lined the inside of the gazebo. It was open on all sides with a clear view of the sea from each section. How wonderful it must have been here during my parents' time. I wondered about that hot summer's night, when Ralph and Amelia had come here as the tide came in and heard the pounding of the sea on the jagged shoreline.

The thought made a chill pass through me.

How my father had loved my mother so. I could not believe that it was he who had thrown her from the cliffs to a horrible death on the rocks below, in a fit of jealousy. And yet, Ralph had loved her too, had given her the betrothal ring. I could not imagine my uncle throwing her over in a fit of rage either.

How parallel it seemed in some ways to today. It was so much easier to believe my uncle had killed her than my beloved father—so much easier to believe it was Charles who had thrown the torch through my window rather than my beloved husband.

Just then I heard a noise and I turned away from the sea to spot Charles coming along the path I had just cleared. I stood stiffly and watched silently as he approached. It was early afternoon, and I suppose he hadn't had a chance yet to take a brandy or whatever it was he had been drinking since the wedding, for his step was sure and his disposition sunny.

His blue eyes twinkled with mischief when he saw me and I remembered that first day we met, when he had said, "It's easy to be charming to someone as pretty as you are." It filled me with sadness to think of the time when I was naive and everything was as it appeared. Now I knew much better, and I stood on my guard when he took the steps up into the gazebo.

"Charles." I nodded to him politely then turned again to face the sea.

"So, that's how it is, is it?" he bantered lightly and stood alongside me. "I fancy you want to fix up this old

219

rotting place too, I suppose?" His tone held a trace of boredom and I became defensive.

I made the decision on the spot. "Yes, is there something wrong with that?"

"No, no." He held up his hand as if to fend off my remark. "But the household is all abuzz with the changes you are making. All the servants are worried you may make changes with the staff as well."

"Really?" I asked, concerned. "I have never had that intention."

"It's funny how gossip starts." He started to pace about the gazebo with his hands in his pockets. "One word, one glance, taken in the wrong way, and a month's worth of juicy tales can spread through the country-side."

"What is that you imply, Charles?" I knew him too well to think that he was making idle conversation with me.

"Oh, nothing." His voice became very quiet and I was beginning to get extremely uncomfortable. The clack, clack, clacking of his hard shoes on the floorboards was making me even more nervous. I tried to stop watching him as he paced back and forth across the gazebo but I could not.

Finally, I turned away completely and forced my eyes to the sea, gripping the ivy-covered banister for support. And then I heard him come toward me. I stood completely still, frozen, my eyes fixed to the waves and the clouds that moved slowly across the sky. He came right up behind me. I could feel the heat of his body and the warmth of his breath on my neck. And then I felt his hands on my shoulders, caressing.

I was about to move away and ask him what was the meaning of all this when I heard a twig crack and the sound of steps on the pavement.

"It seems I have come at an opportune moment." I

heard Richard's voice and was filled with a strange sick feeling. *Whatever must he think?*

Charles had already stepped away from me and was sitting on the bench when I turned and saw Richard's face. He stood at the doorway to the gazebo, looking at me.

His face was black with jealousy.

"So you and Charles are meeting behind my back?" he demanded.

"Richard!" I cried, shocked.

"This isn't the first time I've found you alone, and his hands on you!"

Tears started in my eyes. I could bear to hear no more. As I brushed past him and started down the steps of the gazebo, I froze. Thinking of that long-ago scene, where my father had come on my mother and Sir Ralph and accused her of dallying with him . . .

Was I now to run down the cliff and fall to my death? I would not act as my mother had.

I turned back. "Richard, I am glad you came. I—"

"Are you now?" he asked and raised his brow, stepping away from me. "I will meet you back at the house, Emily. I do not like this place."

Suddenly, I didn't either. Richard was gone toward the house before I could protest. Charles sat casually on the bench, filing his nails to perfection.

All manner of emotion swirled about me. "Charles, what was that about?" I asked angrily.

"I don't know." He leaned back against the creaking banister and let out a laugh, stiff, shrill, frightening.

"What do you mean, you don't know? You must know how it looked!" I went to the entranceway and threw him a hateful glance.

"I suppose." He giggled again and then I wasn't so sure that he hadn't been drinking, even this early in the day.

"Well, know it. I want you to understand that nothing

221

this nature is to happen again. If it does, I shall banish you from Edgecliff." My voice sounded so firm, so filled with authority that I shocked even myself. Though I knew I could never carry out these threats, I wanted my word heeded. "Do you hear me?"

Charles only nodded and looked at the sea.

I rode back to the manor slowly, with a heavy heart. What was happening to me? Only a week before I was a happy bride on her wedding day. And now I was a woman filled with doubts, plagued by jealousies that came from all sides.

Later that night, when we were alone in our room, Richard pulled me close to him roughly.

"So what was it that I interrupted today, Emily?"

"I don't know what you mean," I replied cautiously and pulled away from him slightly, not enjoying the force of his embrace.

"Don't you now?" The look in his eyes was fierce, challenging.

"Charles was questioning me about my plans for the renovation of the gazebo."

"And that is all?" Richard's voice was like ice. I had never seen him so cold, so distant, and it frightened me, saddened me.

"Yes," I replied, but I knew that my voice must have sounded unconvincing for I didn't believe it myself. I knew that Charles had been up to something. But I had to keep silent. I did not want to foster Richard's heightened jealousy.

"I don't think so!" he said violently. "He had his hands on your shoulders! I think there is something more between you. You forget that I saw him kiss you at the ball."

"I have explained that to you, Richard!" I cried

desperately. "I don't know why he touched me today—unless it was deliberately to provoke you. He must have seen you coming. He was pacing, while I had my back to the house. I was trying to ignore him. It is ridiculous of you to be jealous. You know that I love you . . . why do you suppose I married you?"

"Just do not forget that I am your husband," he warned, and crushed me in a rough, possessive embrace.

That night he took me with all the violence of our first kiss, when he had burst into my room after the ball, and none of the gentleness I had grown used to on our honeymoon. It was wildly exciting, in the dark, but afterward he turned from me and fell asleep, not putting his arms around me as he usually did. And all at once I felt bruised, as if he had used me somehow, and very alone. I felt the tears slipping down my cheeks and wondered why Richard doubted me so.

The next morning I awoke to find Richard already gone. When I went down to breakfast, I learned from one of the maids that he had ridden out early on estate business. I was disturbed. After the storminess of the night before, I had hoped to speak to him this morning, perhaps exchange warm kisses, to reassure myself that our marriage was normal, that he loved me as tenderly as he had during the weeks prior to our marriage. I sighed. As I dispiritedly picked at my breakfast, I wondered how I would fill the day. He had left a message that he would be back late, perhaps not even until after dinner. And it was his first day back! The first day of our new life together. I was hurt that it didn't seem to matter to him.

At length I resolved that perhaps I was making too much of it, being too sensitive. I had my pride. I'd not sit and mope like a wilting flower. Instead, when Richard came back, I decided he should find me full of tales of how I had spent my day, how much I had accomplished. I was mistress now, and he'd expect me to play the part, not cling to his coattails and wait for him to direct me. Hadn't I already asserted myself, with all my ideas for a new and more beautiful Edgecliff?

I pushed away my plate and rose. I decided to go into my room for a pencil and paper. I would sketch some ideas for the renovation of the gazebo and present them to Richard tonight when he returned. We would sit together in the library with a fire glowing and excitedly discuss my plans, our plans. It would help bring us together again, help us forget the doubts and jealousies of this past night.

In my room I found something disturbing. As I looked in my drawer, I found that the burgundy cravat was gone from the drawer where I had hidden it.

I sat on the bed. Who had taken it? There was only one answer. The one who had tied it. No miner, indeed. Someone in this house.

It was some time before I could compose myself to go downstairs.

I called Mrs. Kerrenslea, and she was most amenable to my plans, until I came to the drawings of the gazebo. I noticed her stiffen. "The gazebo is irreparable, madam. It should be destroyed."

"In my opinion it is salvageable, Mrs. Kerrenslea," I said firmly. "I intend to restore it to its former elegance as soon as possible."

"Sir Ralph would not have wished it, madam."

"My uncle is dead, and I intend for the past to be forgotten. The gazebo, when restored, will bring back memories of a pleasanter time, instead of reminding everyone of the tragedy that occurred there."

I could see she was startled that I knew, but then a maid came in, carrying a tray.

"If I might say so, you look pale, madam. I took the liberty of having some of the headache tea made up."

"Thank you, Mrs. Kerrenslea. It does seem to help." I

smiled, ready to forget her attitude about the gazebo. We turned to the plans again as I sipped my tea.

I didn't hear the words Mrs. Kerrenslea said to me just before she left the room. My mouth became dry and my thoughts fuddled. Perhaps the injury I had suffered with my fall was having delayed effects.

I walked slowly through the hall, holding on to the wall for support. My footsteps echoed from every room and there seemed to be shadows everywhere.

Just as I reached the stairwell, I heard a crash and something pierced my cheek. I spun around, looking behind me, reaching up to my cheek at the same time. A huge vase which had once graced the top of the bannister on the second floor was now in pieces on the floor beside me. One of the pieces had flown up to my face and imbedded itself in my cheek. I shrieked, blood oozing onto my fingers. I looked up to the second floor. Had I seen a shadow move? I couldn't be sure as I felt a grayness come over my perceptions.

"Madam, oh my word, what has happened?" one of the housemaids said. "Oh, your cheek! We must call a physician straight away."

I could barely distinguish her words. My head was spinning wildly and I felt a queaziness in my abdomen. I felt myself being led somewhere and then I felt some hands on me, a wet cloth, and then blackness.

I awoke I didn't know how much later, to see the dark maroon floral wallpaper of the drawing room. There was a stiffness in my joints and the unmistakable stretching sensation of a bandage across my cheek.

Then I saw Richard bending over me, looking very concerned.

"You awaken." He smiled then kissed my forehead. "The sleeping beauty, awakened by a kiss."

"Oh, Richard. I am so glad you're home early."

"Early? It's already past lunch. The doctor has been

with you all morning. He was most concerned due to the accident, and now another. You must be more careful, Emily." He sat down next to me on the daybed and took my hand.

Then I saw Mrs. Kerrenslea in the doorway, holding a tray. And I remembered.

"It wasn't an accident," I whispered into Richard's ear.

"What?" he questioned.

"The vase." I looked over at Mrs. Kerrenslea. "She did it. She purposefully pushed it."

"Nonsense," Richard whispered back to me.

I waited to reply until Mrs. Kerrenslea had laid the tray on the table beside me and left the room.

"Thank you, Mrs. Kerrenslea," Richard said and then turned toward me with a disbelieving eye.

"We had an argument, about the gazebo," I said excitedly, taking gasps of air. "When I said that I wanted to restore it, she was completely opposed to it."

"And you think she would stop you by dropping a vase on your head?" His eyes held a flicker of amusement and I realized how ridiculous I must sound.

"Yes . . . no," I muttered and closed my eyes.

"This has been a very trying time for you this past week, Emily. What with the accident and the new responsibilities of running a household of this size. And I must admit to not being of any help by my jealous outburst yesterday. I apologize." He raised my hand to his lips and kissed it tenderly. "You must not have recovered completely from your fall. I suggest that you have something to eat and rest. I enjoin you to take things much more slowly until you are well." He kissed me then, gently on the mouth, and left me alone in the room.

I heard voices in the hall, one of which was distinctly Mrs. Kerrenslea's. And I listened very carefully to what she had to say.

"How is the madam?" I heard her ask him.

"Not well, I'm afraid." I heard sadness in Richard's voice and felt a tugging in my heart.

"Is the injury that bad then?"

They moved down the hall then and their voices became quieter, more difficult for me to hear.

"It is not her physical health that I'm concerned with, Mrs. Kerrenslea," Richard said distinctly.

"You think that she is her 'mother's daughter' then?" The implication in Mrs. Kerrenslea's voice was clear. But what shocked me was Richard's response.

"Perhaps," he muttered. "Perhaps the injury sustained in her fall has triggered something."

So he thought me mad! My own husband thought me mad! For that is what had been suspected of my mother so long ago. But there was never any truth to that, I knew for a fact.

But they did not. And now they believed it was happening to me. The dizziness seemed to engulf me then and the last thing I saw in my mind's eye before I drifted off to sleep was the memory of Mrs. Kerrenslea's shadow on the staircase above me, just before the vase crashed down. I had seen her there, hadn't I? My thoughts were disconnected, confused. Maybe I hadn't seen her. Maybe I was becoming mad. For what possible reason could Mrs. Kerrenslea have to kill me?

Chapter Seventeen

The next morning, I rose to find everyone tense at breakfast. The looks that passed between Richard and Charles were almost unbearable and I welcomed the news that they both planned to spend the day away.

After breakfast, I went to my room. It was then I noticed. The ring was not on my finger. Had I taken it off when I became ill? I could not remember. I looked on the dresser, in the drawer, in the jewel box. Then I pulled at the bellrope fiercely. "Nan, come at once!" I cried and scrambled from the bed going down to my hands and knees, my fingers searching through the thick Persian rug. "Madam, what is the matter?" Nan approached me, eyeing me strangely.

"It is my ring. I can't find it. Please help me look for it." She looked at me again with a strange look in her eyes.

"Nan, please. Stop staring at me like that and help me. I must find it."

She knelt down beside me and said, "Don't you worry now, madam. Why don't you lie down and rest, and I can search for it. It is probably under the bedpost or in the corner."

But Nan had no success. I was too uneasy to lie down and helped in the search.

"Are you sure you had it yesterday?" she asked at last.

"Yes, I am sure. It must be there!" My voice cracked. I let out more emotion than I had intended and it gave Nan a start.

"Well then," she said, clasping and unclasping her hands. "It must be there, mustn't it? I'll have Penwillen organize a move of the bed so we can get a better look."

"Thank you, Nan, that is an excellent idea. But please announce his arrival so that I might watch as the bed is moved to see for myself where it has fallen."

The bed was moved later that morning and the ring was nowhere to be found. It disturbed me greatly and the afternoon was a blur of confusion and suspicion for me. The servants all treated me very delicately, as if I would break at any moment.

I awoke, and I wasn't sure how much time had passed, but I could see by the long rays of light streaming through the windows that it was late afternoon. My mouth was very dry. The lunch tray rested on the bedside table, untouched. I felt much better, though extremely hungry. Sleep had cleared my muddled thoughts slightly and the pain had all but disappeared. I rose carefully from the daybed and smoothed my skirts, planning to ring Penwillen for some tea.

I had just reached the bell pull when I heard loud voices traveling down the hall. They sounded as if they came from the smoking room.

"I shall not stand for your incompetence!" It was Richard.

"*My* incompetence. That is nothing compared with all of your business over the hill." It was Charles.

What did he mean by 'business over the hill'? I stepped as quietly as I could into the hallway in order to hear them more clearly. My heart was beating fast. I couldn't bear to hear anymore but I could not pull myself away.

"I shall lend you not another shilling until you have reformed your ways," Richard said sharply.

"Reformed my ways? I would say that the little time I spend at the gaming tables is far less serious than the time you spend in the house of a woman who is not your wife!" Charles growled.

"You insolent little brat of a boy. Just leave your false speculations out of this house. You are the last person I wish to speak to about my relationship with—" Richard stopped in midsentence just as the floor creaked beneath my feet.

I held my breath, waiting for them to continue.

But it was silent. A few moments went by and then Richard said, "We shall continue this talk later." Then I heard their footsteps and the sound of the door closing not so delicately.

Charles gambling?

I went to the bellrope and summoned Penwillen, lest Richard return, wondering why I had been moving about. My mind was filled with questions and I considered how I was going to discover the answers. I knew that I must speak to Charles about what he had said to Richard. To ask him the meaning of "the time you spend in the house of a woman who is not your wife." Those words burned in my mind and I had to know the truth. I needed to speak with Richard as well, but I feared it. Better to question Charles and risk estrangement from him than that of my husband. But the difficulty would be in finding the opportunity to question Charles in private, without risking the wrath of Richard's unfounded jealousies.

I ran to the window and saw Charles going out with a gun. There were some targets set up in the woods where he often went to practice shooting. I would follow him out there. Although I felt better than this morning, I was still slightly dizzy and had to move more slowly than I would have liked. It was a short distance away, but I decided to ride there, not trusting my legs.

I rode to the shooting range and watched as Charles raised the rifle to his shoulder and carefully pulled the trigger. How concentrated he looked. I almost hated to disturb him but my thoughts would not rest until I had the answers that I needed.

I crossed the field quietly behind him. "Charles, I must speak to you." I said, stepping up to his shoulder.

He swung around, surprise in his eyes. "Why sister, you startled me. You look . . . out of sorts. Is there something wrong?" he asked sarcastically, one eyebrow raised. I was certain that the servants' talk must have reached his ears about my "condition."

"There might be. We must talk and I wanted to speak with you alone. That's why I've come here."

"Alone? Why Emily, aren't you afraid that I might steal a kiss?" He laughed and stepped toward me, lowering the rifle to his side. "For that is what your husband thinks. You know, I have been doing very well in my shooting today." He swung around and aimed at the target. "I've been pretending the bull's-eye is your sweet Richard's face. So what must you speak to me about?" He placed the rifle back into the rack.

I frowned and took another step backward, disconcerted by the strange gleam in his eyes. "First of all, I would like to know what you meant by what you said about Richard's face," I said firmly, feeling more at ease now that the gun was out of Charles's hands.

"Come come. Haven't you ever heard of rivalry between brothers? It isn't serious, let me assure you. But he has been a thorn in my side recently."

"It is about the gambling, I take it. It bothers you that he disapproves." I said this wondering in the back of my mind about another kind of rivalry, afraid of Charles's response.

"So that's it, is it? Who would have thought Richard would go crying to you about it? Sending his wife to do

231

the dirty work for him. But then, you are the one holding the 'purse strings,' aren't you?" He snickered and it made me shudder. I had never before experienced Charles without his cloak of charm. If he could change so easily, I feared what Richard could have lurking behind his charming surface. Richard with the famous "temper."

"I have not spoken with Richard since this morning. He left Edgecliff when you did, after your meeting with him in the study."

"So you overheard us then."

"Yes, I did. Most of it anyway. I don't approve of your gambling, Charles," I said with as much sternness in my voice as I could muster.

"You—dictating to me?" he snapped. "You who have been at Edgecliff less than a year. You come and disrupt the entire household and steal everything that is rightfully ours!" He picked up the rifle again. "The riflery isn't a safe place for troublemakers like you." He whirled around so that the rifle was pointed directly at my heart.

"My God, so that's how you feel about me?" I ran toward a tree and hid behind it, shaking.

"Don't be a fool, Emily. I was only playing a game with you. Isn't there more you wish to speak with me about?"

I cautiously peered from behind the ancient tree, just with one eye, to see him seated on the bench with folded arms. The rifle was again in its resting place. His golden hair glowed in the sun and his eyes glittered.

I stepped toward him with trepidation. "So what is it that you really want to ask me?" His sarcastic tone was gone and he seemed warmer. Was this another facade?

I sat down on the bench as far from him as possible and folded my hands in my lap.

"I . . . I would like an explanation when you said 'spending time with a woman who is not your wife' to Richard." My voice shook a little as I spoke.

"I am not sure what to tell you, Emily. Most of what I said was in anger, just to get Richard's goat. But if I were

232

you, I would watch him more carefully. If you value your marriage, that is."

"I see." I felt a tear coming to my eye and looked away into the distance. The sky was darkening and I knew it was growing late. "Is there anything specific you can tell me that I should be aware of?" I asked urgently.

"No." He shook his head. "Just unfounded suspicions on my part. It is a pity though," he said, looking into my eyes, and the force of his gaze unsettled me.

"What is a pity?"

"That Richard was the victor. Even though you don't approve of my 'vice,' a woman with a figure such as yours could keep me from the gaming tables. I am sure of that." He smiled, catlike.

"If those words were meant to make me feel better, let me assure you that they do not. I will hear no more of it." I stood and made a start to leave.

But Charles stopped me. "You must," he chided, grabbing hold of my hand.

I shook free of him and looked at him coldly.

"It is a pity that Richard is showing his true colors so soon. Even I would have been more circumspect than that. And it is a pity that we both had the same idea and that he won the prize."

"What are you getting at, Charles?"

"When you first appeared on the doorstep, I'll admit I was angry that there really was a 'blood' niece still in the family. But after a few days I decided that it wasn't so bad at all. In fact you could have made it lot better for me at Edgecliff."

"Please, Charles, stop. I don't know what you are trying to say to me, but it does not bear on the problems we were discussing."

"But it does, and when I'm finished with my tale, you might understand more than you bargained for."

I sat down on the bench once more. I feared his words but I was desperately curious. What new information

233

was I about to discover? What new things to hurt me and cause me to worry?

"You see, being the second son, I was entitled to none of the wealth of Edgecliff. I was resigned to entering the army next spring. I knew that Richard would take control as soon as Uncle died and a few of the mines would be left to William. I, Charles, the happy-go-lucky, would be left with nothing. Or as close as mattered."

"Charles, I don't want to hear this. I—"

"Quiet, Emily, let me finish." His eyes were brilliant, filled with a strange glint and I feared him now but I dared not move.

"What news it was when Edgecliff was left to you! I had a plan all worked out. It would make me a very rich man indeed. But Richard somehow won you, like he always wins. Firstborn, first with my uncle, and now first with you. He has Edgecliff and his mistress as well. But what about you, Emily? There is still you. Do you not miss him when you are alone in your cold bed?" He smiled a bittersweet smile and touched my cheek with his curved fingers. But I snapped my face away from his touch. It burned me, sickened me, and I needed to get away.

I was confused by his confession. I recalled that he had made his intentions plain long before the will had been read. Which was the truth? Had he really cared for me and was now so filled with pain for his unrequited love that he chose to deny it? Or was he truly the opportunist that he was representing himself to be? I shook my head in disbelief.

"I see from your actions that my plan may have been difficult. But there is nothing I like better than the chase." His fingers clutched my arm and tightened as he drew my face toward him, trying to kiss my lips.

"Charles, stop this! I am your brother's wife."

"And a fine husband he is leaving you alone while he spends his time at the house across the hill."

234

"Let go of me!" I cried. His words stung me more than his actions and I felt hot tears welling up inside me.

"No," he said flatly. "You're much too lovely to be ignored. Such a pity. It could have been I running Edgecliff now and sharing your bed."

His lips reached mine and his kiss was a hateful thing, without a hint of tenderness. All of his anger and jealousy of Richard was somehow being vented upon me with the force of his cruel lips. What did he hope to accomplish?

"Stop!" I cried, pushing him away with a sob. How I found the strength I would never know but I pushed him away from me.

I ran from him, mounted my mare, then turned to look at him. He stood calmly near to the rifle case and I couldn't read his face. I considered riding away with not a word but I knew that I could not do this. Charles would have to realize that I was mistress of Edgecliff and I demanded respect.

"You shall regret what has just happened, Charles. I shall tell Richard and it shall be his decision whether or not you are allowed to stay at Edgecliff or will be asked to leave." I rode from him then, into the forest.

The trees closed darkly around me. Where was I riding? Away from the house. If I was not careful I should become lost. I stopped by a great fallen tree, covered with moss, and looked through the forest gloom, searching for the right way.

There was a sharp crack. It sounded like a rifle shot. The mare reared, lifting her front legs and fighting into the air. I was thrown onto the fallen tree. Just before I lost consciousness, I thought I saw a glimmer of golden hair in the woods. Charles?

Chapter Eighteen

When I awoke, it was to bright sunshine peeking through the shutters of my own room, basking my face warmly. I opened my eyes and saw Richard sitting next to the bed with a sad, concerned look on his face.

"Oh thank heavens!" Richard said and touched my cheek.

"What happened? How did I get here?" I asked. My voice was weak, only a whisper, and I felt dazed. My head pounded with a thudding pain and I could hardly turn to look at Richard when he gave his reply.

"When I returned last night, I found that you had been missing for some hours. Penwillen informed me that you had gone riding and had not returned at the dinner hour. I just arrived when the search began."

"And you found me." I smiled and reached out to him.

"No." He took my hand and stroked it and I felt comforted. "It was Charles who came upon you like a druid in the forest. You must have taken quite a fall."

"Charles found me?" I questioned, my voice quivering. "I fell because of a rifle shot. Charles knew where to find me because it was he who fired the shot! He . . . he deliberately tried to kill me!"

"Stop this, Emily," Richard said firmly, taking both of

my hands in his. "Why would Charles want to harm you? How could you get such a mad idea? Yesterday, you believed it was Mrs. Kerrenslea who was trying to kill you. Today, Charles. I fear the blow to your head has affected your mind. You must rest."

I took a deep breath and braced myself. "Charles shot at me because I threatened to banish him from Edgecliff."

"But Emily, why?"

"Because . . . he . . . he tried to force his attentions on me. You must send him away immediately, Richard, you must!"

"Now my dear," he said just a little too sweetly, brushing my hair from my eyes. "You must rest. Tomorrow you might feel more yourself and we can talk about this then. I cannot believe that Charles would do such a thing without encouragement." The tone of his voice was harsh and reprimanding. "Perhaps your perceptions are confused from the incidents of the past few days." His face suddenly looked sinister to me.

"No! Richard, someone is trying to harm me! I . . ." I started to say and then my lips froze in place. Was it possible they were all working together to rid themselves of me? My eyes opened wide with fear and recognition. Richard looked down on me coldly. His face was a mask, unreadable, but I thought I detected a slight hint of disdain, impatience. I realized then that I must escape this place, leave Edgecliff and everything I loved in order to save my very life.

I smiled up at Richard, feigning compliance, deciding that as soon as the house was quiet for the night I would set off. But should I confide in William first—or Annabel? For surely they were the only ones I could trust.

"Perhaps you're right, Richard. My thoughts have been confused of late. Rest is what I require. Perhaps tomorrow at breakfast you can help me to understand all

237

that has happened."

"I am sorry, Emily. But I must travel to London for an important business matter and will be off before the dawn."

I frowned and turned my head away but he knelt down by the bedside and stroked my cheek. "Don't be sad, my love," were his lying words. "When I return, you will be in good spirits once again."

Or conveniently out of the way, I thought. He was going to London, or perhaps the house on the hill? Charles's ugly words rang out in my mind. I loved Richard so and I could not bear the thought of running away from him, losing him forever. But if all of my suspicions were correct, I had no choice.

Richard stood and left me then. Tears came to my eyes. I would probably never see him again.

Then I heard him speak, his voice like ice traveling through the hall.

"Humor her, Nan," he said. "Smile and pretend to believe her wild ramblings. She is not well, we shall call for a doctor again. I am going to London to bring back a doctor who specializes in—this sort of thing." There was a great deal of pain in his voice.

Then Nan came into my room in her normal good cheer. "There, madam," she said and smiled. "You are looking well. I've brought you some tea. Drink it up now and rest."

She poured me a cup out of the porcelain pot. Its deep herbal aroma filled the room. I sipped at the tea, enjoying its complexity. As soon as the house was quiet for the night, I would slip away. And then I would be safe.

Nan closed the curtains and left my bedchamber. I mentally planned what I would take along with me in the piece of baggage and waited. But I could hardly keep my eyes from closing. I blinked two or three times, each time my eyelids feeling like heavy weights had been placed on them. Then the blanket of sleep came over me, smothering me, sending my mind into oblivion.

"Madam, it's time for some breakfast," I heard as if from a cavern and I woke from a fog to the black, unsmiling eyes and thin lips of Mrs. Kerrenslea. They floated in space before me and I couldn't stand to look at them, so I turned my face to the pillow.

"Come on, mistress, sit up and drink your tea," she commanded.

I opened one eye.

The thin lips moved. "Hot tea is very good for you." She put the cup against my lips and some of the hot liquid spilled down my throat and down my chin, staining my nightgown.

I coughed. "Richard, where is Richard?" I heard myself ask.

"He is away." The lips seemed to surround the room. They flapped at me as if from the end of a tunnel. "He has been away for a long time. No one knows where. Could be with Evonne. What did he tell *you* before he left, Emily, business or pleasure?" I thought I heard but it was dreamlike, hazy. But no. She would never call me Emily.

The lips floated away and left me swinging my head from side to side on my pillow muttering, "No, *no!*"

And then I disappeared into a tunnel of my own.

The next day—or it could have been even the next, for I had lost my sense of time—I woke again to see those black eyes and thin lips.

"You didn't finish your tea, drink it up now."

My hand moved as if uncontrolled by me. I lifted the cup and the tea spilled onto my bedclothes. I tried to mop it up with my fingers but I could not, and those black eyes

239

stared at me unflinching.

"Annabel, I want to see Annabel," I mumbled.

"She has been gone for weeks now. Don't you remember? Are you losing your mind like your mother?" Weeks? I heard a shrill laugh and then tumbled again, falling, falling.

"Drink some more tea, Emily," said a voice.

"I will. It helps my head. Your tea helps my head, Mrs. Kerrenslea."

"Oh, but this is not my tea. It is a special tea. A special recipe of your husband's—of Richard Woodstock's. To help you get better, he says."

The room was filled with clouds like cotton, spinning round and round. I stared up at the sky for hours and watched the lights as they bounced around my head and through the clouds.

"What are you laughing at, Emily?" I heard from a distance.

"Oh, the bouncing lights. Amusing, aren't they, Richard? That is you, isn't it, Richard?"

Then I heard the loud banging of an iron door and tiny voices muttering behind it.

"She has been getting stranger each day." It was Mrs. Kerrenslea.

"I thought she would improve with rest." It was Richard and his voice sounded sad, almost in torment.

I wanted to leap from my bed and comfort him but I found I couldn't move. "I'm all right, really I am!" I tried to scream but the words came out a croak from my lips.

"It may be more serious than just the accident." Mrs. Kerrenslea's voice was cold, shrill. "She might have inherited her mother's sickness . . ." Her voice trailed off and I felt a nausea overtake me. Their words became a muddle and I sank back down onto my pillow, exhausted.

The days passed. Everything was calm and peaceful. Richard was gone, Annabel was gone, and I rarely saw William. I missed them all so much. Where were they? I asked myself. Why hadn't they come? The only company I received were those horrible black eyes that woke me everyday and the bony fingers that were making me eat and drink things that I had no taste for.

Through the haze I heard a voice, a strange deep voice reassuring me, asking me about the clouds and everything I felt and saw there.

Sometimes the fog would clear slightly, the clouds seemed to disappear. I wondered where they went to and I would be frightened. I needed my husband! "Where is Richard, in London? Why isn't he here with me?" I screamed.

My mind was filled with swirling images. I saw Richard with his arms around Evonne DeVere, dancing with her in the ballroom of Edgecliff, laughing. Her bosom blossomed above her low-cut gown. Around her neck, on a chain, was the ring, my betrothal ring, "The blood and the tears."

"Madam," I heard the stranger say. "Richard was just here. He comes to your bedchamber every night to see you."

"It's a lie!" I screamed. "I haven't seen him! He's with that woman DeVere! I know it, I know it!" I sat up from the bed and clutched at a strange man I had never seen before.

He pushed me away from him and reached into a black bag. With one swift movement he grabbed me by the chin with one hand and pried my lips apart with the other, forcing me to drink a bitter liquid from a tiny bottle.

I pictured myself in a dusty old attic locked in chains, wearing rags, with only Mrs. Kerrenslea's threatening face to keep me company, before drifting off into a dreamless sleep.

I awoke much later to see a tray before me and the crowlike Mrs. Kerrenslea leaning over me, shaking my shoulder.

"You should try to control yourself, my dear. Another upset such as that one and the doctor might send you away. You wouldn't want that now, would you?"

"No!" I cried and took the tea she offered me. It was soothing warm and my body began to feel like cotton.

I heard a woman's voice calling to me. "Emily, come Emily. Come to the cliffs. They are beautiful and the sound of the sea is so inviting."

I saw my mother standing on the cliff's edge, her hand outstretched, reaching out to me. But then I blinked and all I could see was Mrs. Kerrenslea's dark figure bending over me with a strange grin etched across her face.

A flicker of sharpness and clarity entered my brain. Memories came back to me. The night of the fire, the vase, and the incident in the forest. It could have been Charles who shot me in the forest, but he couldn't have dropped the vase. They must all want to be rid of me then! I felt a sense of panic in my throat. Yes, I remembered having that thought once before. But my thoughts were all jumbled, strange. I had just seen my mother, at the cliffs. The sound of the waves was so loud in my ears that I wanted to reach out and touch them. But this was all in my imagination. I was lying in my bed. Could it be that my mind was distorting reality? That no one was trying to harm me at all. Perhaps I was only filled with delusions? Was this madness? I asked myself and then plunged again into the darkness.

Then one day I could see the shape of my window when I opened my eyes. The sun streamed in brightly through the gauze curtains. The room came into focus, it had ceased its endless spinning, but my head still pounded.

242

I turned onto my back and looked up. "Malvina?" I couldn't believe my eyes. Was Malvina really sitting there? I wondered and reached over to touch her arm.

"Aye, child. It's me. And I've only a short time with ye. They let me in because I was yer mother's maid—and because they have tried every doctor and despaired. Still, I had to wait till yer husband was gone. He'd not hear of it. It was Miss Annabel who let me in, for once I healed her of a rash when she were a child."

"But—but Miss Annabel was gone."

I could not get over how clear my head felt.

"Nay, she'm been in your room every day. But then, I don't doubt they been fillin' yer head with all manner o' nonsense, to make you believe you were mad."

"Was I—am I mad?" I whispered.

"Made mad—with a potion they'm been givin' ye in the tea. It's a plant I know well."

I caught my breath. "How do you know?"

She smiled, her old mocking smile. "I know because I have the sight, but I'm also an herbalist, child, and I know the scent and taste of this one. I tasted some of yer tea."

"Then—then—" I could not quite take it in. "Someone was trying to make me seem mad? But why?"

Her face was suddenly harsh. "Because when ye jumped from the cliffs like your mad mother before ye, everyone would have believed you a poor suicide. Not murdered."

"Murdered! Malvina, I knew someone was trying to kill me—but—"

The tea! I had a vague memory. Had not Mrs. Kerrenslea told me Richard changed the recipe for the tea?

"I must get away from here!" I gasped, sitting up.

A wizened old hand shot out and stayed my wrist, vise-like. "Ye must do no such thing. Ye must pretend to still

243

be ill, and mad, until we find out who it is. For then yer safe. If you get well, they will kill you another way."

"I know who it is," I whispered through cold lips. "My husband."

"Did I not warn ye against marryin' black Richard Woodstock? And of the curse?" She did not seem surprised.

"But Malvina—I have lost the ring. Is it at an end?"

"Perhaps. But if it's found again, someone will die. I feel it."

"Malvina, I must get away. Help me."

"I shall, child. But he must not suspect. I think he plans to have ye locked away in a lunatic asylum. Then mayhap see ye kill yourself in yer madwoman's cell. For the time being, all that matters is to get away from here. Trust Malvina. I shall watch over ye. Go along with their plans. And eat or drink nothing I do not bring ye myself, or that ye see others eat and drink!"

With that, she was gone, and I sank back on the pillow exhausted.

But feeling delivered. I had been delivered from a certain death.

From murder.

By the man I loved.

Chapter Nineteen

"Drink it all down now," Mrs. Kerrenslea said and looked at me with concern. She seemed so kind now. Where was the nightmare woman of the past weeks? Or was that simply part of the drug-induced delusions I had suffered? For Richard and Annabel had been to my bedside, and yet I did not remember their visits.

I lay weakly against the pillow with just barely opened eyes. I sipped slowly at the tea until the cup was empty and let myself fall against the pillow, faking a lapse into a deep sleep.

I could feel Mrs. Kerrenslea's eyes upon me for a moment, then she turned and left the room, carrying the breakfast tray with her.

As soon as the door was closed behind her, I slipped from the bed and let the contents from my mouth empty into the potted fern, now totally withered. I had been spitting the tea into the fern since the day before . . . and it had promptly died. I shivered to think I might accidentally swallow some of the tea, but there seemed no other course. If Mrs. Kerrenslea were to report to my husband I was refusing the tea, the drug might be forced on me—or other, more drastic means taken.

And then, I heard voices.

"She's just down the hall." It was Mrs. Kerrenslea.

"Has she exhibited any self-destructive behavior?" said a man's voice, unfamiliar.

"No, but her despondence, her lack of comprehension, is total. I can hardly bear it, doctor. I don't know what to do with her." It was Richard. He sounded too calm. His voice betrayed no sadness.

As the door to my room opened, fear gripped me. I didn't know how I was going to act, what they were going to do. But I suspected it was something horrible.

I lay perfectly still on the bed. Someone approached and sat in the chair near my bedside. I felt large strange hands on my face. A finger pulled open my eyelid and I stared straight ahead with a blank expression, trying not to focus on the man with a short-cropped salt-and-pepper beard and wire-rimmed glasses.

"How long has she been in this condition?" he asked.

"Weeks!" Richard blurted. I could hear him pacing across the room and my heart leapt out to him.

"Oh, Richard, I am all right!" I yearned to say but I knew that I could not, for though I loved him still, I believed he wished me harm.

"Has there been anyone else to see her besides the family?" the man asked and touched my forehead. I suspected that he was checking for a fever.

"Yes, one of your colleagues from London—an eminent specialist—has come but he is baffled. I had hoped that she would come out of this state on her own. That is why I waited to call on you. I pray you can help, doctor." Richard's voice had softened. I heard those familiar footsteps that I had longed to hear come up to my bedside. I felt his warm hand take mine and a tear nearly escaped.

"I am afraid she needs professional care." He sounded so final. I held my breath waiting for Richard's response.

"As I suspected," Mrs. Kerrenslea said. "I am sorry,

246

sir. But surely you see she would be better off where she can be cared for."

My heart started to beat faster. Please Richard, I wanted to scream, don't do this! I wanted to leap from my bed to declare myself but I knew that action would seem too sudden, too strange. They would never believe I could recover in a matter of moments. Whoever was responsible for drugging my tea might recognize my game, take immediate action, and do away with me once and for all. I could not take the risk. I could do nothing until Malvina returned to help me.

And so I lay perfectly still and malleable as the doctor examined me. He pulled at the skin on my arm, lifted my wrist, and let it drop on the bed lifeless. He checked the reflexes in my knees, through the coverlet, of course, and inquired about my diet.

"She eats very little," said Mrs. Kerrenslea. "There are days when we can hardly force a teacup to her lips."

"Does she speak?" The doctor asked.

"No," Richard said sadly. "She has not even acknowledged my presence during any of my visits this past week."

"Then I suggest you have her committed to my care as soon as possible." The doctor's words pounded in my brain.

Committed! So this was his plan all along! Not to murder me by poisoning—he only wanted to make me delirious and send me away to a hospital, never to return.

"Today then." Richard's voice sounded like stone. "May she ride in your carriage? It won't take long to have her things readied and have her dressed for travel."

My heart was broken. He couldn't wait to be rid of me.

"Of course," the doctor replied, and his words felt like a sentence of death. "She will be better off under professional care, Mr. Woodstock. And you must not give up hope."

But well I knew that those committed to asylums never returned to see the light of day.

They left the room then and within moments Nan came to start packing my bags.

My mind raced. I had to do something. But what? I could not just sit up and say, "I am all right, really, I was only joking."

I watched from the corner of my eye as Nan removed my lingerie and nightwear from the bureau and placed them into my suitcase. She mumbled to herself as she packed.

"Oh, mistress, a sorry day at Edgecliff is this day. The curse, the curse could not have been broken, not even with the ring gone." She reached into the armoire and removed two simple dresses, folded them neatly, and packed them. Then she took out my traveling suit, the deep red one trimmed with black velvet that I had worn from London for my arrival at Edgecliff not yet a year before.

How much had happened since then. I seemed to have lived an entire lifetime. I had gone from a pauper to an heir and now, to what? Locked away and judged insane? Maybe I should allow it, I thought. Maybe I would be safer in a hospital than in this ominous house.

I let her lift me from the bed then and let myself hang loosely while she dressed me.

After I was dressed, she rang for Penwillen, who appeared with two footmen. They helped me from the bed and I assisted them by placing my feet on the floor and opening my eyes. They were startled at first but then continued as they were when they realized that I still held a blank expression and did not acknowledge them.

"Let me," Penwillen said gravely and took one of my arms. Nan took the other and I walked slowly, blindly down the stairs with their assistance. The footmen

248

followed carrying the bags. As we passed the study, Richard appeared and walked alongside of me to the waiting carriage.

The doctor was already seated inside, impatient to be on the way.

When the door of the coach was opened, the panic seized me with such an intensity that I could not move. My hand instinctively shot out to grip the side of the carriage, making it impossible for Penwillen to put me into it.

"No!" involuntarily escaped my lips.

"Emily!" Richard cried and looked into my face. But again the mask came over me and he shook his head and pried my fingers from their grip on the carriage. *Take me into your arms*, I implored silently, *Kiss me goodbye*. But he only took my hand that he had so forceably handled and held it up to his lips for a brief kiss. *Goodbye, Edgecliff, goodbye, Richard my love*, I said to myself and allowed them to lift me into the carriage.

But with my first step there came a disruption.

"*What is this?*" I heard a harsh voice cry. "Where are you taking her, what is this about?"

It was Malvina!

"She is hopeless. We are sending her away," Richard said. "And what concern is it of yours, Malvina? Take your false cures elsewhere!"

"No, you can't do that, she—"

I lost my footing on the step. Though I regained my composure, this gave me an idea of how I could be saved without arousing suspicion.

I purposefully slipped and let my head fall against the carriage, faking a horrible blow. I let myself fall to the ground and everyone surrounded me.

"Emily!" Richard knelt beside me.

I shook my head, very slowly, then opened my eyes. At

first, I looked at him with a dazed expression but then I let my eyes focus.

"Richard?" I said—and smiled.

That night I dined with the family for the first time in weeks. I took my chair at my end of the long dining table. Richard sat at the other end, directly across from me, and watched me closely as I picked at the sumptuous meal. I could not read his thoughts and it disconcerted me. I felt that I was on display and that I had to take care of my words or actions lest they decide that I had not recovered yet after all.

The doctor whom Richard had called, Doctor Sherman Fielding from the Lunatic Asylum at Bedlam, was seated next to Richard. Throughout the entire meal he was silent. I feared his calculating gaze for I guessed that he had been asked to stay for the evening to test me. I was nervous of his perceptions of me and I thought of the fine line between sane and insane behavior and how such judgments were made. Even though I knew myself to be well, his doubts made me mistrust myself, and I had to prejudge every word, every movement, before taking action, lest it be misinterpreted.

The entire family was in attendance, including the much absent Annabel, who had been spending much time at the Polkerris house trying to catch the eye of Timothy Odgers. She sat next to me on my right, hardly touching her food, looking dreamily into the sterling silver candelabra that graced the center of the linen-covered dining table.

"You look so far away, Annabel," I ventured to say. "What, or may I say 'who' is it that you seem to be dreaming of?"

"Oh Emily, it is so wonderful having you be your old self again. Nothing misses your watchful eye." Annabel sighed and took a sip of her wine. "I must admit thinking thoughts of Timothy Odgers much more interesting than Richard's talk about the mines in Penryn."

"I'm not sure that Richard or William would agree with you." I laughed and I felt that all eyes were upon me. "Do you think that Timothy Odgers will offer for you?"

"I'm not sure," Annabel answered. "I think that he is fond of me and yet I feel that I am being taken for granted, for there are times he hardly notices me at all."

"Though I am not an expert on the subject, I have heard that a woman attracts more through elusiveness than availability."

"I am an expert on the subject," Charles said from the other end of the table. His voice was loud and boisterous and tinged with not a small amount of wine. I noticed that the decanter was placed within his reach and he had poured from it often during the course of the meal. "But I can tell you that there is nothing more exciting to a man than the chase." He looked up at me then and our eyes met briefly. "Especially when there is competition."

I avoided his gaze, allowing Penwillen to give me another serving of fish. Would his insinuations never end, I thought.

"Then perhaps Timothy should see how popular you are with other suitors," I said, my eyes twinkling.

"What? Do you have an idea that will help me to win him, Emily?" Annabel's eyes lit up.

"What say you to having a Harvest Ball?" I looked directly at Richard, who was watching me closely. "I think it's a splendid idea!" I continued, before he could reply. "It's the perfect opportunity to show the world that the mistress of Edgecliff is well and happy. And besides," I added, "a romantic Harvest Ball will give Annabel the opportunity to show the smug Odgers that he is not the only eligible man in the province."

"Yes, let's!" cried Annabel. "I shall be the belle of the ball and all the handsome lads will pursue me. Then Timothy will not treat my attentions so lightly."

Immediately there was a buzzing at the table with excited talk of the preparations for the ball, what the theme would be, who should be invited. I noticed a silence at the other end of the table and looked up to see both Richard and Doctor Fielding eyeing me intently.

"Emily, are you sure that you are well enough for all of this excitement?" Richard's voice sounded grave, much too serious, and I feared his implications.

"I am fine, Richard, truly." My hand shook as I spoke. Richard turned to look at Doctor Fielding, and the doctor glanced at me.

"Do you feel any dizziness or disorientation?" he asked me, speaking directly to me for the first time since my fall from the carriage and my miraculous "recovery."

"No. Though I must admit to a slight throbbing in my temples due to the blow from my fall this afternoon." I folded my hands in my lap and sat perfectly poised.

"That is to be expected." Doctor Fielding nodded. "With another day or two's rest and unless anything changes, I feel a Harvest Ball might be a happy antidote for the entire family, as well as you, Mrs. Woodstock."

"If you are positive in your evaluations, doctor, I cannot be the one to put a quash on such an event," Richard said. "I agree to a Harvest Ball, to celebrate health, happiness, and all of our blessings." He raised his glass for a toast and the clinking of glasses could be heard all around the table.

Though I knew I was still in danger, I felt relieved in Richard's granting me his confidence. It seemed perilous to stay, and perhaps be a target of another murder attempt—and yet where could I go? This was my home. I thought that if I were very careful never to be alone, careful to eat only what others were eating, I would be safe . . . for a time. And then I could decide how to confront Richard with my knowledge of what he'd done. I didn't want him arrested. Just . . . to go away. Leave Edgecliff. Even though at the very thought, my heart squeezed in pain.

How could I still love a man who had tried his best to kill me—or have me committed? It seemed fantastic.

But even in voicing my suspicions, I must be careful. Though I longed to confront him, I knew it would be folly. For he would only accuse me of returning to madness. Had I not already accused Mrs. Kerrenslea, and then Charles, of attempts on my life?

I needed an ally, and one more believeable than Malvina, whom everyone thought to be mad. I glanced at Annabel. Would she help me? It had been she who had sent for Malvina, so surely she was not in on the plot. But how could I ever convince her that her beloved brother Richard was a monster, with murder on his mind?

I needed proof. It was that simple. With proof, I could quietly confront Richard and force him to leave.

He was speaking now, and I forced myself to smile at him as if I were still the same besotted wife he had married. "But Emily"—Richard's eyes were commanding as he spoke directly to me—"you must promise not to be involved in any of the ball preparations for at least two days' time. Two more days of rest with my special tea recipe is all that you'll need."

I almost dropped my wineglass. His tea! So he still meant to drive me back to madness! *Oh Richard*, my heart wailed silently, *you never loved me at all!* and a picture of the beautiful Evonne flashed before my eyes.

"I promise to rest," I said weakly and took a deep drink of wine, wondering what course of action I would take. I needed a sample of that tea, so it was just as well he meant that I should still keep drinking it. Perhaps it was all the proof I needed.

"Just to be safe, Doctor Fielding," Richard continued, "I must insist you stay at Edgecliff for several more days. We must be sure there will be no relapses."

Relapses. His words chilled me. He was plotting still.

"If you'll excuse me, I think I shall rest now. I feel very tired," I said as lightly as possible, standing slowly and turning away from the family, not wanting them to see my disturbed state.

"I'll help you, Emily," Annabel said, and took my arm. We walked in silence from the dining room, through the long hallway, up the winding staircase, and into my bed-chamber in silence. I knew that I was in more danger than ever. Richard was not going to give up. He wanted me gone and he wouldn't stop until he had achieved his ends.

And I alone must find a way to stop him.

Chapter Twenty

"Ready the carriage, Polker," I said, drawing on my elegant lavender gloves and peering around the corner for any stray cousins that might be listening.

"Yes, madam. Where do you desire to go?" inquired Polker with respect.

It warmed my heart. It had been a great strain lately to act as if I were mistress indeed, ruler of the household of Edgecliff, when I knew that all the servants and most of the village were still whispering about me, wondering if I had lost my sanity.

My manner lately, I knew, had been chill, imperious, and brisk, modeled on my long-ago memories of Lady Heathfield's comportment. She had struck such terror into my heart when I had been in her employ. By adopting her manner I hoped to strike terror into my servants' hearts and scotch any rumors as to my failing mind or ill health. And I used her manner to mask my fears of Richard.

He had not come to my bedchamber since I had recovered, saying only that he felt he must give me time to recover. Except once. One night I had been lying in bed, watching the moonlight stream into the room in great silver bars, when I had frozen at the sound of my door softly opening, the key turning in the lock. For of course I had locked it. And only Richard had the key.

I had lowered my lashes over my eyes, forced my breathing to be deep and even. I could see him as he came across the room to stand at my bedside, and my heart had pounded in terror.

For a long time, he had stood, looking down at me. And then he had done a peculiar thing. He'd reached out and gently smoothed a lock of my hair away from my face.

I let out my held breath as he turned and left the room.

I'd hardly been alone with my husband since. As I stood in the front window, surveying the sunlight, I wondered where he was right now.

"Where will 'e be goin', madam?" Polker repeated, and I smiled at him.

With Polker I was more my old soft-spoken self. For although he might be taciturn and even a bit grim at times, he had always treated me with the utmost respect. He made me feel that I truly belonged as mistress of Edgecliff. For this my manner with him was always sunny and even more familiar than one should generally be with one's servants. Indeed I kept him near me, almost constantly at my beck and call for I feared being alone.

"I'd like to drive into St. Just this morning, to Madame Vesey's, the dressmaker. I've heard she's very good," I remarked as I breezed through the hallway, Polker following. "I want to have a special gown made for the Harvest Ball. But I don't want anyone to know of it, the gown I mean. So you must tell no one where you've taken me, particularly not Miss Annabel."

"Yes, madam. I will have the carriage at your disposal shortly," he said. "And, I'll utter not a word to where we be headin'."

On impulse, I pushed open the great doors myself and went to stand in the sunlight that shone on the great stone steps. It was a beautiful day and how wonderful it felt to be out in the fresh air after my long "illness." I felt whole and new. To be dressed and about and "aback to her senses" as I'd overheard the servants say, seemed a great blessing. My fall and illness and doubts seemed far away on this sunny day, the way that evil dreams that have haunted us in the night can be laughed at in the morning. Suddenly it seemed so possible that I had been only having wild imaginings, spurned on only by the ravings of a wisewoman, probably mad herself. Perhaps I had been delirious with fever, or that I had been in truth dangerously unstable, on the brink of losing my mind. These explanations seemed much more probable in the light of day than that my husband was trying to cause me harm, contriving "accidents" and drugging my tea.

Was he guilty or not? One incident had made me doubt whether the tea was his doing. For so many people could have touched the tea. At one time or another, they'd all brought it up to me.

It was lunchtime, the day after I'd recovered. The house was quiet and so I could hear the soft footsteps on the carpet in the hall coming toward my room. I watched as the door slowly creaked open and the breath caught in my throat when I recognized Richard's familiar silhouette in the doorway.

He came into the room alone, with not even a servant to help him carry the tray. On it, along with some sandwich triangles, was a small silver teapot. So, I thought, he is about to administer the poison himself.

"Richard, I thought you had plans to travel to London?" I asked, my voice shaky.

"I had, but I canceled them." He seemed so sure of himself as he laid down the tray and carefully poured me a cup of the steaming brew. "I wanted to attend to you myself today, to make sure that there are no mishaps."

No mishaps in what regard? I asked myself. Mishaps in my annihilation? Terror gripped me. My eyes fixed themselves on the teacup and I watched as the steam rose and turned in the air. Its aroma infected my nostrils and sickened me. What could I do? How could I stop him from forcing me to drink his abominable tea?

"That was not necessary." I smiled. "You don't have to watch over me, Richard. All that I need is a day or two's rest and I shall be my old self again. Really, I am fine," I said, trying to talk him into leaving me alone so that I might spill the tea into the potted fern. But by his expression I could tell that my words were in vain.

"Nonsense," he said, with an incredulous look in his eyes. "Today, I want to take care of you myself. You may fear to eat it when you hear that I have personally prepared this luncheon myself."

How handsome he looked, his black gypsy hair falling on his wide shoulders, his skin browned from the sun. He smiled, teeth flashing white, as he handed me the teacup.

My hand shook as I took it. I lay back against the pillow and looked into its contents, seeing my doom there before me. I could feel Richard's eyes upon me and yet I could not bring myself to drink it. Just when I thought he would say something or force my hand, he reached over to the pot and started to pour into another teacup that I had not seen previously on the tray. So lost in my own foreboding was I that it had escaped my notice.

But I watched carefully then as he poured the tea to the top of the cup and brought it to his lips. I held my breath when he took a deep drink.

"Mmm, this is a wonderful tea." Richard rested the cup back in its saucer. "Drink up now, Emily. It will help you regain your strength."

"Of course, Richard, of course." I laughed then before taking a deep drink of tea, my suspicions gone.

Richard gave me a curious glance and asked me what I had found so amusing.

"I am happy," I replied. "Happy to be well and happy

258

to have my husband at my side playing nursemaid."

Then he laughed with me and we exchanged some light banter about the ball to come while I ate a few bites of the sandwiches that he had brought. I drank the tea at the same pace as Richard, just to be safe, but I knew then that I had nothing to fear from him. At least at that moment.

"The tea is unusual though I quite enjoy the taste," I ventured, after setting the empty cup in its saucer. "How did you acquire the recipe?"

"I once had a riding accident in Polruan. Not a serious one, but I hit my head quite hard. I was taken care of by an old Cornish woman who made me drink this tea three times a day for an entire week. And when I left, she gave me the recipe in case I would need it. And it looks like I do."

"Did," I corrected him. "By tomorrow I shall need it no longer."

How true my words were and how happy I felt now that I stood waiting for Polker with the sun in my face, in excited anticipation of my first venture from Edgecliff since my illness befell me.

I smiled as the carriage pulled up. Won't the tongues be wagging this day in St. Just, I thought, as Polker extended his hand to me, helping me deferentially into the carriage. "It's a lovely morning, my lady, if I may be so bold, and since you haven't had an airing in a time, might I suggest the coast road? It's a bit longer, but it's early for the shops yet, and I thought you might enjoy the country a bit."

"How thoughtful of you," I replied, pleased. "Yes, and if any of the cousins ask, you may say that you merely took me for an airing. It's a splendid idea."

I was gratified to see one of Polker's rare toothless smiles, then he mounted the box and we set off. Though the rolling hills were still green, the trees and flowers were beginning to betray the season's change. The

259

summer roses had long since withered and the gardener had already pruned and mulched them for the coming chilly nights.

The leaves on the ancient trees had begun to change colors, deep yellows and browns, and soon they would be covering the drive and lawns of the manor.

We passed through the gates and I settled into my seat. I felt the cool sou'westerly wind coming in from the shore and I sat farther back into the carriage, denying myself the view but intelligently avoiding the chill moist breeze. I would have no more illness this year, I decided. My thoughts turned to the ball ahead and I wondered if the dressmaker at Madame Vesey's could capture and create the ball gown that I envisioned in my mind. It had to be magnificent. I had to be shown off at my best advantage in order to quell all the horrible gossip that was continuing to spread about my "condition." When they saw me in health, it had to stop. Even if I was forced to personally talk to or dance with every member of the Cornish gentry!

For once I would not allow another woman, even Evonne DeVere, to throw me into the shade. Even though she had been friendly toward me and I had heard that she had visited several times during my illness, she was still, in my mind, a rival. I was too well aware of the charm she had, of her effect on other men, my husband Richard not withstanding, not to feel still threatened by her.

I pictured myself in the ball gown—it would be sparkled with glitter and cling to my body in such a fashion that it would accent my every move. It would be made of cream-colored satin with silver spangles and cut daringly low in the bodice, a dress that Evonne would envy. A dress that would make her think twice about the powers of her rival, if she still thought me proper and insipid.

I frowned as I looked at my diminished figure. I had lost considerable weight during my illness, and I was reluctant to be measured, looking as I did. But there was nothing for it. I would have to start making cook happy by demolishing her rich meals, and gain it all back before the ball. I would gorge myself on Cornish cream and jam and scones this very day at tea, I thought. And if it meant extra fittings, the cost be damned.

Polker set me down at the dressmakers, and I bid him to return in an hour. That should be long enough for me to consult with the modiste and tell over fabrics. The shop was not at all prepossessing from the outside. It couldn't have held a candle to the magnificent shops in London, but I had good reports of it and hoped it would serve my purpose. Oh, for a dress from Worth! I sighed as I approached the doorway.

A flash of brilliant violet caught the corner of my eye, and I turned my head. Down the street, making her way through the crowd, oblivious to the other heads besides mine turning, was Evonne DeVere.

At first I was tempted to bid her a good morning but something about her quick pace and the flush to her cheek stopped me. And by her attire I surmised that she was dressed for a rendezvous.

She wore a dark violet pelisse, inset with bands of lighter violet satin, frothing with swansdown. Her flaming hair under her wide hat caught the sun. She looked as vital and magnificent as a tropical storm as she sailed down the street, chin high, full red lips arrogantly set. Before I could stop myself, involuntarily I ducked into the shop.

My breath was coming in short gasps as I stared out the window, waiting for her to pass. Where was she going wearing such a dress at this hour of the morning? She looked dressed for seduction. Richard? Richard had left before I had, "business in town" he had said.

"Madam? May I be of assistance?" A voice behind me made me turn, startled. I had forgotten I was in the dressmaker's shop. I reddened as I looked at the older woman who stood before me. All I could think of was whether Evonne was in town to meet Richard. And then suddenly I knew I had to find out!

"Yes, Madam Vesey, I believe?"

She nodded her assent.

"I am Mrs. Woodstock, of Edgecliff," I continued. "Tell me, is that hat for sale? I have taken a fancy to it." I pointed to a large hat with a quantity of veiling. It would do to obscure my face.

"Why, yes, my lady, it is for sale," she replied, surprised.

"Then I will take it at once," I said as haughtily as possible. I reached for my reticule for the money. She was picking up the hat as if to take it back and box it. "No, I mean to wear it. I've taken a frightful dislike to my hat. I can't bear it at all. If you would toss it out for me and give me the other, I shall pay you now and take it."

Inwardly I fidgeted, in agony to be on the street. If I had lost Evonne!

"No need to pay me now, madam. I will send the bill on account," she said and watched me strangely as I put down my own hat on the counter and donned the veiled one. Not without a pang—the hat I was sacrificing was from Paris, and quite the most fetching and fashionable one I had. She must think me mad, I thought hastily, for the hat that I bought was a dowdy puce covered with disagreeable brown veiling and didn't even match my dress!

But I hardly cared what she thought as I thanked her and left the shop in haste. I only took a moment to reflect that if I was trying to convince the townspeople that I was not mad, that exchanging a Paris hat for a monstrosity fit for a dowager was scarcely the way!

I emerged onto the street and I was just in time to see a

bright flash of violet enter a doorway not far away and across the street. I adjusted my veil determinedly so that no one might recognize me and set off in pursuit.

It was a teashop that she had entered. I paused a moment, looking in vain through the window, but no sign of violet. I almost turned then and left, afraid of what I might see if I entered. What if she was with Richard? I would surely faint. I would not be able to bear the sight. Even the thought of it was like a knife in my heart. Then I steeled myself. I had to know once and for all if Richard was still seeing the widow DeVere. If he still was entranced by her charms, for charms she did possess.

I stepped inside and spotted her at once. She sat at a table for two facing me and I almost flinched when her eyes swept over me. After a moment passed and with nary a blink, I had no fear that she would recognize me in the hat. But my heart was still beating fast at my daring and at my fear of what I might discover.

I desired to be shown to a table behind hers in an imperious tone and I sat with my back to her. I was certain that the table I was shown to was close enough that I would be able to hear all. Hearing would be enough. I was too timid to sit facing her and watch what transpired.

I disguised my voice to order tea and it was only a moment before I heard footsteps approaching. Then Evonne spoke, her voice low but clearly audible. "And here you are! For a moment I feared you would not be able to escape Edgecliff. But I am happy that we arranged to meet here, at least we can be private together, and we have not been seeing enough of each other, have we?"

I could not restrain a gasp, for the agony almost overwhelmed me. It must be Richard, for who else would have to "escape" Edgecliff? There was a scrape of the chair, someone sitting down, and I squeezed my eyes tight against the tears as I waited for his reply. I knew it would

263

be words of love, words he had not spoken to me for so long now.

"My darling girl, how lovely you look," said a familiar female voice that I couldn't place.

I sat bolt upright.

"Thank you, Mother," Evonne replied. "How do things fare at the household?"

Mother?

"It seems Emily has returned to health and we shall be holding a Harvest Ball this month."

And then it registered. So relieved was I to discover that it was not Richard who had come to meet Evonne that I had failed to identify the voice. But I knew all at once that it was Mrs. Kerrenslea—and that Kerrenslea was Evonne DeVere's mother!

What did this mean? What dark secret had I stumbled upon? Filled with shame for eavesdropping and afraid to move lest they discover me, I sat silent and listened.

Evonne asked the date of the Harvest Ball and where I was to be fitted for my gown. I was surprised when Mrs. Kerrenslea answered her.

"I believe Madame Vesey's boutique," she said.

How had she known?

"So . . . she is better," said Evonne. "A pity. I had such hopes when I learned she was to be put away."

"Hopes! You should have more than hopes, yet if you are not more discreet, you shall gain nothing in the end," said Mrs. Kerrenslea angrily.

"I don't know what you mean," said Evonne haughtily.

"Yes you do, daughter. Meeting him at all hours of the night and day. The whole village knows you are lovers."

"And what difference does that make?"

"If you have hopes of marriage, behaving like a wanton will not forward them."

"Perhaps you are right, Mother. Perhaps I shall be

264

more discreet. But it is difficult when one is in love. And he is as mad for me as I am for him, I tell you."

They fell into silence then, sipping their tea, and I did not make a rustle lest Mrs. Kerrenslea turn and recognize the dress I was wearing.

Her lover? Who was it? Not Richard, I prayed. How I hoped she had found a new lover since his marriage. A mad hope, for was I not planning to send him away and never see him again? Questions filled me, the answers to which were beyond my imagination.

Was Evonne DeVere truly Mrs. Kerrenslea's daughter, and if so, who was the father? And why was this kept a secret?

My questions were not to be answered that day for soon Mrs. Kerrenslea bid her goodbyes and left the restaurant, Evonne DeVere to follow shortly.

But my surprises were not over for the day. I sat while they went out, planning to let them both get well away before I left the teashop. And then I heard voices, the woman who owned the shop and the girl who waited tables.

"Look at her, shameless hussy! How I wish I had the courage to bar her from the shop!"

"It's a disgrace, that's what it is. When everyone in the village knows that she has Mr. Woodstock wrapped round her littlest finger, and he in her bed every chance he gets. I hear he's there every day. And I hear they spent a few days together in Falmouth."

I was sick. I could hardly stand. I don't remember leaving the shop.

Now I knew who Evonne's lover was. And knew that my husband had spent what should have been my honeymoon . . . with her.

Chapter Twenty-One

"Why madam," Nan exclaimed as she walked briskly around me smiling. "You will be the most beautiful woman of all tonight. That is the most unusual shade I have ever seen in a gown, and the bodice—cut so low!" A sigh escaped her and I had to stifle a laugh. For I, always the proper one, would be sure to turn a few heads this night. Though I hoped I would not catch a chill. I was unused to having so much skin exposed.

Just a touch of rouge rid me of my pallor, and I looked at the glass and almost felt I was looking at a strange and mysterious woman there. Surely it was not I, so exotic, so sophisticated. The color of the gown cast a soft rosy glow to my skin and I seemed to radiate in its light.

Ordering a gown made with an experimental new dye had been a risk. But Madame Vesey assured me that there would be no other gown like it in all of Cornwall, at least for another two months or so. Blushing cream it was called, for the cream-colored satin was tinged with just a touch of the rosy hue of spring pink roses and the color did make one blush!

Though I was filled with excitement, I felt an apprehension about that night that I could not explain as if all the events had been building up to this moment, that somehow my moment of triumph would in fact become my hour of defeat. I could not understand this turn in my thoughts but I could not dispel them.

"The night of the great ball and my hands are shaking." I found myself speaking aloud and I stopped short. My, if Richard heard that! He would think I was returning to my former state.

I clasped my hands together and stared at the moon through the open shutters. It was giant orange balloon floating with a sea of dusty clouds surrounding it. I was afraid to move, afraid to walk downstairs and see all the people who still frightened me so. Mrs. Kerrenslea and Evonne DeVere, they would both be here. It would be interesting to see how they reacted in each other's company now that I knew their secret.

And Richard. We had not seen each other alone since I was in my sick bed and we drank tea together. The tea— the special tea that had made me so ill. His frequent absences filled me with suspicion still and I wondered if I would be able to detect anything in his expression when Evonne DeVere's name was announced while we stood together at the receiving line. I knew that I would watch his face closely.

And Charles, womanizer and gambler that he was, who showed his true colors just before my "accident" in the woods. Could he have fired that shot? Though I knew the house would be filled with people, I felt frightfully alone.

There was a knock at the door and I started and accidentally dropped my reticule to the floor.

It was Annabel, coming to take me downstairs. She whirled about for me in her new ballgown, made of white silk imprinted with thousands of tiny violets and green leaves. It was caught up over a petticoat of violet satin, and she wore the Edgecliff emeralds.

"Timothy will be hard put to keep his eyes off you tonight," I said gaily.

"And Richard will surely be able to see no other when he sees you in that gown. How very daring it is, Emily—and how unlike you!" she exclaimed.

I had kept the gown's design secret until now, and Annabel's eyes were wide as she took in the low bodice.

"Ah, but I have changed since my illness," I said lightly.

"Do not change too much, for I have come to love my sister," she said warmly as we walked together down the long hallway to the mahogany staircase. Our dresses made a sweeping sound as they brushed against the railings.

Richard was waiting for us. He stood by the entrance-way with Penwillen, looking so handsome in his dark gray waistcoat with the ruffled sleeves of his shirt extending from the cuffs.

I almost laughed wildly at the sight of the cravat, remembering the one that had disappeared from my grasp after I fainted at the inn. The same one?

"Good evening, darling," he said and kissed my cheek lightly. "You look lovely this evening." His voice was even and betrayed not a hint of emotion. He sounded as if he said the words not in sincerity but out of duty and I felt a gray cloud come over the evening. The dress had no effect whatsoever on him. I dropped my hand from my husband's arm, wondering if any more "accidents" were being planned for me. Tonight is the night—the thought entered my mind as certainty.

"Sir Neville Trewithyian," Penwillen announced, taking his coat and hat.

"Neville, the first to a ball, or so it seems," Richard said as they shook hands.

"And I daresay the last to leave one!" Sir Neville's hearty laugh cheered me. "Emily, you look ravishing!" He took my hand and kissed it warmly in the European fashion. "Gad, Richard, but you are the lucky devil. You

268

must have the most smashing woman in all of Cornwall on your arm this night." He winked at Richard then bowed to me.

"Sir Neville, you charmer. You certainly know how to get in the good graces of a hostess. And such a kiss . . ." I looked down at my hand where I still felt the impression of his lips.

"I may have picked up more from the French during my time in the continent than just a few extra pounds from the fine cuisine, I daresay." He laughed and patted his abdomen. "Though my words are not empty compliments but a true expression of what I feel in my heart."

I laughed. "Your charm is well noted in this corner, Sir Neville. It was quite evident even at that first ball where I met you." I smiled at him with genuine affection. I might enjoy this night after all, I thought to myself.

Sir Neville bowed and made his way into the ballroom, no doubt to be first at the banquet tables.

But not everyone was as warm as Sir Neville. In fact, few of them were. I was subjected to many searching glances, and questions about "how I felt." And Richard received not a few pitying looks. It seemed that everyone knew I had lost my mind, and most were not prepared to believe I was actually well again.

At last, some friendly faces greeted me at the doorway—Roger St. Hilary, Hetty Lerryn, and Margaret Odgers—and I was pleased to finally meet her much-talked-about brother.

"It is so good to finally make your acquaintance, Mr. Odgers," I said. He was a handsome lad, with curling light brown hair and brilliant blue eyes.

He took my hand tentatively and looked at me strangely. I wondered how much Annabel had talked about my "condition," for I knew her tongue to be much too loose.

"Mrs. Woodstock, you are much different than I

269

imagined," he said in a shocked whisper.

"And how did you imagine me?" I made my voice low, playing with his apprehension.

He shook his head in wonder. "I . . . I don't know. But you are . . . beautiful!" He stammered and I feared the young lad might be developing an infatuation for me.

"Thank you. My husband often tells me so," I said, firmly putting him in his place. "I think that I see Annabel at the punch bowl. She has mentioned your name more than once in this house."

He turned and saw Annabel surrounded by the sons of some of Cornwall's oldest and most respected families.

"So she is, and with Jonathan Pierce on her arm, my word!" He stalked off toward the punch bowl and I couldn't help thinking that if everything else went wrong this night, the ball would be a tremendous success in Annabel's eyes. Timothy Odgers's jealous attentions were already coming her way.

"Mrs. Evonne DeVere," Penwillen announced and my head snapped back to the entranceway.

"No, Penwillen, I shall keep my cloak a moment—I feel chilled from the ride," she was saying. The cloak was of scarlet satin, and swathed her from head to heel in a brilliant flame as rich as her hair. Her eyes locked with Richard's.

I watched closely as Richard took her hand and kissed it. "Good evening, Evonne, you look lovely as usual," he said.

As usual? I wondered.

"Thank you, Richard." She batted her long dark eyelashes and dropped her handkerchief. As she bent to pick it up, the V-neck of her scarlet cloak gaped to show an expanse of creamy white bosom.

She stood slowly. "Emily, you look well. I am so pleased." Her voice was sickeningly sweet and had I been mistaken or had her voice suddenly paused on the word "well"?

I took her hand and forced a smile to my lips. When she curtsied and flounced past us, I could not help watching Richard's eyes as they rested upon her figure for more than a moment. Her voluptuous curves, not hidden by the cloak, were an enticement to any man save a monk. And that was something I knew Richard could never be accused of.

I greeted the rest of the guests as if in a daze and soon the ballroom was crowded with people all dressed in the finest in fashion, color, and style. The ladies wore silks and satins, with ruffles and low-cut bodices of the latest style accented with soft lace dyed in autumn colors. Everyone commented on the gown that I wore and I was proud to be admired instead of treated with too much care. The rumors of my illness, as I had hoped, were already dispelled.

I caught sight of Evonne from the corner of my eye. She stood at the entranceway to the ballroom speaking with Charles and slowly they made their way to the center of the ballroom. At the moment I was wondering why she still was wearing her cape, she undid the clasp with a dramatic gesture, turned to look directly at me, and allowed Charles to take the shining satin cape from her shoulders. There was a hush and a few gasps and I couldn't believe it when I saw that she was wearing an exact copy of my blushing cream, one-of-a-kind dress! It seemed that the entire room was whispering and I felt the heat in my cheeks.

I turned to Richard who, mouth agape, stood transfixed with her beauty, with the way her voluptuous figure spilled from the dress. I in comparison looked like an undeveloped girl, no longer the belle of the ball but a laughingstock.

I caught Richard's eye and I knew my eyes were pleading.

Richard came to my side and took my hand but it offered me little comfort. The tears were already filling my eyes.

"Let the dancing begin!" Richard's voice boomed across the ballroom and he motioned to the minstrels' gallery.

"Dance with me, Emily." Richard started to pull me to the ballroom but I stood fixed, struggling with his grip.

"No, I can't . . . I'm so humiliated. I—"

"Hush. Do not let your womanly vanity spoil the evening. It would be bad luck for the hostess of the Harvest Ball to cast a dark shadow for the coming season."

I allowed him to lead me to the center of the polished wood floor and he pulled me close. I rested my face against his shoulder as much to hide my tears from all the eyes that were upon us as for its comforting warmth and solidity.

Soon the dance floor began to fill with dancers and I felt my tension lessening. "Richard," I whispered into his ear. "How did she know? How could she do this to me?"

"What is this about, Emily? I am sure that it was a coincidence. No woman would purposely wear the same dress as another to an important occasion such as this one."

"No, I know that she did it deliberately. I could see it in her eyes when she looked at me just before she removed her cape. It was an evil look, a challenging look. I know what I saw!" I said louder than I had intended and the couple who was dancing next to us gave me a curious stare.

"Quiet, Emily. I do not want our guests to hear your delusions."

I blinked in disbelief. He still thought me filled with delusions. Or was that part of his game? My heart sank, as the song ended, and when the musicians began to play another, I stopped in midstep.

"I am sorry, Richard. I cannot dance anymore," I said, and walked from the ballroom with all the dignity I could muster. My eyes darted around the room for an escape but there were people everywhere, even on the stairs leading to the West wing. I didn't want to face any words of condolence or worse, their polite denial of my predicament, but there was nowhere I could run to.

Then I looked up to the minstrels' gallery. Of course. The musicians would be too busy to pay me any heed and I could be alone with my thoughts.

I rounded the narrow curved staircase to the gallery quietly. The musicians played in the balcony and I stood behind them in the hall. The party was joyful and I watched the happy guests as they turned around the ballroom floor and ate from our bountiful buffet.

It was a painful thing to watch, for my evening was ruined and I saw no way to remedy it. If only I had another magnificent ball gown to change into, the night and my pride might be salvaged. But what silly thoughts to be having on such a night when doom seemed so near.

I turned away from the glittering ballroom and stepped into the gallery. I looked at the portraits one by one. The Edgecliff brides, how beautiful they all were, wearing the ring. The cursed ring that was now lost again. Was the curse upon me, upon all of us, Richard and Charles and all the Woodstocks unto eternity? I quailed at the thought.

The sight of my mother's portrait stilled me and I cried silently, "Oh Mother, help me break this curse. If there is a chance, give me the help I need!"

There would be no way to compete with Evonne DeVere on the terms she had just stacked in her favor. I

273

thought of her trick and I seethed with anger. How dare she humiliate me so, she who knew how much better she would look in the gown with her voluptuous breasts and thin waist? What man could resist a woman such as that? I wanted to strip myself naked of the hateful dress. And then my eyes focused on the painting once more. Of course. The deep red dress that I had had refurbished. It would suit me and it was the only way I could reappear downstairs.

I rushed into my bedchamber and quickly changed into the deep red dress that had been my mother's. How lovely it looked on me, but an eerie sense of foreboding clouded over me as I stared into the glass. Could history be repeating itself?

I shook the thought away and rushed to the gallery stairs. The dance floor was crowded with people.

And then I saw them. I felt all the blood drain from my face and my hand dropped limply to my side. There, behind the alabaster post to the right of the ballroom, a place obstructed from view—except from the gallery where I stood watching—there stood Evonne DeVere, and she was with Richard!

Her arms snaked around his neck and her white hands went into his black hair as she pulled his head down to hers for a hungry kiss. He put his hands on her shoulders and pushed her away, but gently, as he looked around. Afraid to be seen.

"So you saw them as well?" I heard from behind me. I turned abruptly and saw Charles, his charm dropped from him. His face was twisted in an angry smirk.

"Saw whom?" I lied and looked away from him into the ballroom, hoping to catch a glimpse of red hair, or gray waistcoat. But the lovers had vanished.

"Whoever it is that you are looking for at this moment, your husband and the widow DeVere." He sipped the champagne loudly and came close to me so that I could feel his breath against my cheek.

"What are you talking about?" I tried to back away but succeeded in only inches, my back pressed against the column.

"How can you not believe me now, how can you not believe your own eyes?" Charles goaded me. "I know that you saw them. I saw you watching from the gallery."

"Yes!" I admitted.

"So do you not trust me now? It has been for your own good all along that I have warned you, and you never listened."

I closed my eyes and his words rang true.

"What am I to do, Charles?" I cried.

"You must go and confront them, divorce Richard, and start anew." His words were like stones. I did not want to believe him. I still loved Richard and could not believe Charles and yet hadn't I seen the proof with my own eyes? "Don't be a fool anymore, Emily. Marry me. I will make you happy. Happy as Richard, who loves another, never could. Did I not beg for your hand long before I knew you were to be rich?"

"How can I confront them when they have disappeared?" I barely choked the words out through my tears.

"I overheard them. They are having a rendezvous at the old gazebo, at this very moment."

My hand flew to my throat. The old gazebo. Could I dare go to such a fateful place—wearing my mother's dress?

But I had to go there. I had to confront them once and for all, with Charles at my side. He would protect me. He had truly cared for me all this time, had he not? Hadn't he asked me to be his wife before the will was read?

"All right, first let me go and get my cloak. I'll meet you outside," I said and went to fetch my cloak.

I turned into the hall and saw Mrs. Kerrenslea staring

275

at me. Her eyes were wild with a strange glow. Her mouth twitched and the words that came out were senseless, almost as if she were in a delirium.

"You have come back!" she cried and came toward me.

I ignored her. I had to get to the gazebo straight away. I had to catch Richard in the midst of his tryst with Evonne so that I could forget him. So that my love with him would vanish like the mist in the sun. And so that I could divorce him. Charles would be my witness. Then he would have to leave, and the danger to me would vanish as well.

I stepped out into the cold dark night and saw Charles's shadow. I steadied myself as if going into battle and stepped toward him.

"Are you ready, Emily?" Charles said softly. The concern in his voice warmed my heart.

"Yes, Charles. Thank you," I answered and he took my arm and helped me along the gravel path. "Shan't we take the horses?" I asked.

"No," he answered. "We do not want them to have a warning. Hooves on stone would alert them. The element of surprise is all-important."

Though I had known what we were about to do, his words were like a knife in my heart. Oh Richard, I thought. How I had loved him so, and how he had deceived me.

Charles and I crossed the thick lawn that was moistened by the evening mist. I felt the wetness on my shoes and wrapped the cloak more tightly around me to guard against the evening chill.

We walked in silence and after a few moments my eyes became more accustomed to the dark. Closer and closer we came to the copse. I could hear the great roar of the sea and the sound of the powerful waves as they crashed on the rocks below. I shivered, whether from the cold or from fear I knew not which, but I trudged along, feeling

276

safe in Charles's care.

We came to the rough path that led to the gazebo and I stopped to take a deep breath.

"We must go on, Emily," he said forcibly. "It is the only way."

And then I saw it ahead of us. The tumbling octagonal building that had played such a part in the Woodstock past, and its present. I pricked up my ears to listen, hoping to catch a phrase of Richard and Evonne's conversation.

But of course I would not hear them speaking, I admonished myself. Surely, they would be in a lovers' embrace.

Charles tightened his grip on my arm and I was about to say something to him when we reached the gazebo.

My eyes, now totally accustomed to the darkness, could discern no voluptuous figure there. There was no red hair and blushing cream dress. There was no gray waistcoat with burgundy handkerchief.

The gazebo was empty.

"Charles?" I said. "Charles, they are not here."

"Then come inside. We will hide and surprise them," he said, taking my arm and drawing me inside.

It was pitch dark, lit only by a shaft of moonlight. And then Charles's arms came around me, hard, and he pulled me against him.

His lips came down on mine as I turned my head away, then he covered my face with kisses. "Emily, Emily," he was murmuring.

"Charles!" I cried. "What is the meaning of this?"

I tried to push him away but it seemed my struggles only inflamed him and he held me tighter. "The meaning, sweet Emily, is that I can wait no longer for you. You are going to be my wife when the divorce is final, and then it will all be mine. You . . . and Edgecliff. And Richard, at last, will lose."

277

In the darkness I felt his hands on the bodice of my gown, tearing it. The old material parted easily and he was yanking down my corset, his fingers tracing the bared swells of my breasts. His lips were hot on my neck as I twisted in his arms, trying to free myself.

I panicked. Did he mean to force me? And then at once I went cold. As my uncle had forced my mother? The past seemed to be repeating itself tonight in the most hideous way.

"Do not resist me, delicious Emily, for I mean to have you. I must have you!"

"Charles—Richard—he was never coming here with Evonne?"

"No. I don't know where they went."

"But Charles—we must find them and catch them—for otherwise how shall I get the evidence to divorce Richard?"

It worked. He set me from him then, and raked me with his eyes, seeming to enjoy the sight of my breasts through the tatters of my gown. I pulled my cloak tightly around me to cover myself. "You are right. Sensible as usual, my darling Emily. It is just that I have waited so long to have you, I could hardly wait longer. Then you will divorce him—and marry me?"

I had stepped back until the center bench was between us.

Never, I thought heatedly. But I was afraid to voice the truth aloud. He might try to force me again. But he must have seen something of my repulsion in my face, for he stepped forward, his face suddenly menacing.

"You will marry me?" he insisted.

"I shall divorce Richard, yes, but first we must find them, Charles!" I cried in fear.

He stopped, and his eyes glittered in the moonlight. "I can see that you have no intention of marrying me when the divorce is final. Don't be a fool, Emily—as you have

278

been a fool from the first. I mean to have you, and I mean to have Edgecliff. As I always meant to, from the first. And I love you, you see. Oh, at first I didn't, I admit that. At first I only wanted to marry you for the house. You see, I used to listen at the door when you were talking to Uncle, so I knew long before he died that he meant to leave it all to you."

Charles! Charles had been the shadow at the door—not Mrs. Kerrenslea!

"And why not?" he went on, pacing up and down. "Why should Richard get it all? Edgecliff . . . and then you. I tell you, it drove me nearly mad when I saw that you preferred him to me. He'd won again, as he always won. I hated Richard Woodstock's black soul, and I knew then that I would stop at nothing to get what I wanted."

"Stop at—nothing?" I said weakly, backing against the rough boards of the wall. A sudden suspicion plucked at my heart. It must have been something I saw in his face. "Charles—you haven't been—you haven't been trying to harm anyone, have you?"

He laughed, and it chilled me. "You never were stupid, were you, Emily darling? So you see what lengths I will go to to get you."

"Charles, tell me! I—I will never marry you if you do not. I will know the truth about the next man I give Edgecliff to."

He considered this, and the bait of Edgecliff seemed to move him. "Yes—and why not? Why shouldn't my wife know the truth? For when you hear the whole story, you will see that I never really meant any harm . . ."

The moonlight streamed into the gazebo and lit his face as he spoke. "After you were married, I followed you to Falmouth. I didn't mean any harm then . . . I just wanted to prove to Richard I could help with the miners. And then . . . the miners' unrest seemed too good to be true. It was an impulse I followed. I was so angry at Richard, you see . . . and at you, for marrying him instead of me. So I jammed the door shut and threw the torch through the window. I knew I'd never be blamed. With both of you gone, I'd inherit it all. But Richard, curse him, was gone."

I listened in horror. It was Charles! He'd tried to kill us both!

"And that day in the woods—you shot at me?" I gasped.

"No—that was an accident. It was Richard I wanted dead then, not you. I didn't want to hurt you, Emily," he said, his voice strangely tender. "By then, you see, I was beginning to love you. The next day, I was so relieved you were unharmed! And then Richard was a fool from the first, neglecting you. I don't know why he is so indifferent to women. It was after the wedding that I started seeing Evonne, another beauty he'd thrown over."

"You—you and Evonne?" I gasped.

"Yes, for I had need of a woman and she of a man." He laughed again, harshly.

"Was she with you in Falmouth?" I whispered, through cold lips.

"Yes, of course. I'd spent too many nights at her house recently, and there was beginning to be talk. Though she never knew I started the fire."

"Then Richard is not involved with her."

"You saw what he did tonight! Damn the bastard, he has you—and now he has stolen my mistress! Evonne always loved him and was bitter he'd not marry her. So you see, my darling, you must marry me. I am a cleverer man than Richard, and if you divorce him, there will be no need for further violence."

He was advancing on me relentlessly. I groped behind me and my fingers closed on a loose board.

"Kiss me, Emily," he said huskily, standing over me.

I pulled the rotting board free and brought it crashing

down on his head.

He slumped to the floor of the gazebo. I threw away the board, horrified, and stooped to feel his pulse. It was even, his breathing regular.

I stood, drawing the cloak tightly around my torn dress. Charles would doubtless wake soon.

I ran down the gazebo stairs. I had to find Richard! Oh God—he'd never meant to kill me at all!

The cliff path was the shortest way back to the house. I started running down it, through the darkness, to find the man I loved.

Chapter Twenty-Two

I ran through the darkness down the cliff path. I could hear the crashing of the sea below me, knew that the waves foamed over jagged rocks.

Richard—Richard! My heart was singing. *Richard— you never meant to hurt me! My heart could not be deceived! Oh, Richard—you love me after all!* Oh, I had to find him—find him before Charles awoke and could do more harm.

"Amelia!" a deep voice called from the darkness on my right, and I stopped, frightened.

Just then the moon broke out from behind tattered clouds, and I saw a dark shape standing at the cliff's edge.

It was Mrs. Kerrenslea.

"Amelia—what are you running from? From Ralph? Or from your husband? You shall not have Ralph anymore, Amelia. You left him and married another, and now he belongs to me!"

I stood frozen as she advanced on me, her eyes wild, speaking, she believed, to my dead mother.

And then her hands closed on my shoulders as she sprung on me with startling swiftness.

"You shall lie in a watery grave this night, Amelia, as you did once before," she cried, raving. "You have come back to haunt me, but you shall lie this night in hell!"

"Mrs. Kerrenslea!" I gasped. "It is I—Emily! Not Amelia! My mother is dead!" I struggled with her but she had the terrifying strength of a madwoman.

"I know only that you came back. Wearing her watch the way she always wore it! Wearing her dress! Her twin! I tried to poison you with the tea, and then convince you to jump, for I knew you were in truth Amelia's ghost come back to haunt me for what I did!"

"You—you poisoned my tea—not Charles?" I cried, confused. "What did you do?"

"I killed her!" she screamed into my face, and I was looking into the face of a raving madwoman. "I killed her that night when she ran down the cliffs, for I'd followed Ralph. I heard him say he still loved her. But she had Thomas! And I was pregnant then, pregnant with Ralph's child! She wasn't to have him back. So I ran after her in the fog, and when I found her, I threw her off the cliff and listened to her scream! Then I hid in the woods. They never knew I was there. As I shall throw you off again tonight! For if you are no ghost, but Ralph's daughter, why should you have it all when his other daughter—my Evonne—has nothing? And then she shall marry Richard at last and take her rightful place as mistress of Edgecliff!"

She flung me to the cliff's edge, and I crouched there, panting. "No, Mrs. Kerrenslea—no!" I cried. "I am Emily, not Amelia! Thomas's daughter—not Ralph's!"

She leaned forward and pushed me, and I was falling.

I screamed and lashed out with my hands, which found the edge, slipped, then held.

She stood above me in the moonlight, her gaunt face like a skull's burning with madness, her black garments flying in the wind.

My fingers slipped, and the cliff crumbled. I knew I could not hold on long. And at any moment, the cliff itself might give way.

"Mrs. Kerrenslea—help me," I pleaded. "Help Emily."

"Help you, Amelia?"

I was about to speak when a strong voice rang out behind us.

"Amelia, as she ever was! She has come back from the grave to torment you! See, she wears the dress, Mother!"

And Evonne DeVere was at her mother's side, looking down at me with a look of mocking triumph and evil.

"She cannot hold on much longer," Evonne said.

And it was true. My arms weakened. But just then, I slipped a bit, and my toe found a purchase in the rock. A narrow foothold, but I worked the toes of both shoes onto it. I was precariously balanced. They had only to shove at me and I would fall. Even the wind, howling now, seemed strong enough to blow me off the ledge. I could never get up without help—and neither of those above me would offer any help.

Evonne! She had given me the watch. Worn the dress, perhaps knowing the other had been refurbished and that I might change. Egged her mother's madness to the breaking point. I could imagine Mrs. Kerrenslea's secret guilt all these years. Seeing Sir Ralph keep his shrine to his lost Amelia, and never marry her. Then seeing his perhaps-daughter by her hated rival come back, looking so much like Amelia it must have been a torment. Until at last, in her mad confused mind, she did not know if it was today . . . or the past. If I were Emily . . . or Amelia.

Yet she was my only hope.

And as Mrs. Kerrenslea looked at Evonne, I saw her face change, become puzzled. "Evonne? What are you doing here? You are not born yet—still a child in my belly." She looked down at me, and frowned.

"Mrs. Kerrenslea . . . I am Emily," I pleaded. "Emily. Please do not kill me. I never meant you any harm."

She seemed troubled. "Emily—not Amelia? It must be

so, for Evonne is here. Let me help her up, Evonne," she said uncertainly.

"No, Mother!" Evonne's voice rang out. "Do you not want to see me take my rightful place as mistress of Edgecliff? When she is dead, Richard will marry me! He only married her for the house! He loves me! And then—then—I shall wear the ring of the brides, Mother!"

I watched in horror as Evonne reached into her bodice. And there it was. She held it aloft where the ring caught the cruel empty light of the moon and sparkled, like drops of blood and bitter tears. In triumph, she set the circlet on her finger and stood outlined against the sky.

"I will come into what is rightfully mine—as this ring—which *you* took for me, Mother, is mine!"

Then she turned to her mother and said in a low and commanding voice, "Push her, Mother."

For a long time, they stared at each other, Evonne seeming to will her mother to do the evil deed. I dared not speak.

"No." The answer was low, tortured.

"No?" Evonne's voice was a whiplash of scorn.

"I—I killed once. I am sorry for it. It has haunted me, all these years. I will not kill her daughter, too."

And Mrs. Kerrenslea, looking old and broken, turned toward me and bent to extend a helping hand to me.

"No, Mother—then I shall do it myself!" Evonne screamed, laying her hands violently on her mother's shoulders and pulling her away.

There was a struggle, at the very edge of the cliff. I did not look away until suddenly a pair of strong, warm hands clasped mine.

And as he had that very first morning, Richard Woodstock pulled me up over the edge of the cliff.

He pulled me hard against him, then turned to shout at Evonne.

"Leave it, Evonne! It is finished! For even had Emily

died, I would never have married you! I love Emily—I always have. Did I not tell you so when you tried to kiss me this evening?"

Evonne and Mrs. Kerrenslea both turned, startled, and saw that I had been pulled to safety. For a moment, they stood frozen, grasping each other's shoulders, staring at Richard and me where we stood clasped in each other's arms.

And then the cliff gave way beneath their feet.

Epilogue

I pulled the soft blankets over Richard's tiny frame and smiled into his face. Richard Woodstock the second, the image of his father with a down of black hair and eyes as green and sparkling as emeralds.

It was a year to the day since that fateful night on the cliff's edge. I felt a chill as I looked through the windows to where the sea crashed. I could hear them still, their chilling screams, as they fell to their deaths on the rocks below.

Richard had turned to me then, and in his hand was a note he'd found when he'd looked for me in the bedroom during the ball. "I can stand it no more, to the cliff's edge I go, like my mother. Emily."

Thank God he had come in time.

Evonne had written it, I knew.

Now I looked down at the ring that sparkled on my left hand. One pure white diamond in a band of gold. Richard had placed it there, telling me it symbolized the purity of our love.

The ring of the brides had fallen with Evonne over the cliff's edge, and when they found her body, it was gone from her finger. The sea had taken it, and the curse as well.

Malvina said the curse was lifted now and I believed her. I would always believe her.

Charles had gone to America, and I knew we would never see him again. Annabel was married, to Timothy Odgers at last, and William had married too. And Richard . . .

I turned, to see my husband coming into the room. He crossed the room and stood beside me silently, taking my hand as he looked down at our sleeping child.

All had come well in time, the curse ended, and together we shared the great house that we both loved so much, that we were born for.

"My darling," he said then, looking at me with his beautiful eyes so that my heart turned over, "have I told you yet today how very much I love you?"

"Not yet," I said and smiled. I was the happiest woman on earth, an Edgecliff bride.